CB Barrie

The Odessa Bride

Éditions
DÉDICACES

Contents

1

He looked down on the grey speckled concrete, watching his feet cover the same five-yard track he had been repeatedly treading for the last forty-five minutes.

The tightness from his left shoe had swollen his foot and it had just started to throb; his right dragged slightly as a touch of cramp reminded him of his long and anxious pacing. He bent down, stiff with tension, loosening the laces on both shoes and feeling some relief as the pressure lessened.

Why, he asked himself, do disasters always seem to come in three's, and why were all his disasters predicated by a profound lowering of his spirit. God knew he had weathered many grim adversities in the past, but of late, they seemed to be swamping his resilience like avenging demons. How easier it would be to cope if he had more of the optimist in his nature, rather than what now amounted to a paranoid pessimist.

But even the most optimistic soul has a limit of endurance before optimism succumbs – often to be replaced by a grim stoicism. Indeed, he found it hard to remember a time when he didn't survive on sheer bloody persistence and stamina. That was it – all he could do was to keep going – somehow.

Looking up from the garage floor, he sensed the presence of the shop supervisor.

"Mr Enfield?"

"Yes, what's the news?"

"Pretty good sir! You'll be on your way in an hour - we've found a new alternator for you, we're fitting it now."

An hour!

Well, he knew now that the good news was bad news.

The car had ground to a halt on the way to the hospital. On his way to be with his wife Betty as their son went into the operating theatre. He should have taken a taxi, hired a car or pleaded with the garage to provide an unofficial courtesy car - but it was less straightforward than that.

His employers electrical business had stalled over the last three months and even the senior men like him were being reduced to short time attendance (and a much reduced salary). After months of trying to pay for domestic bills and constant hospital visits, resulting in outgoings far exceeding income, his personal finances had collapsed just a week before. He had too little credit left to deprive Betty and their boy - their welfare came first, even if it meant he was absent when Betty was in need of support.

His mouth - dried of saliva - felt swollen and sore. A drink would have been welcome but in the circumstances, even a vending machine coffee was an extravagance.

"Oh, Mr. Enfield, reception has your keys."

He looked up; the foreman was smiling a smile of 'didn't we do well - forty minutes instead of sixty'.

He forced a smile in return to the foreman and fumbled for his wallet. At reception his hand shook slightly as he handed over his last credit worthy piece of plastic. It was typical - had he been nearer home, he had the tools and the expertise to have done the job himself, and it would have saved so much precious and vital money, but as usual fate created the worst of circumstances.

To his relief the card transaction went through without embarrassment and in minutes he was in his car and fitting the seat belt.

As he twisted the ignition key the dash lit up and the engine fired. Now the alternator warning light extinguished, so all was well. He sat motionless for a moment listening to the tick over as he re-checked his bearings; then, engaging first gear he rolled forward out of the service yard.

A gap in the main road traffic allowed him a smooth and unhurried merging into the traffic stream and, as he picked up speed, he was suddenly aware of his stupidity in not using the garage's phone to contact Betty and tell her he was now on his way. Thirty minutes and he would be there to hear what the surgeon had to say. Betty was probably frantic, her worry compounded by his absence and the outcome of the operation.

Christ, but it never let up did it? All he needed...!!

He never heard the impact as such, just an overwhelming force that slammed into his back and whipped him forward. After that it was all blackness, filled with a small voice that kept shouting at him not to let the dark void swallow him up and turn into oblivion. It shouted and shouted again, and only abated when he began to notice that it wasn't so dark any more and a dim light was coming from somewhere.

He opened his eyes to find himself strapped onto a stiff platform of some sort with his head and neck pinned into position by compressible pads and straps. Likewise, his lower half was immobilised with more straps and cushions around his torso and legs. Above him bright actinic strip lights bathed everything in a shadow-less artificial daylight. Around him, he saw three figures inspecting parts of him with a serious, unwavering concentration, while another, white masked and dressed in clinical green, appeared to be absorbed by something to do with his right leg.

"Mr Enfield...Peter...can you see me - is your vision okay?"

His mouth hardly worked but he managed to mumble a response to the man with the stethoscope who suddenly towered above him.

"Good - do you hurt? Have you pain, if so can you tell me where?"

He thought for a short moment.

"What happened - what the hell am I doing here? Got to get up...Betty..."

"Calm yourself - you've been in an RTA. Everything is under control - please answer the question - any excessive pain? Do you hurt?"

He had to get to Betty, had to tell her he would never desert her, had to know how their boy was doing, had to get up no matter what!

"Let me out of this bloody thing - I have something to do - it's bloody important, I don't care what you say, let me out or I'll break out."

The three gowned figures surrounding him turned towards the stethoscope man with perplexed looks and then, as if on que, walked off.

The stethoscope man looked down at him. "Alright Peter, we'll have you out of there in a moment - just let us do a final check on your leg, it appears to be a bit cut up at the moment and you will need some work on your head - it'll require some surgery I'm sorry to say. We've given you a touch of morphine, you may not be feeling or thinking too clearly...okay?"

He tried to turn his head as a smile from the man said goodbye and he suddenly disappeared from his field of view.

He sank back, retreating from panic into uncomplaining anxiety, resolving to give them two minutes to keep their word.

As he became more aware, the idea that he was in a hospital A&E department was no surprise given the term 'RTA' that the doctor had used, that (he remembered) meant Road Traffic Accident.

So – another piece of foul luck!

He'd somehow been involved in a collision, though for the life of him he couldn't work out how. Jesus Christ! How the fates laughed at him. It was all he needed.

At that instant another body appeared above him, a bespec-tacled man dressed in a surgical gown and armed with a very comforting and disarming grin.

"Mr Enfield – seems you aren't having the best of days! I'm Davis, senior surgical registrar here. I thought your name was familiar when I overheard that a patient was causing a ruckus here in casualty and staff were being urged to sedate the individual in question. I don't think that will be necessary will it? I've met your wife by the by – that is, prior to your son and I becoming acquainted."

A wave of relief overwhelmed him; it was sheer joy to hear the words the man spoke. This man knew about his son and Betty – please God it wasn't bad news.

"Oh Lord! Please – what's the...situation. Is my son okay, is my wife...where is my wife?"

"I'm here."

Her concerned angelic face framed by long dark hair came into sight below the shoulder of the man above him. As the two bodies exchanged, one pirouetting away from the other, she was leaning down on him kissing his lips.

"You've been in the wars my love – I was so worried..."

Delight replaced relief as she came close to him and in the massive respite of the moment he allowed his head to collapse back on to the pillow. As he felt the softness of his wife's lips on his, the pent up tension began to drain away and he silently thanked heaven for his reprieve.

"Betty –how is...."

The man in surgical green reappeared – and interjected.

"Fine – a tricky procedure but we won through. Your son will be fine I assure you."

The thought that the spinal tumour on his son had been removed without the risk of permanent paralysis was another massive plus – worth all the trauma he had been through. He suddenly felt elated and exhausted in equal measure and could do little more than smile up at his wife's lovely face. Drawn, and showing all the signs of a long physical and psychological ordeal, she was now beaming with the same sense of release and hope that he was.

"Sorry to interrupt but I'm taking you into surgery."

The green man with spectacles loomed above his wife's head, peering down with a knowing expression.

As they both became silent and their heads turned towards him, the surgeon continued in a brisk business–like manner.

"Got to get your leg and skull sorted out I'm afraid – taken a bit of a bashing."

I didn't think I was...that...bad!" he anxiously choked out forcing his voice outward against the numbing of the morphine.

"You're in need of a 10,000 mile service I'm afraid – I'm going to have to fix a good deal of tissue loss on your right leg and pin your right tibia before the day is out, not to mention a touch of cranial depression of the right side of your skull. But don't worry, I appear to becoming your family surgeon and I appreciate the privilege."

The surgeon smiled, and as two other nursing staff responded to his nod, they collectively began to pull his trolley out of the trauma cubicle. He suddenly found his right arm in the hands of a male nurse who took the canula tube leading to his drip and started to inject into it with a syringe.

"Pre-med okay." He said looking at the surgeon who then nodded an acknowledgement.

Betty walked alongside, holding his free hand as the trolley glided out of the casualty unit and into the hospital complex. He tried to keep her in sight but the restraints around his head kept getting in the way. He didn't mind, she was still there - he could just feel her. As they approached the OR he felt another hypodermic prick his right arm.

He tried to lift his voice so the surgeon could hear him.

"Before I get really...dopey, how bad is my skull? Did you say a...depression? I can't feel...anything."

The green man was walking on the opposite side of the trolley to Betty and half a pace in front. He slowed and looked down.

"From your verbal and physiological responses, and with no sign of serious concussion, I suspect it's no great shakes. The CT scans we took while you were unconscious show cranial damage, but there is no sub-dural bleed or any sign of compression on the brain so we are dealing with direct impact damage to the skull. I'm simply going to brace any skull fractures and leave your body to repair it - permanently that is." The surgeon's eyes twinkled behind his spectacles in the half shaded corridor lighting and he said no more, concluding his remarks by grinning reassuringly.

It fell on deaf ears - his patient had already drifted into anaesthetic oblivion.

2

It had been a nightmare of circumstances to get where he was now. He had been discharged from hospital only a day later than the time Betty had arrived to take their son home. She had too much to contend with given his son's needs, and for all his own incapacity, he resigned himself to being as independent as possible; so as to give her the smallest possible work load.

She somehow found the time to help him back from the hospital, but he refused any further support once he was home. The agency nurse who had stood in for Betty while she came for him, smiled sympathetically as she saw him limp in through the front door.

"Good to see you on the mend Mr. Enfield. I'll stay a while longer to give Betty a chance to organise things. Want some tea?"

Betty smiled a thankful smile as she took his arm and steered him into the lounge. He propped the walking stick alongside one of the fireside chairs. Gripping the chair arms from behind he flopped down into the seat and wondered how long it would be before he was completely mobile again. The surgeon had given him a "no less than three months" before he could expect to be back to 100% fitness.

"You can't expect to be running marathons straight away!" he'd said, "You took quite a beating in the RTA and although you are recovering very well we have to be realistic. Okay, I know it means somehow you will have to survive without an income for a while, but better that than pushing yourself to the point where your wife collects your life insurance!"

"Yeah - yeah!" he thought, but the one was almost as bad as the other - at least if he was dead Betty and his son wouldn't have to scratch around for money to pay the bills.

But the medical man was right of course, though it was going to be a bloody difficult few months.

Betty had borrowed from her parents while he was in hospital and had worked herself into the ground holding things together while their son Bobby recovered from his 'op. As to that, he had the momentary realisation that Bobby wasn't in the house to greet him as he returned.

"Get you some tea." Betty said as she fussed over his cushions and backrest.

Before he could quiz her about Bobby she hurried off to the kitchen where the agency nurse was supervising the kettle. He heard the two women chatting in the kitchen - not in any excited way but with a subdued and friendly tone. Snatches of the conversation flowed out of the half closed door and it was clear that his son was in no condition to see his father.

"Turn him every two hours - bedsores are a bugger, get him to try and wriggle his toes every hour and make sure he gets his lower joint exercises. Mind his support cushions - try not to let him load up the spinal area where he has the stitches. From what I can see he should be starting his bed exercises very soon, but as to that, when he's ready, and only when he's ready...okay. That's as soon as he recovers full control of his bladder, bowels and can wriggle his legs and toes voluntarily. Give it ten to fourteen days."

He sighed inwardly; he was no more than a stairway from his son but the chances of him seeing him anytime soon was remote. He was hardly mobile, while his son was bed-bound for the interim. Each of them was too early into their respective recoveries and recuperation to bridge the gap – each of them might just as well be at the other end of the world.

Damn! No communication was unthinkable.

What he needed was a pair of megaphones; he could call up to Bobby and tell him how much fun they were going to have when their ills wore off. With his bedroom door open Bobby in turn could shout back.

It sounded stupid, but he desperately needed to restore contact with Bobby and Betty, to tell them how sorry he was for all the misfortune that had descended on them, and how he hated watching them having to be brave and stoic.

Perhaps hate was too strong a term – resented was better. He resented their silent compliance because he had never heard a word of complaint; they never blamed him for all the misfortune or expressed any bitterness. Neither gave a hint of how easily it would be for one to say 'it's your fault – your fault because you brought me into a world of pain and discomfort" and the second to remark "and your lack of care in your choice of employment, coupled to your thoughtless driving, brought us to the edge of domestic and financial ruin.

He was guilty as hell, guilty enough to want their absolution, guilty enough to want to demand that they didn't bury their feelings, and guilty enough to want to rail against the world, against fate, and above all, God!

Just one small shift in the chaos that engulfed his life could have changed everything, but it seemed that on his Lotto ticket was the inverse of the big prize – his prize was misery, and he kept on winning!

He wanted to feel something more than the enclosure of his

house, of the impending and predictable difficulties the next months would throw up. He wanted just a taste of complete freedom from worry and concern – enough to kill his depressed state and refresh his buoyancy and optimism.

He grabbed at his stick and hauled himself to his feet. The lack of muscle strength in his right leg was still pronounced but he was going to ignore it. He limped out of the lounge and into the hallway making a snake like route to the front door. He was through it and onto the front lawn at a pace. Propelling himself forward he almost fell, staggering back up to an upright position using his stick as a crutch.

He waited outside the door, looking around at the neighbour-hood houses and his long front patch of rampant grass that spoke volumes about the neglect two months in hospital could create. Even the fencing had weathered badly in the short time he had been away; or perhaps he had never noticed it when he had been around. His job had been a massive and soul-destroying distraction – he seemed never to have the time to think of other things. Now, as he thought on it, he resolved to change everything. Betty, Bobby and he would cope, he would find another occupation, train if necessary, start a new life.

Yes – that was it, be positive and insist on something better.

He slowly limped towards the front gate, running his hands over rough, weather beaten wood. He saw himself with the time and the enthusiasm to commit a Saturday morning to repairing the hinges and then slapping wood preservative onto the fencing. His imagination saw a refreshed fence and a refreshed life – that was if he didn't let circumstances rule him and betray his determination. No, he was not going to sink under any more...by all that was holy, he damn well wouldn't!

As the thought passed, something sucked the air from his lungs like a huge vacuum cleaner and a massive, searing hot force picked him up and slammed him into the fencing.

3

Everything considered, he had come out of it relatively unscathed. He should have been killed or at least crippled. The skin grafts on his back and legs had healed well and he was walking virtually unaided now. Even the hair on the back of his head had re-grown enough to cover the scars and indentations the surgeon had left after removing the debris that had punched into his back and skull. How he had survived was a miracle, but not one he was inclined to boast about.

The fact that he remembered nothing of the colossal explosion that had gutted his house, or the weeks of semi-coma, was, so they told him, a good thing. You couldn't have nightmares about something you didn't witness or were unable to recall they said.

They were wrong!

Not only that, they had no answer to the numbness in his soul that kept pulling at his emotions and making him yearn for a time when things were bad, but at least offered a world that was recognisable, intact and mutable. Now Betty, Bobby and the district nurse were gone – as was his world. A world of disappointment and pain certainly, but one he had once vowed to restore to full life.

Now there was only himself – with a severely damaged body and soul to mend.

The police had asked him for a statement – he'd told them all he knew which, in truth, was very little. As more information

filtered through to him, after months of treatment and conva-
lescence and visits from faces he didn't know and never saw
again, it seemed that the explosion that had nearly killed him
had originated in the kitchen.

The experts had concluded that a gas leak, from an unlit gas
ring, had filled the kitchen with enough gas to create an explosive
atmosphere. Unnoticed by the two women occupants, the gas
concentration ignited from the newly lit rings. The resultant
explosion collapsed most of the kitchen side of the house and
exposed a gas main. This, leaking volumes of fresh gas, had
momentarily delayed its out-gassing just long enough to provide
a second massive eruption. He'd been on the receiving end of
both shock waves, the first being the most destructive. They
found him halfway into the street, having been lifted off his feet
and blown through the rickety garden fence.

Half the time he'd spent in hospital had been a dream like
sequence of catheters, surgical masks and injections. Not
to mention being wheeled for the umpteenth time into the
operating room, only half conscious or aware of the glowing TV
monitors, the gleaming white walls, and the blue white of the
overhead strip lights each glinting and reflecting off the laid out
racks of chrome-steel instruments.

But, now it was done - he had been discharged with only
periodic check ups to bear; and those not for a while yet.

He sat outside the hospital main entrance; now free from the
vague smell of methyl alcohol, disinfectant and open toilet doors.
The day was breezy but bright and he welcomed the wait for his
taxi.

A small gaggle of nurses, patients and visitors were hogging the
side screens to the Perspex covered entrance, furtively puffing
cigarettes and glancing nervously at the main doors for sight of

any officialdom.

He remembered how he too had distrusted his luck when it came to contravening the rules of his job, and how early in his career he was always disciplined for stepping out of line just a fraction. Even to this day he still felt massive resentment for the time he had sacrificed hours of unpaid overtime for his employers only later to be torn off a strip by his supervisor for just once arriving at work fifteen minutes late.

But now – he was free.

In his inside pocket was his safety net, a cheque for £650,000 and a letter of condolences from the insurance companies. All the damages and personal injury claims, the letter added, had been settled to everyone's satisfaction.

It was funny how, without him raising a finger, everything that followed the disaster had been superbly organised, apparently without the slightest hitch or mishap. His story had been a major news item for a short while, but interest had waned quickly and, except for the local papers, the aftermath to the disaster wasn't particularly newsworthy. The houses adjacent to his, those damaged in the explosions, were being restored and refurbished. His old house, so he understood, had been completely demolished and the site cleared. He had absolutely no intention of revisiting the site to see progress – he feared the emotional reaction.

Even the funerals, attended by a myriad of sympathetic faces (which, again, he had never seen before) had in retrospect, been run like a military exercise.

Looking back, the funerals had torn his heart out – the coffins of Betty and Bobby were so bedecked with layers of flowers they hid the fact that there was little inside the caskets which resembled, or could be recognised, as those he'd loved.

The hospital had grudgingly allowed him to attend the funeral in a nurse chaperoned wheelchair, and it was all he could do not to wrench at his wheels, turn away, and escape the grief and torment that filled his soul.

Part guilt, and part fury, his emotions had battled to maintain his sanity, and it was only through the intervention of his personal chaperon and nurse, the amazing Isaac, that he had survived the day and all the days that followed.

4

Recalling the day, that terrible day, the time spent at the funeral had eventually come to represent a soul-restoring episode.

As the sad trail of mourners and casual spectators trudged away from the crematorium, he found his wheelchair suddenly accelerating away from the gravesides and then racing in an entirely new direction.

"What you need my friend," said the now familiar voice behind him, "is a touch of the dog you haven't been bitten by yet". He tried to look round at his companion. God almighty – after all the bitterness and sadness, the man's only thought was getting a drink!

He felt himself instantly rebelling against the idea of trundling into the busy, bustling bar of a pub. Not while he was struggling with a deep and abiding sorrow, not while his face showed obvious signs of grief and tears.

"No – it's not right – I don't feel...Christ, I'm only a few weeks from a my last serious op'. I'm bloody well not up to it."

"You might not be – but I bloody well am!"

Yes, he remembered it all very well, his name was Isaac, and Isaac was all he would answer to.

Isaac obviously had prior knowledge of the geography of the crematorium and all the alternative exits and entrances. As he bumped uncomfortably and precariously in an almost out of control wheelchair, they began to narrowly negotiate a paved path flanked by memorial stones. As the set of stones came to an end he could see that they were making for a metal gate set into birch-bound hedging marking one boundary of the crematorium.

He'd protested again, had even pleaded, but to no avail.

His wheelchair kept moving at a pace – out of the bushes that bordered the railed pathway and on to another that lay behind what seemed to be a continuous close-boarded fence separating the gardens of a housing estate. Soon they were skuttling down yet another perilously bumpy pathway that divided two houses and their gardens. As they left this new lane, they suddenly exited on a broad tree lined road with a service station immediately opposite, and to its right the unmistakable architecture of a purpose built public house. An extensive, but sporadically occupied car park surrounded the building that was fronted by a high, black painted gibbet, carrying a hinged panel painted with a white hart deer.

"God – you're a bit of a load!" he heard Isaac gasp.

He tried to twist round to look up at Isaac.

"What are you doing, I told you, I'm in no mood for a pub."

Isaac was not easy to forget, he had olive skin, dark brown eyes and a heavy thatch of glossy black hair. Gleaming white teeth showed as his widening lips revealed a combination of manic grinning and the physical exertions of a rapid wheelchair transit from crematorium to pub.

"Come on – it'll do you good. A couple of stiff ones will take the edge off of everything. And believe me, my need is as great as yours!"

Impotent and bound to a wheelchair, he gave up any thought of resistance there and then, for in a sense Isaac was right – a distraction of any kind would be therapeutic.

Physically, he was stiff and bruised from Isaacs furious ride.

Some of his stitches were still sore from incomplete healing but more importantly he was a spiritually broken and emotional wreck. He knew that unless he was going to find a way to cope – he wouldn't.

That frightened him.

In all the years that his confounded, malevolent luck had plagued his life, he had at least held on to his sanity and resolve. Now, seeing how misfortune had had the last laugh on him, he felt depressed beyond redemption.

"Here we go – and you're buying!" Isaac sang out as he felt the wheelchair suddenly gather speed, jump the curb and dash across the street.

Getting in to the saloon bar was a small miracle as Isaac pushed, and he pulled on his wheels, in order to get over the threshold step of the entrance. It was clearly intended to deter wheeled and inebriated customers.

Once in, they discovered a cavernous seating area, all fronted by an endlessly long, highly polished bar. The rear of the bar was festooned with inverted bottles of spirits, rosettes and ephemera from past football matches interspersed with bank notes from every corner of the world. The bar top was littered with strangely contoured white china ice bowls, each gleaming with a deep glaze and each nestling into a thick, red bar mat, woven along its edge with a brewery's name, and advertising one of the house beers.

To his relief the pub was virtually deserted. The whole seating area was empty except for one corner table occupied by a couple face to face in intimate, whispered discussions. They were utterly engrossed in each other and made no effort to even turn their heads. Further forward of the table area was a small disc of open floor intended for those brave enough, or drunk enough, to have a dance. This area, in turn, preceded a small stage, elevated some

19

three foot above the dance floor and still with its curtains open. A well worn and somewhat distressed drum kit sat in the middle of the stage, each drum and its mount battered into irregular angles by the most recent rebel against noise abatement.

Isaac had negotiated them through the vast layout of tables and chairs taking the shortest route to the bar. As they approached the bar an apron fronted figure appeared at the far end and began to walk towards them.

"Good morning gents, what would you like?"

The barman, tall and lithe, was in his twenties and had a serious air about him. Looking down at the wheelchair he offered a sympathetic smile.

He shifted his weight in the wheelchair trying to find a less uncomfortable position and was slow in attempting to answer the query.

"Two double scotches and a...." Isaac hesitated. Turning back, he gave a slight nod of his head, inviting him to have a say.

He was suddenly caught in mid-thought – standing on his dignity was no therapy, He decided that Isaac probably knew best and he had to face it, he had nowhere else to go.

"Four double scotches and two pints of lager."

The barman smiled in surprise, "Starting the day well then boys – okay, coming up!"

Isaac said nothing but turned around behind the wheelchair and pushed it towards the nearest table. He stepped forward and pulled back two chairs enabling the wheelchair to roll up to the table. As he felt Isaac release the wheelchair's push bar, he held out his arms, buffering himself from the edge of the table. The chair started to slow and then stopped. Isaac appeared from behind him and quickly took a chair on the opposite side of the table.

"You're paying." Isaac said with a slight hint of amusement.

Somehow he resisted the temptation to allow his sorrow and baseless resentment about the pub to be taken out on Isaac.

"Thought as much," he grunted, "what if I haven't brought any money?"

"You'll have to owe it to me then – with interest of course!" Again Isaac smiled a rueful grin, "Not too onerous – I only charge five percent...and I promise all my clients that they will cheer up."

Indignant at the observation, he looked hard at his companion – the resentment momentarily replacing the chasm of sadness that had occupied him since the funeral.

"Bloody easy for you to be flippant – your world wasn't destroyed by more stinking luck than you could imagine."

Isaac lent forward, promising the beginning of a more intimate exchange, but was interrupted by a shout from the bar.

"Four doubles and two lagers gents."

As he watched Isaac rise immediately to retrieve the drinks, he wriggled unsuccessfully in his wheelchair to achieve a less irritating and uncomfortable position. All the wounds and skin grafts on his back and lower thighs were healing well but at times, they were healing with intense itching and it was all he could do to cope with it. He knew that as far as healing was concerned it was a good sign, but he longed for the day when it would all stop. It was simply impossible to ignore. Just for a moment, and rather guiltily, he realised that he was actually looking forward to being alive, to actually having a future; and that added remorse to his already miserable state.

Of course, it was guilt and blame he'd always had to contend with wasn't it?

Guilt made the loss of everything that more acute, and more

mortifying. The grief was one thing; the fact that he was responsible for it was another. It was too much, and it was more than life was worth. There was no way he could detach himself from his history – and no way he could be absolved from his guilt or blame. In short, and in reality, he saw no prospect of anything changing.

With that realisation, he felt the utter desolation of his spirit and unable to contain his emotions anymore he buried his head in his hands and wept.

5

The clink of glasses and spare coins on a tray brought him back to his surroundings and what to him amounted to a disgraceful reality. Isaac stayed silent, looking pensive as he distributed their glasses of spirits and ale at each table place and sat down.

"Try a scotch - come on, you could do with it".

But he couldn't respond. Shattered and ashamed, and desperately trying to hide his tears, he turned his head away.

Isaac seemed to ignore him for a moment and appeared to holding a small liquid filled glass tube, which he promptly emptied into his mouth.

Now Isaac spoke - a soft, gentle almost cautious tone that struck him, even in his distressed state, as mellow, empathetic and undemanding.

"You know, they told me what you had gone through when I volunteered to bring you to the funeral - your whole history that is. They said you were very fragile and needed to be handled carefully. Now that was strange, because that's exactly what they told the hospital porter who had charge of me when I was given day release to visit my new foster parents. I was eleven at the time."

Through tear-obscured eyes, he turned in time to see Isaac throw back a double scotch in one mouthful.

"You've been through this kind of b...bloody nightmare?" he stuttered.

Isaac allowed his lips to widen; not a smirk, or a grimace but an unspoken confirmation. "I'll tell you all...on condition you match me drink for drink."

Isaac eyed him without blinking; it was an inflexible condition – he couldn't refuse.

He reached for the glass and sank the scotch in one throw. His already tear saturated eyes reacted again as the fiery spirits burnt its way down his gullet.

"Good – next one we down together." Isaac said, pausing for a reply.

"Yes, together." he croaked wiping the stream of tears from his eyes and cheeks with the back of his hand.

Isaac smiled as he watched the tears flow, and waited until the glistening eyes and rivulets of sadness had abated a little."

"I'm Lebanese," he said, "oh don't be fooled, I was educated in England and arrived here from the Lebanon as a boy – that was after the first civil war and during the Israeli invasion in1982. My family were Maronite Christians, living in a small Christian enclave just to the south side of Beirut. We managed to avoid the conflicts for some time and tried to maintain a routine life.

My father was a lawyer, my mother a trained private secretary. She handled all my father's administration. When the shelling started to move into our district we decided to try to get to a safer area. We ended up near a place called Damour, the scene of an earlier massacre of Christian Phalangists, and when that became too hot we started to move again – just our luck! A Palestine Liberation Organisation militia group caught us on the road. They treated us, and all Lebanese Christians as infidels and sworn enemy. They had no mercy. My two sisters and my mother were beaten and raped constantly. Over a period of two days my brother, my father and I were forced to watch this brutal, pitiless and dreadful treatment. My older sister was forced into oral sex with one of them in front of us. She resisted as hard as she could and finally bit down on his penis. In his rage, he dragged my courageous sister away. He made sure she didn't die immediately – using a handgun he aimed at her limbs – her arms and legs were hit first and then the *coup de grace* – he forced a rifle barrel up her anus and fired. I remember him telling my mother and my other sister that the same thing would happen to them if they didn't 'co-operate' with the militia band.

My father was driven to despair, and when his pleading for pity resulted in a vicious beating, he swore in the name of God that he would see them go to hell. They laughed, telling him that the death of any one of them would be the death of a martyr and would result in a personal paradise – not hell. Still, they said, if hell is where you want to meet your family, we will accommodate you. They cut off his hands and feet with a meat clever and over the next half hour they let him bleed to death in excruciating pain."

Isaac hesitated for a long moment, his voice becoming suddenly husky and his eyes misted. He wrapped his hand around the pint of lager and drank half the contents.

Isaac's flat, monotonic voice and terrifying story had driven away all other emotional preoccupations that had wrapped itself around his thinking. He was so gripped by the unfolding horror of Isaac's story that he sat unmoving in his wheelchair, no longer aware of the punishment it delivered to his damaged body.

Isaac's rapid disposal of the lager was accompanied by a twitch of his head, aimed at the untouched lager on the table in front of his wheelchair.

Swig for swig was the deal, so he lifted the glass and sank half the contents. Replacing the glass on the table he saw that Isaac was patiently waiting for him to turn his attention towards him again.

"So - my brother and I suffered the ordeal of all helpless captives, fearing for ourselves, furious and appalled by what we had witnessed and certain that it was far from the end of our torment. There was a kind of table or bench in front of us and rather than have to hold the women down they tied my naked mother and remaining sister to it like pack animals, with their heads hanging to the ground on one side and back and legs the other. It meant the men could have intercourse from behind and not have to look at the two women. We cried out to our mother and sister not to despair or give up, that God would help them and that we were praying for salvation. My mother was stoic and virtually silent but my little sister was in agony - both of my sisters had been virgins and as the constant rapes continued on both of them their agony had increased. After they killed my big sister the rapes continued - my little sister became silent and would simply pass out. In a way it was a blessing, but one morning one of the PLO creatures withdrew from my sister with blood all over his penis - she turned her little head and gave us a last mournful smile, after which she closed her eyes and didn't stir. She had been so damaged internally that she had haemorrhaged; she bled to death. My mother died the next day - I suspect she simply gave up and stopped trying to survive.

My brother and I were still chained up and hoping for a clean bullet to the head. It was on the night of the fourth day that half the PLO were called away and we were left in the hands of a murderous few who were now without any leadership. They wanted some fun, so they unchained my brother and me and told us to run. They gave us twenty seconds to escape and then they were going to hunt us. My brother and I were too weak from our treatment and starvation to have any chance, but even so my brother started to make a break for it. They laughed and mocked him even more when they saw how he had soiled himself from the past day's terror. As he stumbled away most of the men had turned to sneer and insult him, and I suddenly found myself behind the throng of militia. For that moment I wasn't under surveillance any more. I noticed one of the men had three grenades linked to the waist of his camouflage jacket through the detonator rings. It was a kind of bravado – if God chose to accidentally pull a grenade out, and it detonated, it didn't matter; they were destined for paradise anyway – or so they thought.

I was very weak and felt terrible, but I fixated on the three grenades and made sure that if I were to die, I would take all the PLO bastards with me...and not to paradise!

I stepped forward, crouched a little, and grabbed two of grenades with each hand. I was ten years old but I knew how to detonate a grenade and where my duty lay. As I pulled at the detonator rings on the little pineapples I prayed, and swore vengeance for my sisters, my mother and my father. As the grenades became primed, I gently rolled them forward into the jeering mob intent on watching my brother limp away. I was certain of my own imminent death but regardless; I was hoping my brother might survive. The animal who had lost his grenades suddenly realised what was happening and shouted a warning as he turned on me with his AK47 rifle."

Isaac paused, looked at the table and the remaining scotch and beckoned him to match it. He was becoming utterly numbed by what Isaac was recounting, but managed to respond. He watched Isaac lift his glass and simultaneously downed the last measure of scotch in one go. Somewhat theatrically, he slammed the thick-bottomed glass back onto the table as Isaac did the same.

Isaac licked his lips, "Glad I'm not Muslim!" he said. He smiled appreciatively and continued.

"The animal with the AK47 never got it near me, the grenades exploded virtually at the same time as he had turned, and now he was directly in front of me with the first grenade behind him. The last thing I remember is his body lifting towards me and overwhelming me with enormous force – so much so that when I regained my wits I found his remains spread all over me. Though I was still dazed and soaked in blood, I had just enough strength to push what remained of his torso away from me and stand up. Most of the militia were dead – those that weren't I left to die of their wounds in as much pain as I could inflict. The one that had finally killed my big sister was happily for me still alive – I told him what I was going to do and let him suffer a little more. Then I poured petrol over him and ignited it.

I found my brother, rather bloodied but very much alive, behind one of the armed Land-Cruisers the militia transported themselves around in.

We found some food, made shallow graves for our family, grabbed a couple more handguns, and started learning to drive one of the Land Cruisers. A battalion sized Israeli unit picked us up the next day. They had just engaged the first PLO militia group and wiped them out."

Isaac bent his head, as though in contemplation. He ran his finger around a small pool of slopped lager on the table and stayed silent.

Transfixed by his story it took a second or two to ask the obvious question.

"My God Isaac...how did you get to England – is your brother still okay?"

"Uh – oh yeah...my brother... well, the Israelis' sent both of us to a UN resettlement camp. Refugees, waifs and strays were being shipped hither and thither and my brother and I were supposed to go to Canada. That never happened because of a quota limitation. Instead, we were routed to a Greek Orthodox missionary group who then handed us to a UK Christian charity who shipped us out - we were told no other refuge was available. We were lucky. We were taken in by a wealthy Christian Lebanese family living in Bath and because they had lost their two sons fighting Hizbollah they came to dote on us. We were adopted by them and they sent us to private schools - they said a good education was paramount. They were right, at first my brother and I floundered with our non-existent English but we had to learn quickly or go under. We had learned to survive against bigger odds than an English public school - and survive we did. On graduation, my brother left the country immediately and went to Israel. He later joined the Israeli air force as a fighter pilot. I had no such ambition - I found satisfaction in helping people and because of a curious sense of guilt from my past life, I went to medical school in Southampton and qualified as a physician."

The revelation was a complete surprise. "You never told me you were a doctor - I thought you were on the nursing side."

Isaac nodded, "What's the difference? I saw your notes and thought it a good idea to offer you a different perspective. It was that, or refer you for psychiatric support. If I've given you any food for thought, and its positive, then I've done some good. If not, its time for a long course of psychotherapy preceded by a heavy dose of anti-depressants."

The anguish he'd felt as Isaac recounted his experiences displaced much of his self -pity. As they finished their drinks, and said their goodbyes to the now empty pub, he mulled over his options and decided that if Isaac could overcome massive bitterness, and rise above adversity, disasters and tragedy, then there was hope for him too.

As Isaac pushed his wheelchair away from the pub, skirting the housing estate and taking a longer route back to the crematorium car park, he knew he was no longer the unluckiest man in the universe.

6

Now he felt a deep sense of resilience, a grim determination to survive and make good; not merely through a conscious renaissance, but by augmenting his self worth; by knowing that no matter his history, he was worthy of life and happiness. Isaac had shown him that it was possible not to be soiled, soured or corrupted by the experience of horrific events. Isaac was the living testament to the good that could be salvaged from even the most evil of circumstances.

"Isaac, when did you last see your brother – does he visit at all?"

Isaac paused. "No...I haven't seen him for twenty years."

"That long? You don't keep in touch then."

"No – he's dead."

He turned in the chair, his horrified look asking the question he wasn't able to articulate, but Isaac ignored him and remained mute.

Isaac stopped the chair just as they reached the mini-bus in the crematorium car park.

"You've drunk as much as I have Isaac – I'm really fuzzy, are you okay to drive?"

Isaac smiled, unlocked the side door and pressed a lever to operate the powered lift. Unspeaking he pushed the wheelchair onto the platform and started the lift.

Waiting for the motor to disengage, he dropped the lever to

neutral, allowing him to swing the platform and chair into the minibus. Isaac then entered through the second sliding door and checked the safety harness that held the wheelchair. After locking the wheelchair brakes he began interlacing the safety straps around the wheels and tightening them with the ratchet. As he finished he gave the wheelchair a push and, satisfied there was no free movement, grunted with approval. As Isaac did so he looked up and caught his eyes.

"I will be driving with little alcohol in my system – I have a friend, a biochemist who supplies me with yeast derived alcohol dehydrogenase ampoules. It degrades alcohol when it gets to the bloodstream. I'm virtually un-inebriated if you will – I had a dose of ADH earlier, before we started drinking, and with downing only a couple of scotches and a lager, my blood alcohol will by now only amount to drinking half a pint of beer." Isaac lifted his eyebrows as if to say 'now shut up'.

He'd sat there, glum and pessimistic and somewhat befuddled as he watched Isaac methodically check the safety harnesses. As Isaac looked up he wanted to say he was sorry he had doubted him and had been too nosey in asking him to recall another bad memory. But Isaac sensed his diffidence and spoke first.

"Incidentally, you were entitled to ask the question about my brother. I gave you no indication of his history and may well have implied he was alive and well. My fault! Okay, it went like this. When we left school I was aware of my brother's burning hatred for the PLO and Hizbollah, indeed anything that represented anti-Christian or pro-Islamic extremists. Since the Israeli's were the enemy of his enemy he was happy to enlist. He flew many missions against various anti-Israeli targets and was happy to do so because he knew who it was he was attacking. Then, one day on a routine low-level reconnaissance sweep over the west bank he was fired on. He got back to his base and landed normally but when the ground crew got to him he was dead. A single bullet had hit the aircraft as it banked. The bullet pierced the cockpit canopy and hit my brother in the neck. He managed to hold back the blood loss for the return flight but in the end it had been too much for him. And, before you ask, yes, I miss him terribly. Except for my foster parents, I have no one left now... I prefer to remember him as....well, I don't have to tell you what I mean."

The harrowing experience of Isaac's disastrous story now left him with mixed feelings. There was optimism now, and though Isaac had displaced his misery with an example of how tragedy and overriding personal hardship could be mitigated; it had also shown him that some catastrophic events left their mark – no matter what.

As the minibus moved off he needed to know; there was something that would make the decision for complete renewal easier – it was imperative.

It took time; time for him to phrase it in a way that would provide an unambiguous answer. He just hoped that Isaac would be honest.

"Isaac – Isaac–" he called out but Isaac appeared not to hear him. He tried again. This time the head turned slightly away from watching the road.

"Got a problem?"

"I need to ask you something."

"Go ahead."

"Please be honest with me."

Isaac paused, then laughed.

"No way are you getting my bank details and PIN!"

He smiled at the riposte but wasn't going to be deflected – the question had to be asked.

"Isaac – are you Jewish? Is your name Jewish? You said you were Christian. Why? Were the stories you told me true or fiction. I just want to know the truth – no recriminations, no complaints. I know you are – you have – helped me so much today and I understand that sometimes the ends justify the means. But I must know everything!"

Isaac said nothing. The minibus drove on and he felt suddenly abandoned. Isaac was not going to respond and as his query died in the roar of the engine, the tension heightened.

Suddenly he felt the minibus swerve to the left and as the brakes bit hard they were abruptly stationary in a roadside–parking bay.

Isaac undid his safety belt and twisted around in the drivers seat. He looked harder and more careworn than an hour ago in the pub.

"Picking holes in my story now are you? What part of "it's true" don't you believe."

He shuffled his backside to relive some intense itching and get a less paralysing position in the wheelchair.

"I want to believe you, but it's the name – just tell me."

Isaac looked at him hard and then relented.

"I was adopted as a small baby by a Christian couple when my biological parents were killed. They knew only that my given name was Isaac. They had no wish to take away my birthright, and kept my name. They were murdered too. The people I saw killed by the militia were my second family; without any question I loved them no less because I was of different blood. My brother and sisters and my adopted parents were as much my kin as if we were bound by blood. Can you understand that?"

It clicked.

"So – you had two sets of adoptive parents?"

"Yes, and I loved them all." Isaac turned back in the driving

34

seat.

"Is that why you have a more empathetic and more tolerant view do you think?"

Isaac considered the question as he re-started the mini bus engine.

"I suppose so – But I also had the advantage of meeting a kindly hospital porter when I arrived here in England. He had lost his whole family in a wartime bombing and he felt my pain and understood what could be a salve. He saved my sanity. But don't mistake me – I can't forgive all the evil I remember and even now I would cheerfully send every one those bastard, ungodly Hizbollah and Islamist fanatics to the most miserable, lingering death I could think of!" –

7

It had taken well over ten weeks for him to battle through all the physiotherapy and get back on his feet. Even so, it was an exhausting and heartbreaking process, and only his fortitude and grim determination to respond to Isaac's miraculous example made it possible.

Janet, his daily physio', was a stoic, patient and unwavering tutor in how to be as single minded (and objective) as he had hoped to be. She knew what was possible in his physical rehabilitation, she knew how long it would take, and she never relented.

He endured the pain of scare tissue elongation, the stretching and working of excised and atrophied muscles, and the constant extension of damaged ligaments and wasted tendons, never once disclosing Isaac's psychological anchor that kept him from screaming out that it was all a waste of time and he would never stand upright again.

But, he also knew he would never reveal it or dare say it – for apart from the constant presence of Isaac's example, Janet would never allow him to capitulate. Indeed, as the weeks passed she had become his mother and, like a clinging fractious child being disciplined, he was always finally and inevitably, obedient.

And then the day came when he was able to walk twenty paces unaided, and Janet had suddenly stood back – not to give him room on the safety rails, but as though the umbilical cord had been cut.

It may have been an unconscious gesture, a kind of involuntary separation, a Freudian slip, but suddenly she had cut the apron strings of her surrogate son and he of his surrogate mother. Had she dusted her hands, or waved farewell with tears in her eyes, it would have been no less a goodbye. She let him go with a tender touch of the arm and a "We'll done – up to you now." and once again he felt the loss of someone precious.

Now, sitting outside the hospital watching the cigarette smoking nurses drift back to duty, he still wondered why he had been showered with so much pain and grief. But above that sense of resentment, there was now a growing resilience in him – it seemed that the more one experienced and overcame adversity the more a hard core of emotional armour developed. He had been given another chance to find happiness and he was damned if this time he was going to allow fate to rule his life. This time it was he who would decide his future. The £650,000 cheque was a door to a new life, and he was going to spend it wisely.

8

Looking back to the moment he had dived into the taxi on leaving the hospital, armed with a renewed sense of optimism, he knew now that his original ideas about his future were actually indistinct, if not vague. He had immediately instructed the taxi driver to take him to the best hotel in town and had booked in with the idea of beginning his pursuit of a brand new life.

But where to begin?

Laying on the double bed in the quite of his well-appointed hotel room he envisaged the material circumstances and the life he had always aspired to. He had visions of a large, spacious and select house, tastfully furnished and decorated, set in its own well-tended and secluded gardens with a swimming pool perhaps, and a luxury sports car ensconced in a spacious double garage. Additionally, he was going to buy his way out of all the domestic chores and drudgery, by ensuring sufficient money was permanently available for a laundry collection, home maintenance, car servicing and anything else that would constitute a waste of his time. Yet, though his £650,000 was a significant amount of money, it would hardly stretch to meeting all his expectations if he failed to use it carefully. For him to do all he wanted to do, and get all he wanted to get, he was obliged to look carefully at how he was to maintain his expected lifestyle; in short he had to spend wisely and invest even more wisely.

For once he had time to consider his investment options; which approach offered the safest haven for his money and what offered the highest return?

On his next day constitutional after a hearty breakfast in the hotel, he walked through the whole centre of Lidmouth, looking at every advertised investment opportunity.

He agonised over at least five financial management agencies and, tiring of all the local ones, none of whom inspired confidence, he spent the rest of the day working in an Internet café chasing high interest rates and guarantees of secure capital. He fled a host of websites for corporate investment, stockbrokers and personal investment venture capitalists – none of whom encouraged any move on his part to start writing cheques. In the end, he had neither the confidence, nor the inclination, to take a chance with any one of them and simply, with no little relief, handed his local building society a cheque for £300,000.

The dark haired girl behind the counter was so taken aback that she shook slightly and in a husky, awe struck voice called the manager. It was not the reception he wanted, as he found himself being treated as the font of all financial miracles. He eventually escaped the obsequious manager and his sycophantic assistant by insisting that he had little time to consider alternatives to a monthly income account, and given his extremely tight schedule, would they please hurry up with completing the paperwork. However, the figures they gave him for the monthly return on his £300,000 were reasonably good, and he had no doubt it would meet his domestic and personal outgoings for some time. It might even grow, were he able to limit his rate of spend or withdrawal and feed some money back onto the capital.

The finances satisfactorily arranged, all he needed now was somewhere to live!

It proved harder than he imagined. For weeks he traipsed

around town footsore and frustrated. Fixed in his mind was his cherished image, an image which nothing he saw through the various estate agents in any way matched.

It was now almost a month after he'd first arrived in town, and finding himself yet again carried through a series of disappointing house viewings, he finally saw what he wanted.

It was remote – a country house built in the last twelve years with a modern approach, yet classically elegant in its design. If anything it was better than he could have hoped for. The brown speckled brickwork blended beautifully with the soft tones of the roofing tiles and the broad open windows bespoke a kind of gothic charm in their lancet geometry. Its frontage was symmetrical, with two round towers at each corner, their turret roofs complimenting the central roofing that had a similar conical shape. The rooms were large and, because of the broad glazing, well lit; particularly the 20' by 40' living room that, through wide folding double glazed doors, looked out on two acres of well stocked and secluded gardens. Just to the back was a series of formal flowerbeds, all interspersed with variegated blue–green conifers and pebble pathways. More spectacular was a purpose built hardwood chalet, housing a 20' by 20' heated swimming pool. Beyond this, extending to the side was the main area of lawns and arboretum. In the house the kitchen, bathrooms, living room and three bedrooms were equally spacious and well equipped. By just sacrificing some of the extensive internal space, the house could easily have accommodated five bedrooms instead of three.

The property was accessed through a gravel drive which joined a relatively short lane, connected on the west side to the main road leading to Lidmouth town, the other eastern stretch meandering through the country for two miles before meeting the small hamlet of East Linkin.

The estate agent guided him around the house and grounds with the air of a museum curator, every now and again exclaiming with delight as he came to either 'a splendid view' from one of the windows, or a particularly 'fine architectural feature' of the house. The agent was wasting his time – there was no need for persuasive or flattering terms; what he saw was far more than the estate agent saw – it had the all the qualities implicit in his dream, and now he faced a dilemma.

"What did you say this property is priced at?" he asked as the agent invited him into the second on-suite bathroom.

The agents black-rimmed spectacles gave him the air of a frozen scuba diver, especially since the glasses were set against a puce white skin and thin bloodless lips.

"Well, Mr. Enfield, somewhat above your instructions I'm afraid, but I thought this property might interest you just the same."

Yes it did, but interest was no good if the bank balance prohibited further involvement.

"Tell me, what's the history of this property, I note it isn't furnished so I assume the owners have gone to greener pastures."

The agent paused in front of the pristine, chrome filled shower cubicle.

"Not pastures green I'm afraid Mr. Enfield – rather a disastrous story altogether. Without going into details, the property is in the hands of the crown agents – there were no family beneficiaries you see – no extant wills."

It was a chilling statement. His heart sank a little; reading between the lines was a tragic story that for him could change everything. Perhaps it explained the atmosphere that pervaded every corner and empty room in the house – was he being oversensitive? To him there was a definite sadness in the air, as though he was in the company of something that harboured a deep and abiding sense of loss.

"I'm interested in this house but unless I know it's full history I can't even begin to think seriously about how I might purchase it. Please, tell me everything."

The agent looked away for a moment, licking his lips and reluctant to begin a tale which could jeopardise a potential sale.

"If you are really interested in this house – I'm sure things being as they are you could secure it for a very reasonable price. Crown estates have no objection to an offer well below the asking price; it has been on the market for some time."

"Yes, that's good to know, but I have no intention of making an offer of any kind unless I know what is behind the current situation with the Crown estates. Please, disclose the history and background, or I'm afraid we are going nowhere."

The agent seemed to brace himself, a perceptible stiffening of his body accompanied by an even greater whitening of his already colourless face. He visibly, and somewhat theatrically, took breath.

"The Ferguson family, two parents and three children, all girls incidentally, were on Flight 554 – perhaps you will remember the news from about six months back? The aircraft went missing over the north Canadian wastes. The crash was in such a remote location the search aircraft took eleven days to find it. Only the dead were located at the spot, fourteen passengers were unaccounted for and when at last the remnants of the party made it south a month later there were only nine left. Apparently the whole Ferguson family were among the first victims – need I say more?"

It was an horrific story and needed no embellishments.

"No kith and kin?" he asked.

"None that I know of, it seems both the father and mother were orphans from childhood and had no known living relatives."

"I see."

They both stood silently for a short time in the shower room, both in their own way considering the outcome of the revelation.

He was at first alienated by the horror that had befallen the owners of the house – it explained why interest in the house had waned when prospective buyers learned what the house represented. No doubt the house was viewed by many as tainted by the tragedy that was attached to it. Yet he knew what many could not, that there was another side to the coin. That regardless of the depths of misfortune that could so easily mar life, hope sprang eternal and from ruin. No matter cataclysm and disaster, there was always the promise of salvation, redemption and renewal.

"Look – tell me what figure might be acceptable, if it's close to what I can afford, and that includes running costs – I will seriously consider it."

The agent smiled, it was an unexpectedly pleasant smile and had no indication of being triumphal.

"Unfortunately I can't tell you immediately Mr. Enfield. The one great failing of this location is that there is very poor signal coverage for mobile phones. "However, I will let you know very soon – I'm sure something can be arranged."

9

As he negotiated the short lane up to the drive and dropped a gear he realised that he had somehow started to experience a significant change in his luck.

The 'E Type' Jaguar, which he was now driving, had appeared before him as he had meandered around Lidmouth. Even now he felt his finding it was manna from heaven.

He had been killing time furniture hunting in yet more charity shops while he waited for developments. The chance to buy a car never occurred to him. The chance to become the owner of a car he would ordinarily only dream of, was so distant a thought it might well have been at the other end of the universe.

Its nose had been protruding from what appeared to be the side garage of a sizable terraced house, buried down a narrow off-the-road lane on the outskirts of town. He had just vacated the premises of a small second hand electrical dealer and, as he passed the lane, had stood captivated, having espied the unmistakable feminine contour of the vehicle's front third.

Curious to know if his observation had been right, and wanting to satisfy his interest, he wandered down the lane and stopped adjacent to what was in fact an open carport. To his astonishment he found himself staring at a 1963 series1 3.8 Le Mans 'E Type' convertible. As far as he could see it still presented a virtually unblemished condition; the chromium spokes on the wheels gleamed, the tyres were immaculate and the bodywork had no obvious deficiencies other than the rather dirty, somewhat tired surface of the metallic red paintwork. He stood and enjoyed the elegant streamlined shape for a good five minutes, remembering how as a younger man he had dreamed he might one day be the owner of such a beautiful car. For at least five minutes, he inspected the car from the lane and, reluctant to go closer and risk the owners wrath, he satisfied his interest with one last look and grudgingly turned away. As he was about to return along the lane, the curtains of the bay window in the house moved and a woman's face appeared.

He waited, intent on staying long enough to apologise to her if she came out and complained he had disturbed her.

The front door opened and a tallish, dark and very attractive women in her middle years, dressed in a beige, figure defining two piece suit, appeared. She had a wide, open, face, broad lips and blue, almost turquoise, eyes. Her make up was simple but complimented her natural skin tones.

"I hoped you would be here earlier." she said "Was the train late?"

He was taken aback - there was no reprimand in her voice, only a certain disappointment and a clear misapprehending of his status.

"I'm terribly sorry...I only stopped to look at the car. I always loved E Types...I don't think I'm the person you think I am."

She froze for a moment, her face suddenly caught in embarrassment.

"Your not Mr. Laithwaite then - the classic car dealer?"

"No, I'm sorry - was he due here to see the car?"

She nodded. "I was hoping for a good price. It was my husbands - his pride and joy. My husband John spent years keeping it up to scratch. Mr. Laithwaite was going to value it and have it moved

45

if he could find a buyer at the right price."

"Have it moved? It has a fault then – won't it start?"

Her lips spread in a regretful smile.

"I tried to get it to start after my husband passed away, but somehow it knew he'd gone and refused to do anything without him."

Again, she smiled. It was a sad but understanding smile – as though she completely empathised with the car.

For a moment, he began the automatic process of a polite farewell and disengagement; of offering his sympathy and condolences and then departing apologetically. And yet, he was suddenly of a different mind.

Why not?

Why not see?

"Have you got the keys? May I try for you?"

"Well...are you a mechanic?"

"No, but I have some experience with cars that refuse to start." and in truth there was no disputing that statement. He'd seldom owned a car that wasn't worn out and cantankerous.

She turned and walked back into the house only to reappear almost an instant later. She handed him a single key attached to a round fob engraved with the face of a Jaguar.

He nodded his thanks and walked into the carport alongside the open car, and lent into the drivers seat. He looked along the dashboard and located the ignition. As he pushed home the key he felt a surge of surreal empathy and whispered, "Come on girl – I know what it's like to grieve. It's time for you to have a new life – come on!"

He twisted the ignition key and as the engine turned over he had a feeling it wanted to oblige, but even though the engine cranked wilfully, for a good ten seconds nothing happened. He was just about to release the ignition when he felt the rumble of the exhaust and the engine fired. It kept going, but after a short time it coughed and began to run erratically, finally stopping with a lumpy resentment that shook the car.

But, it didn't matter; he could see why there was a problem.

"No fuel - the fuel gauge is reading zero. I would guess that with some petrol in the tank she'd be okay."

The woman had stood by, her eyes glistening with fond memories of times past. As the car had started, she had even stepped forward, as if anticipating the same pleasurable routine she had always enjoyed with her late husband. Now she stayed silent and unmoving as he handed back the key.

"Lovely car - original too and very valuable, as it stands you could be looking at £100,000."

He smiled at her and stood back waiting for the right moment to tear himself away from his dream car and the woman's sadness.

"Would you buy it?" she said, almost in a whisper.

There was no argument - if only he could.

"I would love to...but I don't have that kind of money I'm sorry to say."

She stood pensive, as if she was making a profound decision.

"What could you pay for it?"

It was a question he had never contemplated - it was so beyond his resources that he would never have considered it.

"I really don't know, I doubt more than twenty thousand and that, to be honest, would be nothing like what you should expect - it would be criminal - you would be giving it way."

She said nothing for a few seconds and then asked, "If you owned it, would you care for it? As if it was precious - as if you valued it as more than just a car?"

It was a question that he knew for him had only one immediate response, and one that would be the absolute truth.

"Definitely, absolutely – if the car was mine you can be assured it would be my pride and joy too. Were it mine I would even promise you a few jollies in it – we would make a day of it every now and again."

His last remark saw her face brighten and some of the sadness fled from her eyes.

"If you will keep your word on that, come back later and give me £20,000 and the car is yours. It's Ella by the way."

He was staggered and delighted at the same time.

"Oh, thank you Ella – you've made my day. I'm so grateful."

She gave him another mournful smile.

"No, the car is called Ella, I'm Catherine!"

He felt no awkwardness only gratitude. Unable to completely express all his thanks, he leant forward and kissed her on the cheek. Another meek smile came to her lips as he assured her he would return shortly with the money. He turned to walk away, and as he took another unbelieving look at the car, he could have sworn that the paintwork had brightened.

Well, the car definitely had been manna from heaven.

He'd spent more on it than he had intended, but it was all good, solid self-indulgence. What with the twenty thousand payment, insurance, tax and much more work on the car, he had gone beyond thirty thousand; but now it was close to perfection. A good service, including rusted brake replacements after the long lay-up, had restored performance and the body was now gleaming from a paint restoration and re-polish in a professional body shop. It had been valeted professionally too, so that now it appeared to be in better than showroom condition. The engine and transmission were sweet, the previous owner having doted on its servicing and maintenance. He was still unable to overcome the thrill and elation he felt every time he started to drive it, nor the feeling of relief the way other matters had transpired.

As the car was being restored, he was notified that he had bought the house!

His recent acquisition of the house was the outcome of a protracted negotiation by his agent, which had been reluctantly agreed by the crown at almost £75,000 below the asking price, on the basis that he offered immediate cash and seemed the only genuine interest.

Perhaps he'd been the only one that had sensed the depressed aura of the house – the loneliness that had enveloped the whole structure as if it was weeping. But orphaned or not, he intended to form an alliance with the house. In short – he intended to give it a purpose.

The misfortune that had befallen the original owners of the house was for him no ill omen, being simply what he recognised from his own background as someone else's cursed existence. Why other prospective buyers of the property had shied away, particularly because of the way the house come on to the market or its atmosphere, he failed to understand.

Undoubtedly they had a different and far too fearful outlook compared to him. He had experienced too much in the way of tragedy and misfortune to believe someone else's hard luck could make ones own fate any worse.

He was now fatalistic enough to know that although he could not change what was to happen to him, yet as things stood he had an inkling of a revelation, that it was not always the case that ones fate was in the hands of some vindictive force. There was nothing in the house to portend disaster and the future wasn't inevitably, or inescapably, written in ominous terms.

He thought back to his earlier life, of the constant threat of adversity and disaster, financial and otherwise, that had eventually caught up with him. The loss of Betty, Bobby and the time he spent with Isaac and Janet had covered such a traumatic period that surviving it had taught him one salutary thing - that King Solomon's observation was probably true - that *'all things must pass'*.

Deep down in his soul he held on tight to a hunch that any ill-fated life could be rejuvenated, or at least prevented from being predestined as hopeless.

His new 'E Type' exemplified this belief - after all, like him, it had waited a long time in deep mourning before being told that it was to have a hopeful future. The car seemed to respond to his sentiments, seemed to be sentient enough to understand him. Not for one second did he dismiss the view that the car was a conscious entity - that was how he treated Ella, and that was how she appeared to react.

He'd parked on the small circular roundabout at the front of the house. Now with the engine silent and the car facing the front door, he sat staring at the overall structural symmetry of the house, a symmetry that had first attracted his interest. Yes, he liked all of it - the exact fundamental reason why this was so he could not fully identify or detail, but it represented his ideal. The house, or something like it, had always been in his minds eye even in those days when he sweated out the nine to five.

Now, sitting in Ella's enveloping drivers seat, he held the front door key in his right hand and the car's ignition in his left. He kept lifting them both, feeling their respective weights against the palm of each hand. It was, he knew, a kind of ritual, each key signifying a recompense for surviving, for learning resilience, for reaching a stage where all things considered, he should not have been. But, the crooked and painful path to achieving this had been followed, and now he could permit himself some of the pleasure he had been gifted – it was time to live.

He exited the car and took another look at the house, it's boundary privet hedges and the variegated Acers that flanked symmetrical flower borders and open side lawns. Then, in what was the virtual silence of his new surroundings, he slipped the key into the lock of the heavy oak frame storm door, and heard the interlocks smoothly glide back.

Possession of the key meant possession of the house, and as he walked into the hallway and revelled in his good fortune it dawned on him that while the house was empty, he had the opportunity to make his peace with it. He was to do all he could to placate its likely resentment of an intruder, to let it know he understood why it exuded a melancholy mood; that its lost family was, if not mourned by it's new inhabitant, was at least empathised with it.

He let the silence settle over him, allowing the depressing, melancholic atmosphere swell and overlap him.

He then took breath and began his plea.

"I know what happened." he called out – and then he waited, while a few seconds of time limped by.

"You had your happiness and contentment ripped from you when you lost your family – believe me, it happened to me too. Yes, I was crushed by sorrow, drowned in despair, and had my life shattered after the loss of everything I loved. I too know what it is to grieve – to grieve so much that you would welcome death if it came for you. Yet, I promise you now that our collective hurt and mourning is over. We cannot bring back the past, but you and I now have a future. I want us to restore some of the joy we both lost but still deserve to have.

Listen to me house – I feel a bond between us.

You and I were brought together through the agency, and from the proceeds, of misery. But, I know a man who suffered much more than we have, and because of his example I was restored and able to live again. I will make you live again too – that is, if you will let me. Trust me, I mean what I say."

His last words were spoken as loudly as he could without shouting, and they echoed back to him as the sound reverberated through every open door and room in the house.

Inwardly he knew that a neutral observer listening to him would have asked if he had drifted into a kind of insanity. Talking to an inanimate structure and treating it as though it was sentient might mark him out as a suitable case for treatment. And yet, he felt no embarrassment or shame, the ritual was a healing and therapeutic procedure, in short it was wholly cathartic and his emotions told him it was what he had to do.

He waited, as if anticipating a vocal response, but there was none and as his words died away everything reverted to a heavy, if not oppressive silence. For a few seconds he thought perhaps the house might reply; but almost certainly that was too much to expect and truthfully, therein lay madness. It was only as he made his way into the kitchen that he distinctly heard a noise from somewhere above. It was the central heating boiler activating and the water pump starting up. It was followed by the radiator pipes coming to life with a gurgling of running water. The sound was eerie and indistinct, but he could have sworn that as the flow started, what came to his ears sounded like a 'Yes'.

10

At long last he had a bed!

Two weeks of searching the town's stores and shops for all the essential furniture he needed, at a price he thought was affordable, had resulted in a large leather lounge suite (second hand), two elegant sideboards, a coffee table, an intricately carved welsh dresser and an attractive white bedroom flat pack suite; consisting of two bedside tables, a dressing table and two large wardrobes. The house had carpets and curtains fitted and he had no need to decorate otherwise.

A new mattress and some new bedding laid on the bedroom floor had served to provide a comfortable nights sleep for the interim as he began his domestic foray. Now he had a very fresh hardwood double bed, courtesy of a charity shop he had stumbled across. The shop was tucked away in a remote back street that he discovered during his hunt for kitchen appliances. It had everything an ardent cook would want to equip a kitchen. Following the discovery he had been able to stock his kitchen with all the essentials including by all appearances, a new refrigerator and freezer, electric kettle, sundry bits of crockery, mugs, tea services, cutlery and so on. It even provided a farmhouse kitchen table – a hundred years old, it was sturdy and beautifully grained and preserved.

Nevertheless, though he was moving towards the day when he was fully equipped and self-contained, as the deliveries of his items – and the organisation and construction of everything – rapidly overtook his days, he was still obliged to drive into town and order his meals from a café or restaurant menu.

He was now well adjusted to his new environment, and had no sense that the house had not accepted his 'proposal'. It seemed warmer and more inviting than before; even the warm and mellow sunlight coming through the windows seemed that much brighter and, as more and more furniture and ornaments were added to each room, it seemed the house revelled in it. There was even the feeling that the house welcomed him back every time he returned from a sojourn into town; to him the warm reception was virtually palpable. Indeed, now he thought of the house as 'home' and looked forward to making it his ideal.

As all the flat pack construction, picture hanging, distribution of bedding, clothes and so on became less of a chore and less arduous, he had moments of respite. He soon began to think of what needed to be done to keep up the gardens and the swimming pool – he had been so busy, both had been severely neglected.

Equally, as the tedious understanding of all the new remote controls that operated his shiny new video and audio systems started to become familiar, he found himself thinking about what was to be done beyond the upkeep of everything domestic.

He was a useless cook and had no idea how to iron clothing or run a washing machine. Not only that, though he loved the garden with its lawns and arboretum, it was destined to become a wilderness if he left its upkeep for too long. But, more importantly, he needed something else besides managing his domestic duties rigorously – he needed an objective, a long-term purpose.

He had always been aware that though he had gained massively in equity – on what constituted a comparatively tight capital budget – he was effectively of independent means only as long as his disposable income exceeded his outgoings. He had to avoid Micawber's syndrome.

For the moment, at least, he could cope with all household and motoring costs, and still have a reasonable margin of money for all personal and pleasure purposes. However, from a pessimistic standpoint he could see a day when he might be forced to consider gainful employment again and that was, as things stood, anathema.

Every now and again, when he had exerted himself in the house, or attempted to overload his back or right leg, he was painfully reminded of what it had cost to arrive at where he was now. How in every hospital bed, rehabilitation centre or funeral he had occupied or attended, he had sworn that never again would he allow the slavery of a nine to five job re-impose on him the blighted life he and his beloved family had endured.

So that was it – if he had to go back to work, it would be on his terms and for his reasons only, and on no one else's! He would certainly never sell his electrical engineering expertise as cheaply as he had before. There was no Bobby or Betty to support, no mortgage, no un-payable bills and no chance of yet another creaky business likely to force him on to short time or redundancy.

However, for the interim, he had much to do, and as he finalised all the house fittings and effects, he started to list what else he needed to focus on.

The kitchen window looked out on the garden and as the midday sunshine lit up an array of blue and green conifers, exotic shrubs, trees and verdant vegetation, and sparkled off the wet pathways and grassed areas, he realised that he'd had insufficient time to explore the whole area.

He was tempted to enjoy the sunlit moment outside and take the opportunity to attend to numbers two and three on his long list of 'things to do'. That was to check the pool, its glass covered conservatory, and all the gardens, arboretum, outhouses and sheds.

He was praying that all the original garden machinery and suchlike were still intact. He assumed that if they had not been spirited away during the time the house was empty, then they were ensconced in one of the outhouses. He remained puzzled as to why the Ferguson's furniture and all other effects and chattels had vanished from the house before he had arrived. If it were true of all the garden tools and machinery, he was somewhat stuck. After all his self indulgent extravagances with Ella and extensive expenditure on household effects, there simply wasn't enough spare cash to immediately invest in everything that would be needed to tend over two acres of gardens; so as he exited the rear door onto the patio, and made his way to the pool, he had his fingers tightly crossed.

It took him a few minutes to find which of the keys on the many key rings he had inherited fitted the pool double doors. As he finally felt the lock turn he pulled at the door with a sense of expectation. The whole pool housing was wood grain uPVC on the outside, an effect so realistic from a distance he had never suspected it – neither during the original viewing of the house, or currently. Inside the effect was even more impressive, all the inside plastic surfaces being gloriously brilliant white and bouncing light from the extensive roof glazing. The smell of chlorine was evident and the pool itself was full; a still, blue, flat expanse of water surrounded by a two metre wide, slip-proof tiled walkway that led to the diving platforms at the other end of the pool. Behind the diving platforms he could see an end wall of vertical wood-like slats merging into the roof glazing. At ground level were three doors and he guessed that one of them was for the pool filtration and chlorination unit.

He made his way forward and tried the first door he came to. None of his keys would fit but he was luckier with the other two – one duly being the filtration room, the other a reasonably big changing and shower room. The latter he noted with some sense of sadness had a teddy bear and a small swimming costume still laying on one of the wooden wall benches.

All that remained was the one locked door and he was tempted to leave it for another day, wanting to find the garden machinery first. However, he was too curious to know what was behind the door, and too impatient not to eliminate it immediately.

Once again, he tried all of his keys but none appeared to turn or operate the lock. It was only as he pushed hard on the handle in exasperation that he felt it suddenly give way and the door opened. He let out a gasp of annoyance – it had always been unlocked. All the same, his success was short lived.

As he viewed the interior it was with disappointment – just a dark and musty smelling storage room, which apart from a partly inflated life ring propped against the right hand wall, was completely empty. He was about vacate the room when he realised that its dimensions were much smaller than the other two. He assumed that the lost space must be because there was some other area or room to the side of the pool conservatory. Nevertheless, as he began to turn away he caught the gleam of something metallic halfway up the back wall.

There was a light globe above his head and finding a switch to the left of the doorframe, he pressed it.

The onset of bright light confirmed his observation – a small circular metal disc was protruding from the wall. It was similar to a Yale lock but had two slots one above the other. He scrutinized the lock and its surroundings but was unable to discern any reason for it being there, the wall did not appear to be anything but a wall – the disc certainly did not seem to provide access to a door or cupboard.

Intrigued, he began to look through all the house keys he was carrying but none resembled a Yale. Only the two front door keys he kept separately in the house on a hallway telephone stand were Yale's, and he doubted that they would fit. He ran his fingers tentatively over the metal plate, testing the surface for movement, and as one finger pushed forward and obscured the two slots, he suddenly heard the low whine of a motor coming from his left. To his astonishment, the wall to his left began to slide up into the ceiling. He stood bewildered as the vanishing wall slowly revealed another room, with much the same dimensions and panelled walling as the one he stood in. The difference was that the new room contained a desk, a personal computer, a swivel high backed chair and to the right of the desk a three draw filing cabinet. There were pictures on the wall, a filing tray and a desk lamp standing to the left of a desk mounted VDU.

He moved in to inspect his find, surprised that unlike the rest of the house these items had remained 'in situ' while every other part had been emptied. It was strange, in either case. Not least, that the door to the room and the access to this hidden, 'secret', room had both been left accessible. Had they been secured, he would not be standing where he was now.

The pictures on the wall first drew his attention. There were three; family groups in each case and each showing a smiling couple with three children. In the first the mother (he assumed) was a very attractive flaxen haired female in her mid thirties. She exhibited a trim figure and was dressed in a summer frock. The man, maybe a little older, had light, well-trimmed hair; clear skin and a broad, wide lipped smile showing well-scrubbed teeth. He wore Hawaiian shorts and a red T-shirt. The children, all of similar sub-teen age sat at the feet of the couple and were dressed for the beach. The background was not clear but could have been a holiday resort. The other two pictures were matt computer colour prints – apparently the same five but normally dressed and with the side of the house in the background, obviously taken in the garden on a sunny day.

Checking the filing cabinet he opened all three draws to find each of them disappointedly empty. Turning to the computer, he looked to see where the mains lead terminated and noted it was plugged in to a single wall socked with the switch showing red. He pressed the PC power button, being rewarded with the drone of fans and hard drives starting up. As he stared at the screen the motherboard logo came up and shortly after that the desktop background and available applications appeared, The desktop background was intriguing – a deeply attractive dark haired woman in her twenties, carrying a large bouquet of red roses contrasting against her upper half; she wore an elegant cream jacket. The woman was pictured against a park like setting on a bright, leafy sunlit day. She was smiling – a smile of delight and perhaps gratitude – whatever the case, he was captivated, she was lovely.

He scanned the screen, noting what application tiles had appeared. It was a sparse collection; the usual Microsoft applications were there but nothing of any real note. Only the one drew his attention – 'You have e-mails' flashed gently, and without a second thought he moved the mouse cursor over the flashing tile and left clicked the mouse.

The listing was as sparse as the applications – three unread emails were presented and each of them was entitled the same way – 'From Irina'.

11

He opened the most recent email – from some two months back – and after the screen had blanked for a moment it suddenly presented a web page showing a woman's picture against a ochre background and some text. To his amazement, the picture was of the same woman seen on the desktop background, only this time dressed in a swimsuit and photographed against a turquoise sea and a sand covered beach. She took the greater area of the picture and appeared standing in a somewhat erotic pose. Even with the bleaching effect of a powerful sun, her tan and perfect figure made for a stunning appearance. He could not help wondering what connection she had with the Fergusons, the earlier house owners. It was as he saw the website banner – *Eastern European Brides* – that the woman's appearance becameobvious, someone had been in contact with an online marriage site.

Now he was the more intrigued, and yet puzzled.

Standing slightly awkwardly as he bent towards the screen his back and right leg began to remind him of past misfortunes and he dropped thankfully into the swivel chair in front of the desk.

The message, in black medium font below the woman's picture was short and poignant. *'Darling – why have you stopped writing? I'm so unhappy – I thought we were to meet? I have the GIFT. Irina'*

Clicking on the page back button, he returned to the message listing and activated the next message.

'Darling – is there something wrong? I am ready to meet you in

Odessa. Please confirm. Irina'

As he opened the most recent of the three messages he began to understand the implication *'I understand – received your suggestions. I will wait to hear from you via the website for your flight times into Odessa. I cannot tell you how happy I am to be meeting you at last. Thank you darling, I have the GIFT – I 2 will always be yours. Irina.'*

He sat staring at the last message, wondering how it had come to be that he was looking at something intimate and private – something that should never have had been overlooked by the estate agent in his survey of the house.

Come to that, who had last used the system? Regardless of the personal messages, it was a valuable PC system and no one would ordinarily abandon it. And why the strange use of semantic shorthand *"Thank you darling, I have the GIFT – I 2 will always be yours. Irina."*

He couldn't imagine the pasty-faced estate agent daring to use a covert Internet access secretly installed in a house he was expecting to sell; and then forgetting to remove it before being discovered. Nor could he understand how the system had been left intact if neither the estate agent nor the previous house owners had set up and used the system. As his thoughts rambled, he returned to his original query. If the house had been emptied of all commodities and furnishings, how was it that the PC had escaped removal?

It was only as he remembered the tragic story of the Fergusons related to him by the estate agent that a possible, explanation began to form. But the idea had no more taken hold before he heard the whine of a motor and the sliding wall behind him began to move down.

He came to his feet immediately, kicking back on the chair, half in surprise, half in panic. He could still see into the first room and there was nothing there – nor was the metal sensor on the wall obstructed by anything or anyone. But, it was too late. The wall had descended swiftly and smoothly onto the floor, closing off the opening before he was able to react – not that he would have been physically agile enough to dash through the remaining gap, even if he had been in time.

He stood astonished at the event; now, facing a blank wall, he realised that he was confined to the room with no apparent escape.

And yet, he was sure that there had to be a way out. Nobody in their right mind would create a secret room that constituted a trap for themselves. And, since he had not discovered any mummified bodies when the wall had lifted, he was the more convinced of his belief.

Once again he scanned the room, searching for another metal button identical to the one on the first room's wall.

Searching, he found nothing on the walls, behind the filing cabinet or behind the pictures – it had to be elsewhere. Carefully sinking down onto his knees, he inspected the wall area behind the computer desk. As he did so, he was suddenly struck by the maze of wiring linking all the PC units.

One seemed out of place, and as he rolled onto his back and wriggled further in under the desk, he used his fingers to trace its path. It terminated at the under surface of the desktop midway along its length, and as his fingers touched what appeared to be the side of a metal box, he heard the familiar whine of a motor. Twisting his head he looked at the opposite wall and, to his relief, it was lifting.

Now he understood – his electrical training providing the answer. The sensor was coupled to a delay circuit that initiated the wall closing sequence so that it automatically closed the door after a fixed time. By sitting in the computer chair the sensor would normally detect an occupant and override the closing sequence – but he had stood by the computer for some time and had only sat down for a short period. That, it seemed, forced the closing sequence to take priority over the opening sequence.

He took one more look at the messages on the screen and decided he needed time to think – there were too many mysteries about his current discovery, and he had other priorities as yet. His 'things to do' list was overruling his curiosity at the moment, particularly since he had not the slightest idea of what to make of, or what to do, with the secret room and its implications.

No, for the moment, and frustratingly, tracking down a way of cutting the grass was paramount and something that could not be ignored any longer.

Closing the outer door of the secret room he heard the faint sound of a motor and had the satisfaction of realising his hunch about the delayed operation of the sliding wall was right. As he skirted the pool towards the exit, he could not help thinking how odd fate and providence played their game. He was no gambler, but he had a feeling that he could bet on the outcome of his discovery. And for some reason, it felt ominous.

12

The hot water made a comforting gurgle as it slurped into the coffee cup, forming a creamy brown, aromatic bliss as he added the milk.

Cool enough, he sipped it with pleasure as he looked out of the kitchen window on the perfectly manicured garden lawns and edgings.

He'd worked hard over the last few days even to the point of servicing the two tractor mowers and two powered hand mowers. To his absolute delight, he'd found all four crammed – and neglected – in one of the larger outhouses by the garage.

The grass was cut, the house cleaned and even the entrance and gravel driveway up to the house had been raked and tidied. There was hardly a tree leaf out of place (he had pruned diligently) and Ella, his beloved E Type, had been polished until his back ached and the car gleamed. It had all been physically demanding and his efforts had been rewarded not only by satisfaction but also by raw reminders of his past injuries which were only subdued by the powerful analgesics he had been prescribed. Less painful, and the more satisfactory, was his growing confidence in his cooking. His choice of groceries, and a growing independence from convenience foods, had improved with only a modicum of embarrassing culinary exploits, enabling him to reduce his trips to the town's cafes and restaurants to a minimum. He was almost self-sufficient!

Now, as he enjoyed his coffee, he settled back to thinking about the pool and it's curious secret.

As to the pool, he was inclined to drain it and shut off the underwater heating to avoid the forthcoming winter electricity and maintenance bills, but he was determined to enjoy a few swims before the fateful day. While that was open to him, he had to consider what to do with the hidden computer and it's intriguing messages. One thing seemed apparent, a very attractive woman somewhere in Odessa, if she and the content of the messages were to be believed, was deeply disappointed by the non-arrival of the PC's operator. He had to admit it; ever since he had seen the picture of her on the VDU screen, he had held her picture in his mind. She was what he might term 'his type' - a body shape similar to Betty's when they had first met and a very open and natural smile. Her eyes gave a sense of honesty and though her pose was erotic, it was a little understated and a little coy, implying that she never ordinarily paraded her sexuality. That aspect he found even more alluring, and he was aware that the picture of Irina, the lovely Odessa woman, had prompted his recent, somewhat erotic nightly dreams.

However, that in itself engendered remorse; he was grateful that his recent dreams, full of fragments of recent miserable experiences, had been displaced by far more pleasant images. Yet, was he being genuinely realistic?

Part of his reluctance to immediately try to take the place of the girl's previous contact was the chance of rejection. Would she believe his excuse for making contact? Would she be interested in him as a possible partner?

He was quick to remind himself that Odessa, a port by the Black Sea in the South Ukraine, was a very long way off. Not only that, but he had to consider the possible spread of civil conflict. It was pointless him harbouring optimistic thoughts about the Odessa girl if everything he thought might be true about the situation was prone to change and was no longer valid.

In any case, what made him think that the last message was still applicable – unbeknown to him she could (by now) be comfortably, and lovingly ensconced in an Odessa hotel with the phantom PC operator; never needing to send a final message saying *'so glad you arrived at last'!*

But, that was it of course – he didn't know for sure, and he wanted to find out. As to that, he needed to know why the PC had been abandoned as it had, and by whom. Why the secret room – why the need to hide the exchange with the Odessa woman?

The joke was that if his quest did turn out to be futile, at least had had the consolation of gaining a fairly upmarket PC – ironic though it might be.

If not, and she was still anticipating contact, there might be possibilities. Perhaps this time fate would tire of once again handing him the losing card; so far he was starting to win and he liked what was for him a rare sense of optimism.

Yet for all that, there was another impediment to opening contact, he feared allowing Betty and Bobby to become a receding memory. Yes, he missed Betty, and although there was an ache still in his heart, her loss hid the truth that after being stirred by the Odessa woman, he could now see the years stretching ahead with only himself for company. Did he relish the thought of being alone and rattling around in the house forever? No – but there was a distinct chance it would happen! Yet, the alternative, that of finding another partner, would mean harbouring a persistent sense of guilt – betraying Betty's memory and all it represented.

He had reluctantly resigned himself to remaining a widower, having instinctively held on to the belief that to venerate Betty's memory through a solitary life was a noble and proper sacrifice.

But that said, would she have wanted him to die a lonely old man? As he thought back to her gentle and caring nature, he began to think not. He was the one holding candles at her alter, and it was his guilt that governed his thinking. Perhaps she would understand – God knew she had always wanted both of them to be happy. It could be that a little counselling from an impartial source would help.

He was soon to pick up Catherine for the first of the promised jollies in Ella. If she was in favour of him pursuing the Odessa connection, and she gave him her blessing, he would try it. If his luck held, the Odessa woman could be the pathway to another, happier, life.

Dear God, he hoped so!

13

She smiled at him across the tea table, and he had to admit she was a very attractive woman. It was a long time since he had enjoyed the smell of a woman – the hint of her perfume in the car had been cathartic, provoking memories from days he dared not resurrect. And yet, it was wonderful, and as he looked into her broad, perfectly symmetrical, face with its dark eyes, red voluptuous lips and grey flecked hair he could not deny that for a middle aged woman she looked exceptional.

They stopped at a park like garden centre on the outskirts of town and took a leisurely tour through a lush jungle of vibrant blooms, rampant pot plants and blossom-laden late blooming saplings. As the afternoon sun began to beat down they made there way to the garden centre's coffee shop and to their relief found it air-conditioned and cool.

Catherine was clearly enjoying her outing, and as he sat opposite her, he found some pleasure in watching her methodically stir the tea, served to them in a large blue ceramic teapot. They had chosen to sit around a large Victorian cast iron table in the coffee shop, bedecked with a stiff tablecloth sporting a brightly coloured blossom motif. And yet for all their table's cozy location, he felt some regret that their opposite seating positions around the table was a little less intimate than he would have liked. However, the low murmur of other patrons' tête-à-tête's did not interfere with his and Catherine's conversation. He trusted that their own two voices remained equally subdued and private.

"Ella, its the name my late husband gave the car because it was an E Type -E for Ella."

He listened avidly to Catherine's story of her late husband's heroic efforts to fulfil his dream of getting an example of the E Type, a car he had first seen as a boy, and of how he had saved year in and year out for the moment he could bid for a less perfect one but one ripe for restoration. Then the moment of serendipity had arrived, when an elderly cousin told him about a late friend who, bereft of family, had bequeathed said cousin his estate. Locked in a garage at the deceased's home, and untouched for years, was a dust and detritus covered 1963 series1 E type.

Did her husband want the care of it, asked the cousin?

Dear God, she recounted – he would have killed for it.

The money her husband had originally saved was hardly touched even after transporting the car, and so he was able to carry out a reasonable restoration and repay Catherine's years of neglect and financial deprivation with some generosity. She didn't mind that much, she said, she had married for love – even though he was much older than her.

Spreading more cream and jam onto a thickly cut half scone he nodded in appreciation as he empathised with the late owner's single-minded obsession. As she spoke, the rest of the coffee shop patrons appeared to have concluded their conversations. It was not only he who appeared to be enjoying the story – everyone else in the coffee shop hardly made a sound as Catherine cheerfully enlivened the atmosphere with the ongoing tale of her husband's second childhood; of clocking up speeding tickets and repeated police lectures, and how he revelled in the sheer pleasure of outrunning everything except the odd super car. Even into his late sixties, she said, he would think nothing of a midnight run on a nearly deserted motorway, just for the pleasure of seeing the speedometer flick past one hundred and twenty miles per hour. He even kept a reserve of money, just to pay the fines he knew he was likely to attract and to pay for expensive but clever lawyers. His lawyers loved him, they always managed to argue for the minimum sentence on conviction – in fact they never really lost a case – somehow he kept his license. These sojourns with Ella, Catherine observed, were solitary, she would not compete with her husband's 'other' woman. She simply stayed at home and prayed for his safe return.

Catherine had stayed quiet for a moment as her reminiscences came to an end, and he saw in her face what he recognised from his own recent episodes of grief and emptiness; the return of overriding sorrow that only a sudden and colossal upsurge of reminded loss could instigate.

He waited in respectful silence as she grappled with her emotions. When at last she had composed herself and restored her earlier mood, she looked at him and nodded her head.

"More tea?"

He acknowledged by handing over his cup.

"I'm glad to see you are a much less speed obsessed driver than my husband was." Catherine said in a bright voice that reflected her quickly restored outlook. She paused as she poured well-infused tea from the pot. "And Ella, my goodness, she does look pristine and drives so well."

"Well, perhaps it's the fact that I'm too fond of the car to risk upsetting it with aggressive driving – to me she is too beautiful to cane. I want her to be my last car – I'll never want to drive anything else. More to the point, I've had my fair share of nasty outcomes when driving. I don't want to end up in hospital again."

Catherine gave a sympathetic look.

"You've had some bad accidents?"

He hesitated, and then conceded.

"Oh yes, uncountable weeks in hospital after a car collision and on the day I was discharged I was the victim of a freak explosion due to a gas leak in my house. I was re-admitted for another four months; not to mention the months of interminable rehab."

He smiled inwardly, knowing he had made the mistake of inviting many more questions.

Catherine leaned across the table and in a sympathetic gesture put her hand over his. As she let go, she asked,

"Is that the reason you have no family?"

He began stirring sugar into his cup.

"It shows I know - I never told you I was a widower but I suppose you saw the signs."

"Well, we had the limited contact when you bought Ella so it was not completely obvious, but the absence of your better half at the time, and your subsequent failure to mention her did speak volumes. I'm so sorry to hear you lost your wife."

"Yeah, my son and all, I lost my family in the same disaster that resulted in my second hospitalisation. I'm sorry for you too - from what you say your loss was equally devastating. I know that nothing like that leaves us any less than shattered. When I'm a little further from the rawness of it, I'll give you the full chapter and all the verses."

Catherine gave a wane, compassionate smile and stirred her tea.

"Of course Peter, when you are ready, if you want to. Incidentally, where are you living now? Are you comfortable?"

Grateful for the change of subject he nodded his head. "Yes, thank you - found myself a nice place, just outside of

East Linkin, just off from the main road. It's big, and will take a lot of my time to keep it up, but I like it. You must visit one day – have a swim in the pool."

"Pool – did you say pool? Goodness, it must be quite a place!"

"Well, it's not over-big in the sense of being a mansion, but it is well proportioned and has very big gardens. The main feature is that it is very secluded – I needed absolute privacy after all the misfortune I'd experienced, and its setting is very therapeutic. Added to that is the fact that I bought it with a very low bid; a bid I was able to afford. The family who owned it had some very bad luck. It appears the other buyers dropped out because they thought the house was tainted. As to whether I can afford its upkeep is another matter. Ella was a welcome but unexpected outlay."

He saw Catherine's face become preoccupied for a moment, as though searching for the most diplomatic way of asking a difficult question.

"I don't mean to pry, but will you stay single do you think? I mean, you are a comparatively young man and, if I may say so, still deserving of a wife and family."

He shook his head, dismissing both the compliment and any minor offence and dropped his voice so as not to be overheard.

"You flatter me – and thank you. It's opportune that you asked that Catherine – I was going to broach the subject myself after we met today, but never felt the moment was right. Nor was I able to overcome my sense of unease about it. You see, when I first fully explored the house where I now live, I discovered it hid a curious secret – a secret room adjacent to the changing room and filter house in the indoor swimming pool. Even though the house had very little in the way of effects remaining when I first occupied it, for some reason this secret room was still well equipped as an office, with a personal computer and all the functional stuff you might need with a PC. I won't bore you with the details but although there was no sign of paperwork, the system was still connected to the Internet, and I was able to bring up three comparatively recent emails – all from a woman in the Ukraine. She was one of the members of a web–based *'meet me and marry me'* site. What puzzles me is that the three emails were appealing for the person operating the PC to keep to a promise of meeting the woman in Odessa – the Ukrainian port by the Black Sea. Puzzling also is the fact that not only was the secret room apparently undiscovered by the estate agent who sold me the house – I know because I never saw it when I first viewed the house – but according to the estate agent the previous owners family were supposedly all lost in an air crash – he, his wife and three children. I can't believe the PC would have been his if he was married and living in the house with his family unless he was planning an escape from his domestic life."

Catherine shook her head in disbelief as he told the story and remained silent for a brief moment, appearing to let the revelation go un–remarked. Then, as though finally recalling a connection, she asked, "What was the name of the family who owned your house?"

"Uh...Ferguson if I recall correctly...Yes, Ferguson."

Catherine considered for a moment.

"That rings a bell you know – I can't be sure of my facts but I vaguely recall a report in a local newspaper about some local people lost in a plane crash and, if memory serves, they were named Ferguson. But as I remember they were not man and wife, she was a widow with children and he was her brother. Apparently the house was actually hers and he simply moved in when his business collapsed. The brother, so the paper said, was divorced and had been swindled out of everything he had through crooked investments. If I can find the newspaper article, I'll let you have it. If I am right, perhaps the brother was looking for a new wife and a new life – hence the computer and emails."

What Catherine had said shone another light on a possibly intractable problem; if her recall was accurate, the explanation concerning the PC's owner was plausible. But, it did not explain why the PC had been left behind when the house was emptied of its effects – but then, perhaps it did! If none of the original occupants had supervised the house clearance, there would have been no one there who knew of the secret room. Ergo, no one clearing the house was aware it existed. As the thought occurred, he decided to make up his mind if he was going to pursue the puzzle or simply let it drop. The truth was he was distrustful of getting involved in something that could spoil his trouble free and therapeutic existence. It would be better all round if he pretended the secret room had not, and did not, exist. Curiosity aside, it was becoming an unwelcome distraction, if not a fixation, and it all still felt ominous.

"What were you going to ask by the way?" Catherine said.

He hesitated – on second thoughts now was not the time to risk a question that could upset her. Better to find a more appropriate opportunity if need be – after all, Catherine would be a terrible loss.

Catherine said goodbye as he dropped her at the top of her lane. She looked radiant as she gave him a parting kiss on the cheek. She giggled as though the afternoon had taken away the sorrowful years and renewed her passion for life. Indeed, her gushing thanks gave way to even more gratitude when he promised to repeat the outing within the next few weeks. As he drove off, he had the definite impression that from the point of view of emotional sustenance, she'd received equally as much as he'd been given.

Indeed, Catherine was a complete tonic to his own emotional morass – being with her displaced the constant need to find chores and busy occupations that erased the lingering and enduring memory of Betty and Bobby. Try as he might – when it came to his past, it kept slipping into his thoughts and he could not let go completely.

As he nosed the Jag up the short drive to the house, he became preoccupied with the next days visit to the hospital. He was due for a consultants appointment, a recurring three month check up to ensure he was mending okay. As it happened, the appointment was opportune, his back had been a little sore lately and he wanted some reassurance that his injuries were not reverting to yet another booking for a hospital bed; he'd had his fill of hospital life. Even so, he had learnt fatalism – to know that what must be must be. In any case, he sensed that his current complaint was unlikely to be overtly serious – he certainly hoped not!

14

It wasn't exactly good news the consultant had imparted. An extensive area of scar tissue on his back was beginning to contract and the tightening might continue and become very uncomfortable. For the time being he was to apply a steroid cream. When the contractions became intolerably painful, he was to swallow Naprosyn and Tramadol, prescribed anti-inflammatories and analgesics. It was too early for any other intervention such as skin graft surgery, and with luck he might not need it. Time would tell.

When he had complained that it was virtually impossible for him to apply the cream on the affected area, he had been prescribed a small plastic stick which carried a pad – it was akin to a back-scratcher. He was to arrange a pair of mirrors so that he could view his back, and with the pad duly loaded with cream he was to apply it to the areas in question. Regardless of what the pharmacy nurse had glibly suggested about practice making perfect, he had his doubts!

He had a hankering to stay in the hospital long enough to find Isaac, to let him know of progress and an opportunity to express his gratitude for Isaac's friendship and timely intervention. But there was no Isaac to find – he was supposedly attending a university medical seminar and wasn't expected back for a few days.

Returning home in the warm midday sunshine, he left the Jag' at the front of the house and made his way to the kitchen. He intended to slake a thirst that had started to sting his lips and mouth on departure from the stiflingly hot treatment room in the hospital. The kettle had just come to the boil, and his need for a large mug of tea was just about to be satisfied when he heard the front door chimes ring out.

For the moment, he ignored the urgent sound of the repeating tubular bells and stayed where he was, determined to complete the tea making. When at last he had taken the first welcome sip of tea, he held on to his mug and made his way to the hallway, pulling at the ornate brass front-door handle with his one free hand.

He opened the door to find a smartly dressed man wearing a dark grey suit, white shirt and a patterned mauve tie. He was physically well proportioned with shoulders so wide and square they appeared to have been chiselled out of stone. Yet he stood a little distance back from the door threshold intending, it appeared, not to pose a threat.

"Good morning – my name is Charles Ferguson, I used to live here."

The man's voice belied his hard granite eyes by having a soft cadence to it. Indeed, the tone was sufficiently pleasant to invite an immediate and civilised reply. However, he was also conscious of mock geniality in the man's approach, but had no intention of showing it. Indeed, he realised that his momentary surprise and hesitant reaction had to be controlled if he was not to embarrass himself. The sudden appearance of a previous house occupant, someone who might now solve the puzzle of the secret room, was exciting, and he had no intention of scaring him off.

"Ah, at last! I've just made some tea – would you care for a cup?"

He stood back and gestured with his free arm, inviting the man in. Ferguson stepped forward without hesitation and as he passed into the hall there was at least a six-inch difference in height between them. As the door closed behind him, the man's eyes rapidly surveyed the hall and the various rooms where the doors were open.

"I take it from what you just said that you were expecting me?" He turned away from the door to face Ferguson.

"More hope than expectation – come in to the kitchen – do you prefer coffee to tea?"

Ferguson gave the hint of a smile. "Coffee, if it's not too much trouble."

He made a vague gesture along the hallway with his mug of tea. "No problem, the kitchen's this way – I'm sure you know where it is!"

He waited for the man to walk forward with the confidence of someone who knew where he was going.

Ferguson gave a slight bracing of his shoulders as if to say 'I know your game' and proceeded to walk directly towards the kitchen door. It was clear he knew where he was going – there were three doors leading away from the hallway on the left side but he unhesitatingly chose the right one. As he opened the door, he looked back as if to say 'See, I am who I say I am'.

He followed on into the kitchen, allowing Ferguson to wait patiently the other side of the kitchen door as he made directly for the kettle.

The kettle was still hot and it only took a moment for him to find the coffee, a clean mug and to produce a black coffee.

"Milk, sugar?"

"No – you got it right first time – black for me."

He carefully lifted the mug with one finger balancing the rim and three fingers supporting the base. As it steadied, he handed over the mug to Ferguson, handle first.

"Thanks, this is welcome – I imagine you have some questions."

"That's an understatement. As I understand it you are supposed to be dead and the photos I've seen of you don't do your present appearance any justice."

Ferguson let out a dry and humourless chuckle.

"Yes, so it seems... I can't vouch for the photographs but it was my sister and her children who died in the plane crash – I only died on paper!"

"I'm very sorry for your loss, it must have been devastating, but what do you mean you only died on paper? From what I have heard, the newspaper reports seemed to indicate that you were on the same plane as your sister."

Ferguson hesitated for a moment and then replied.

"I don't need to tell you that you shouldn't believe everything you read in the papers. No, I wasn't on board the plane that crashed – I was meant to be there but I missed the take off. I had to be somewhere else at the time. Lucky I suppose, but the newspapers simply reported the passenger list and no survivors rather than the body count found at the crash site. On paper, at least, I was dead!"

"I imagine that caused you some difficulties – how did you get resurrected?"

Ferguson's face became sombre. "I wasn't – it served my purposes to stay dead."

"Why so?"

"That must remain my business but I'm not here to give you my life story, there is something here in the house that I want."

There was a change to the slightly affable tone with which Ferguson had opened the conversation; his last remark was tinged with a certain insistence. The mock geniality had gone.

He was slightly uncertain of how he should respond to Ferguson's implicit demand, but he did not intend to just capitulate – especially since he knew precisely what it was Ferguson was talking about.

" I assume you are talking about the secret room and the computer system. "

Ferguson stiffened as the revelation was made, but said nothing.

"Let me remind you that the PC is no longer your property. When I bought the house any items that remained here when I took up occupation were forfeit. Furthermore, even if you were legally entitled to recover it, you cannot prove it was once yours. In short, you will have to give me a very good reason for me to part with it. "

Ferguson gazed down into his coffee mug for a moment and then lifted his head, fixing unblinking eyes towards his host. His voice dropped an octave and took on a sound akin to gravel being washed forward in a stream.

"The best reason I can give you is that I need what's on that PC, and to compensate you I will replace the existing system with a new one and no questions asked. Fair?"

On the face of it there was no dispute, after all he had no direct use of what Ferguson valued and exchange was no robbery. Yet, truth to tell, leaving the equipment in the secret room would save him a lot of bother and hassle in replacing everything for his own use. More importantly, his principle reluctance in letting it go would be in surrendering his fantasies about the Odessa girl – once he allowed Ferguson to recover his interest in her, his own hopes, tenuous though they might be, were dashed.

" Well, okay, though I can't understand why the PC *per se* is directly of value to you, I could only see a very limited range of software installed and a single internet access to a Ukrainian marriage site. The last three messages I found on it were from a very attractive woman in the Ukraine. She has the gift you sent her and simply appealed to you to do as you promised and fly to her in Odessa."

Ferguson suddenly looked startled. "Gift? What did she say about a gift? How was it presented – what did it look like on screen?" His gravel like speech was now even more insistent and demanding than before.

"Only that she had what she referred to as 'the gift', it was capitalised but the next sentence used text speak in "*I have the GIFT – I 2 will always be yours. Irina.*" She was disappointed you had not turned up in Odessa. Here, I'll write it for you so there is no misunderstanding."

He reached for the memo pad hanging from a wall cabinet and using the attached pencil wrote ' *I have the GIFT – I 2 will –* '.

Ferguson leaned forward and stared at the sheet as it was held up in front of him.

"How long ago was this – when did you see this message and when was it sent?" Ferguson had taken a step forward, his whole demeanour now somewhat menacing.

If he had still been the man he was, before his two shattering tragedies, Ferguson's attitude would have had him submit – even perhaps to the point of him helping Ferguson take the secret PC out of the front door.

However, he was not the same man as before because Isaac and others had rebuilt a much tougher him, and Ferguson's belligerent stance now simply made him resentful and unwilling to cooperate any further.

"Sent about six weeks ago, about the same time I saw it, and before you ask I have not made contact with the lady even though I was tempted. If you have abandoned her, it's your loss. Now I'm going to ask you to leave. I won't accept your offer and I don't like being intimidated by people, particularly those I invite into what is now my house."

He gestured towards the front door and watched for Ferguson's reaction.

For a second or two Ferguson wavered, as if calculating the possible advantage of more aggression. But then with a curt nod of his head, he turned about and walked out of the kitchen, abandoning his coffee mug to a work surface as he exited.

Ferguson arrived at the front door as though hurried by a crisis, quickly extending the distance between the two of them. The front door was flung open and left ajar as Ferguson hurriedly left the house. He skirted the Jag and started crunching down the gravel drive at a pace so rapid it was just short of becoming a run. He never looked back and was gone before there was any time, or apparent intent, for a spoken farewell.

As he stood at the door, watching Ferguson's bulky, striding figure exit the entrance gates, he wondered why there was no car waiting for him, nor any indication of how Ferguson had arrived.

He continued to stare fixedly on the marching Ferguson as he turned past the gates and walked on, the top of his head occasionally bobbing up above the privet hedge bordering the front drive and garden. The head was eventually lost from sight, but as he was about to close the front door, he heard a car engine start up and move off. The car must have been parked near the road junction, and as the engine revs climbed, it was obvious from the combined sound of engine noise and squealing tires that the driver was in one hell of a hurry.

He was virtually sleepwalking on his way back to the kitchen to retrieve his tea, utterly preoccupied with the events surrounding Ferguson's arrival, his departure, and its implications. Not only was Ferguson's behaviour inexplicable, but also underlying the strange behaviour was something apparently more mysterious, if not sinister. Still, Ferguson had not pressed his case to the point of it being overtly confrontational, and with Ferguson now out of the way he was confident the precious computer system was no longer forfeit. He resolved not to allow the matter to fester or through weakness collapse. If Ferguson came back, the front door would remain closed – he had no wish to allow matters to deteriorate so that he became embroiled in something that would blight his existence; he had taken pains to create a simple life devoid of major hassles – and it ended there!

15

He shoved the wire cutters into his back pocket and wrapped the waste wire into a spool around his right hand. The job had taken no more than a minute and it meant that the secret room was no longer going to react to the appearance or presence of anyone wanting to operate the PC.

By shorting out the wall-switch and disconnecting the infra-red sensor, the sliding door would remain permanently open so that there was now easy access to the old, what was, secret room; neither was it hidden from sight. As far as he was concerned the whole business surrounding Ferguson and his curious, if not strange activities was now far too clandestine and furtive to make sense, and his earlier temptation to see if the Odessa bride might still be available had become tainted with Ferguson's curious behaviour. Overall, his decision to reject further involvement with the enigma of the Odessa Bride seemed to him the better part of valour, and from a pragmatic point of view had the benefit of excluding her and allowing him to speculate on whether the lovely Catherine might really warm to him. The latter certainly was a pleasant thought.

However, he was reluctant to delete the information on the Odessa site; it was a selfish contingency, as though if all else failed he could still try to attract the woman in question. Deleting the website and her identity had too much of a finality about it – it left him very limited prospects. He harboured the hope that if he eventually chose to make contact with her she might succumb to the idea of getting to know him, and perhaps agree to take things further. As long as she was there, and he had her in reserve, what happened if Catherine objected to developing their relationship would be less disappointing. If he was honest with himself, it was deeply selfish to think that way, but he had a right to happiness too, and not to be reduced to what could be a futile and forlorn existence. Betty and Bobby would never be put aside, but now he saw he had a life to live.

He gave the now open door and the quiescent PC one last look as be backed out of the cubicle and started to turn towards the pool walkway.

"So that's where it was!"

The voice forced an involuntary spasm of fear and he froze as he realised he was no longer alone. He reached for the wire cutters in his back pocket and turned to the cubicle doorway holding the sharp jaws of the cutters forward and facing the source of the voice.

"I'm sorry – I startled you."

He was tall and in his fifties; well dressed in suit and overcoat, with what appeared to be a very expensive and flattering grey flecked scarf draped over the shoulders of his charcoal topcoat. His dark hair was grey streaked but his deep blue eyes and relatively unwrinkled skin gave a youthful impression. As he smiled broadly at his remark he showed a set of clean white teeth marred by the absence of one upper canine.

"Who the hell are you?" he held the wire cutters like a knife, pointing towards the stranger.

"Rennison...my name is Rennison Mr. Enfield, I understand you recently met an acquaintance of mine – name of Ferguson." The man offered a further smile, somewhat disarming and very slightly unsure.

"How did you get in to my garden – I never heard you arrive."

Rennison held out his arms in supplication.

"So sorry, I did try the front door chimes for a good few minutes. When there was no reply I came around through the side gate – to see if you were in the garden. I saw movement at the back of the pool so I came in...you were probably too occupied to hear me."

Still wary of the man he slowly let the wire cutters drop to the side of his leg and moved towards the newly arrived stranger. Rennison retreated slightly away from the doorframe, allowing enough room for the cubicle door to be closed. For the moment, he had no reason to treat Rennison as a direct and immediate physical threat. More as a gesture of appeasement, and to remove temptation, he returned the cutters to his back pocket.

Now they both stood on the pool walkway as if in an awkward, self conscience tableau, and as Rennison offered yet another conciliatory smile, he decided not to concede or throw the wrong oil on troubled waters, even though it was clear he was not in any immediate danger.

"Okay Mr. Rennison – I met your Mr. Ferguson recently and I didn't like him much. Now I find someone who styles Ferguson as an acquaintance arrives at my house, knows not only my name but the reason Ferguson was here. I assume you have come for the PC – the same as Ferguson. I will tell you what I told Ferguson. The PC was here when I took possession of the house and since there was no immediate claim for it at the time, I have a legal right to retain it. It constitutes a fitting or a fixture and since the house was sold without a listing of such things, I have a watertight case for retention."

Rennison smiled, bowed his head slightly in acquiescence and gave a dry, throat-clearing cough.

"Mr. Enfield, who am I to dispute it – I merely hoped you might show me what Mr. Ferguson had gathered from its use. Allow me to enlighten you a little – I have a story to tell and, if it's not too much trouble, could I impose on you for a cup of coffee?"

For a moment he hesitated, demonstrating to Rennison that he was reluctant to agree, but it was difficult to deflect the courteous request, and given the somewhat appealing and intriguing manner Rennison was projecting, he grudgingly lifted his right arm indicating the pool door and the direction of the house.

"What's you preference Rennison – black, white – with or without?

"Oh," said Rennison" "as it comes Mr. Enfield".

16

The pleasant odour from Rennison's miniature cigar was a surprise. He had always found tobacco smoke distasteful at best, vile at worst, but here was an aroma that was far from offensive. He'd opened a window to allow the kitchen to vacate most of the billowing puffs of smoke that were the upshot of Rennison's obvious enjoyment of his addiction, but he had to admit it, what wafted towards him and invaded his nostrils was far from offensive.

When Rennison had asked if he could light up he had given his okay on condition that it was just the one, and had steeled himself for what was for a non-smoker, a forthcoming ordeal.

"Turkish," Rennison grinned, "the tobacco leaves are rolled and then immersed in a bath of naturally occurring ingredients – leaves, flowers, some spices and herbs. It takes three days for them to be prepared and dried out. I found them by accident, usually they are exported and only smoked by women – but I found them very pleasant so I decided to ignore the gender implications."

Rennison offered another of his wide smiles as he recounted the story, and it was becoming clear that he was trying hard not to appear as a threat.

"Coffee okay – care for another if you have finished?"

Rennison shook his head "Plenty for me thanks. Can we address the reason I'm here."

"Sure, go ahead, but you heard my remarks about the PC a short while ago, I can't change that."

As he spoke, Rennison gave a few shakes of his head.

"No – that's not my intention Mr. Enfield. It's not the PC itself I am interested in. It's what's on it and what Ferguson saw when he visited you."

"If you mean did Ferguson confirm that the PC was still here, yes he did – I told him so. But he never actually had sight of the PC or what messages were on the website he was interested in. I simply showed him the rather cryptic aspect of the last message in question. That seemed to create serious interest – in fact immediately after I repeated the last message I had seen on the website, I had the pleasure of turfing him out. He left very quickly and with no resistance."

Rennison leaned forward.

"The message – cryptic? Can you explain?"

"No – not until I am given a reason why all this mystery is so bloody important to Ferguson and yourself. I'm completely in the dark about this, and as I recall, you were supposed to be enlightening me on the background to all the why's and wherefores. Who or what is Ferguson – come to that, who or what are you? More than that – why is it you have to stand in for Ferguson? After all, he seemed to take with him all he wanted to know – hasn't he briefed you?"

Rennison gave an appreciative grin.

"Well, as I said, that's why I'm here. I did say I had a story to tell Mr. Enfield and since that obligates me, I'll first have to identify myself. My name is Emanuel Rennison. I'm a member of a special operations group allied to a national security agency, and if you must know, that means MI6, the secret intelligence service. My somewhat select group operates very widely, though we are focused on internal security. That doesn't mean we are parochial, introspective or have tunnel vision. If the internal threat emanates from outside our borders, we pursue it wherever it comes from, or wherever it goes. Now, what I am about to disclose to you must be kept strictly confidential, what is more, unless you agree to signing the official secrets act I can only give you the bare bones of what you are sitting on...agreed?"

It was too tantalising an offer, what difference did it make whether he was bound by the OSA or his own integrity, if he agreed to keep silent then silent he would be – regardless. In any case, the only way he was finally going to get the whole damned story was to consent to the condition Rennison was offering. From what Rennison had said so far, the mystery of the hidden room was beginning to clarify.

"I've no objections – do I sign now?"

The MI6 man chuckled. "On the one condition that you don't suddenly dash out of the house and then vanish, I think we can leave it 'til after I complete my exposition."

Nodding in agreement, he looked intently at Rennison as the intelligence agent launched into his briefing.

"You see Mr. Enfield, this house was originally what we call a safe house, owned and used by MI6 and MI5 during and after the cold war years to house foreign agents, intelligence officers, iron curtain defectors and for debriefing teams and interrogations. In recent years it's been used as a refuge for our own people – those recuperating and those we want trained, briefed, kept out of circulation or simply removed from their official habitat for a while. It has also been used as a base for certain SIS strategy meetings and suchlike. However in the last year or two, as our operations took on different needs, this house started to become redundant. We kept it available as an emergency safe haven, or sometimes as visitors temporary accommodation, by installing a caretaker. Now Ferguson's sister – at the time a recent widow, and one of our better administrative people – was not fully trained as a field operative and was willing to establish herself and her children here for the interim. It very much suited her situation and ours. However, we had no future inkling about her brother – one Charles Ferguson."

As Rennison scornfully articulated Ferguson's name, he instantly knew his suspicions about Ferguson were right. Ferguson had left him with the impression of being someone secretive and dishonest, and he was willing to bet that Rennison was about to confirm it.

Rennison paused for a moment, sipped the dregs of his coffee and then continued.

"As far as we can establish, Ferguson found a refuge here after persuading his sister he was desperate for help. Now Charles Ferguson was Secret Intelligence Service too, or at least had been, but unbeknown to us ran a few clandestine business operations on the side. His sister relented on giving him some refuge after some of his so called business interests had collapsed – through his own greed and ineptitude it should be noted. His sister had no authority to offer him a home here but it was probably a case of blood being thicker than water. No doubt he promised her a respite from looking after the children, and that his stay would be brief before he was activated again. However, true to form he stuck like a leech the moment he was ensconced in the house – and why not, he had secured a very comfortable existence. It allowed him the ideal environment to pursue his illegal, not to say nefarious, operations. I say that because we now know that he and his sister were chalk and cheese – she, honest and highly dependable, him charming, untrustworthy, thoroughly dishonest, cunning and a complete parasite. And yet those attributes had, at times, been very useful to the service. To our shame, we made very few checks on Marie Ferguson while she was here. As long as the administrative work she carried out...in the hidden room we both now know about...was completed on time and competently, no one complained. In any case, in the beginning, we were sensitive to her unfortunate status as a recent widow, and no one wanted to interfere in her grief and period of recovery. She was, for all intents and purposes, entirely independent, there was no direct supervision. That was our mistake. As far as we can surmise, Ferguson must have had sight of some of his sister's work. Certain documents, which should have remained entirely confidential, came into view and he decided to try to capitalise on them. I doubt his sister knew for certain if he had seen anything, I'm convinced she would have reported it. In any case, whatever she knew or had suspicions about was never revealed or reported, certainly not before she and her children were lost in the plane crash of flight 554 in Canada eleven months ago. Now here is the rub. When, following Marie's death, our executive decided to put this house on the market through the crown solicitors, we were unaware that she had been using the room I have just seen in the swimming pool as a covert workroom. She must have taken the confidentiality of her work to an unusual level from the beginning, she was not expected to do it - or normally would need to do it. I suspect she attempted to keep people, and eventually her brother, out of sight of her work.

It means that what remained in the room, after her vacation flight to Canada, was sensitive, restricted material no one else should have seen other than our own people. We suppose from airline records that Charles Ferguson should have been on the same flight as his sister but we now believe that he booked in but slipped away before take off. In short, he hoped to disappear – and to all intents and purposes he did. He is officially listed as a victim of the crash. However, we both know that he appears to be very much alive."

So far the expose' was a revelation and if Rennison was unfolding the tale as he expected, Ferguson was going to be the centre of a very nasty set of circumstances. Only the 'why' of it was a mystery.

"Then why haven't you intercepted him and found out what's going on – after all, if he was in possession of restricted material it's effectively espionage. That's grounds for arrest isn't it?"

Rennison paused in mid response and the fleeting silence took on a grim air.

"We got to Ferguson a day after he came here to see you. We began to look for him initially when we were notified of Marie Ferguson's death and the fact that Charles Ferguson had been seen after the aircraft took off – apparently, he had skipped the flight. It was puzzling, and we needed to eliminate the possibility that he was carrying anything that belonged to his sister. He refused to cooperate in any way and we could find nothing on him that implied theft of restricted material or any associated skulduggery. All we found was a note on his tablet giving this address and the term 'Irina – computer contact'. As far as we were concerned his only crime, if crime it was, was skipping the flight he was supposed to be taking with his sister and her children to Vancouver. We know he boarded the flight, we know he was subsequently identified leaving the airport – what we don't know is how he absconded unseen before the aircraft lifted off for Vancouver. Be that as it may, it's rather academic now – we now have the bare bones of something suspicious and we are obliged to follow through. That's why the computer is so important at this time – can we boot it up please?"

Rennison's story was less than instructive, He was holding back more than was comfortable, and taken as a whole, what he had said was *prima face* not only logically inconsistent but lacked what was the obvious approach or strategy. Although he felt obliged to keep his word about confidentiality and non-disclosure, it occurred to him that what he knew now was little more than he knew before, and there was actually very little he could disclose even if he had been confronted with an aggressive interrogation. In truth, Rennison had told him too little for it to be a cohesive story – that had to be said.

"Okay – but there is very little to see. What I said to Ferguson is still valid, apart from the conventional PC software there nothing else on the computer other than a message page from woman on a Baltic bridal mail order website. All I found were three messages from her – from Odessa in fact. The last message seemed to get Ferguson excited. I told him what it said – I even wrote it down for him. He never actually saw the web page itself – he got demanding, wouldn't take me at my word and subsequently got kicked out."

Rennison looked pensive. "Understood – but if you don't object I would still like to see the web page and the office."

He volunteered a nod of his head at Rennison's request and led them out of the kitchen door back towards the pool house. As they walked, Rennison offered what seemed sincere approval for the way the garden was laid out and tended. As they entered the pool house he remarked on the investment Marie Ferguson had made to the estate – it came as a surprise to learn that the agency had owned the house, but she had paid for the pool.

They arrived in the secret room, a term which was quickly

becoming a misnomer in his mind. He certainly had his doubts. Given the number of individuals who now appeared to know about it, it was certainly not now, and probably never had been, entirely 'secret' - the 'hidden' room was far more accurate.

Rennison made no comment on the now quiescent sliding wall, and was quick to scour through all the filing cabinet draws and every other place where documents could, and should, have been left. The complete absence of any remnant of official paperwork, or even a trace of any sensitive documents, seemed to disappoint him. He stood back, looking around the room as if to find some nook or cranny that might be hiding papers, or for some other subtle indication of what the room had once witnessed. It was only as he heard the hard drive of the computer begin to whine its way towards loading the software, and uploading the screen icons, that his attention was distracted from the search.

He brought up the web page and stood back to allow Rennison a full view. Rennison bent forward to scrutinise the screen and as he scanned the last of the three messages he gave a soft whistle.

"Maybe I was wrong - but if I am wrong it's muddied the water considerably"

"What do you mean - what have you seen?"

Rennison lifted himself away from the screen but kept his eyes fixed on it.

"What I mean is that if Ferguson understood what was implied in this last message here, he's not the Ferguson we had in mind."

The remark sounded strange.

"I'm sorry - should I be aware of what that means?"

Rennison turned and smiled. "No, but I'm going to tell you because you will need to know - it's becoming deeper than I first imagined, and anyway, I promised to tell you everything regarding this project on condition you agreed to abide by the OSA.

Well, you did agree, but I never expected to have to tell you things that might endanger you. The first thing you should know is that when we caught up with Ferguson we were only able to hold him for a short time. Even we can't hang on to people because we are puzzled or suspicious. Some time later, having released Ferguson, we received some intelligence that a small arms and ordnance shipment, destined for NATO evaluation trials in Estonia, had found its way to eastern Ukraine. Almost simultaneously our contacts in the Ukraine notified us that they believed the same shipment had been routed through Odessa via a civilian carrier being paid and instructed by a British shipping agent. This, so it appeared, was an unnamed and as yet undeclared operation apparently owned by Ferguson. On the face of it, Ferguson had intercepted some of his sister's classified data, obtained access to the weapons shipping authority, and had rerouted the shipment. Someone was looking for a big payout it seems, and it was typical of him. And yet, from what this message says, something is wrong. This last message is supposedly from a mail order bride in Odessa, someone unknown to you or me but she, or whoever it is, appears familiar with security agency code. The message as such is twaddle, but the bit that says 'GIFT I2' has meaning. Had it been just GIFT it would have signified *'Got Identity - Found Target'* whereas GIFT I2 means *'Group Identification Finalised - Tactical Intervention Imminent'.* That means the Odessa side of this message appears to be *bona fide.* Damn, we should have pressed Ferguson harder while we had the chance."

The use of the past tense was puzzling.

"You speak of Ferguson in the past tense - did you lose sight of him completely"

Rennison pursed his lips and then smiled.

"In a way - we think he's dead!"

17

It came as a shock.

Up to now he had thought of himself as a bystander, an informed bystander granted, but someone on the periphery of a strange set of circumstances in which he was only involved incidentally. Fate, as always, had handed him an unwanted role in a potentially dangerous game, even though he had been minding his own business and had done nothing to invite the course of events he was now embroiled in. Up to now he considered himself immune from any consequences likely to arise from keeping the Odessa bride messages available. Now he was far from sure.

"Dead – how so?

Rennison had turned away from the VDU, giving an almost inaudible sigh.

"He was found dead in a London Hotel by the local police. Pathologist gave a non-committal verdict of an alkaloid toxin – we are still waiting for the toxicologists to establish what the poison actually was. The body was identified as the man we had seen before, the man we believed was Ferguson, but now we're not so sure. Passport photos of the real Ferguson look very similar to the man we interviewed, but 'very similar' is the same as 'very doubtful'."

As Rennison paused it occurred to him that 'if', and it was quite an 'if', Ferguson had been impersonated, he could yet get a visit from the real one asking again about the PC – unless of course the real one was dead too, and thus was the reason for the impersonation. Had the arms deal been, or was it about to be, infiltrated by a security agency? Who was it at the Odessa end organising what appeared to be some kind of mop up operation. That was where the real exposure would come from wouldn't it? And surely if any British intelligence or security agency was involved, MI6 or the SIS would know about it...wouldn't they?

As Rennison cogitated, standing uncommunicative and silent by the VDU, he felt it was an opportunity to give free rein to his thoughts.

Rennison looked up, and listened intently to what was being said; occasionally he nodded an agreement.

As Rennison appeared to give him due attention he finally announced "Is it possible that the man seen leaving the airport and apparently skipping the Vancouver flight was a stand in – a Ferguson look-alike – someone working for one of our security agencies. It could have been a case of the real Ferguson on the plane and somebody else leaving the airport."

With that, Rennison smiled a broad agreement.

"Yes Mr. Enfield, your analysis is reasonable – I think you have inadvertently focused on a specific point. We may be working from the wrong end. Whatever is going on in Odessa we need to find out about it and let it lead us back to the UK. However, whether Ferguson the real, or Ferguson the impostor, instigated this arms diversion, we must assume it originated from here, from this office. Furthermore, which of the two is now lying in the mortuary at Bethnall Green? Likewise, since some messages from Odessa arrived back here it is an odds on bet that the instigator expected to coordinate some of the operation from here. The only thing we don't know is who started it and for what reason. Was this another security agency sting, started to ferret out gun running? From what I can see that appears plausible given the message code –except, being who I am, I should know about it. Or did it start as a typical Ferguson scam and get hijacked by another operation. I honestly don't know Mr. Enfield – but I intend to find out."

Rennison turned about and started to leave the room. As he began to follow Rennison, he had a fleeting thought and turned back to the room. Looking to the left of the desk and above the VDU he rapidly scanned the three pictures.

"Mr. Rennison, before you leave can I draw your attention to this photograph?"

As Rennison turned and came back into the room he pointed to the extreme left of the three wall pictures.

"You may have missed the significance of this."

"What is it?" Rennison said, as he peered at the faded colours of the photo.

He leaned forward and tapped the male figure standing alongside the woman and the children.

"Compare this figure here, and the two on the other photographs."

Rennison stayed silent as he scrutinised the first of the three photographs and then moved on. The second took his attention for only a few seconds and the third resulted in an almost immediate response. "Christ!"

He was pleased that Rennison's sight was as good as his own.

"Yes, that's what I thought too. When I heard your story about there possibly being two Ferguson's something kept twitching in my mind. Then I remembered the photos. As far as I can tell, and I think you have confirmed this by noticing the birth mark on the one, and not the other, there definitely are two Fergusons here – they are not identical twins but very similar to one another, so much so that one could easily be mistaken for the other. I don't suppose you could have detected an upper leg port-wine birthmark when you questioned the Ferguson you arrested, but I'm willing to bet that man wasn't Charles Ferguson but rather a sibling or a look alike."

It was beginning to crystallize, and as they both silently considered the implications it was Rennison who broke the silence and suggested the most plausible sequence of events.

"So, my guess is that Marie Ferguson boarded the plane with her children and either Charles Ferguson or his doppelganger. It may be that it was the mysterious second man who waited around the departure lounge to ensure they were both on the flight and then, confident that the flight was about take off, left the airport. Looking so much like Charles Ferguson, he was picked up on CCTV and was thought to actually be Charles Ferguson. However, the other Ferguson was already a long way from the plane and if that is true it begs a plethora of other questions – and at the top of my list is one I don't like one little bit. Why need to ensure your sister and her offspring were leaving, and wasn't it an unfortunate coincidence that the aircraft crashed? Likewise, which of the two is now lying in the Bethnal Green mortuary and if it isn't Charles Ferguson how is it that we have no record of this look-alike or mysterious sibling? How and why would anyone want to remain anonymous for so long? As I recall from her file, Marie Ferguson's background checks during her recruitment fifteen years ago revealed only her brother, she did not mention, nor did we locate, anyone else in her immediate family. Yet the photographs there on the wall demonstrate the fact that she knew this other so-called brother.

Rennison turned to look at the photographs again and once more lapsed into a silent, brooding air.

It was for both of them a trying exercise – to have assembled some idea of the players and events in the baffling story behind the Odessa messages was satisfying, excepting that it simply led to an even greater puzzle that was unlikely to be resolved without much more work.

Rennison suddenly shuddered and snapped back to life, as if a decision had been made and he needed to move on.

He stepped away from the wall pictures and began to vacate the hidden room. He was on the pool walkway before he turned and spoke again.

"Mr. Enfield – I am grateful for your assistance and I 'm sorry I sucked you into something which may harm your somewhat tranquil life. I am not going to understate matters; to me this looks like a nasty game so I want you to be on your guard. I will give you my details and we'll complete the OSA on the way out.

As they re-occupied the kitchen Rennison simply produced a sheath of papers from his inside jacket pocket and exposing the very last page said, "Sign there if you would."

As he retrieved the trusty notepad pen once more, and signed and dated the paper, he took notice of the final paragraph above the 'To Which I Hereby Do Attest' on the signature and witness lines. It detailed the penalties for transgression of the agreement. He suddenly had second thoughts about his willingness to sign the OSA – but it was too late – he was already committed.

Rennison stood by, quietly watching him complete the signing. As the pen-strokes stopped, he gathered up the papers, folded them, and slipped them back into his inside jacket pocket.

For a moment each man fixed his gaze, the one at the other; then Rennison nodded, offered his hand for a handshake and gave a profound and sincere smile of appreciation.

"You've been a great help Mr. Enfield and I'm sorry if the

exercise has disturbed you. Look, here's my card, contact me anytime day or night and particularly if you get another message from Odessa. That I want to know about as quickly as possible."

He stood and shook Rennison's hand – not a soft hand but one a little calloused and with remarkably dry skin.

"I won't say it wasn't, what shall I say...an intriguing exercise Mr. Rennison because it was. As for being disturbed, I somehow think I'll get over it. Come on, I'll take you to the door."

Holding Rennison's card with one hand, while the other turned the front door lock, he nodded a grateful goodbye as Rennison stepped out onto the driveway. Just as he was about to close the door Rennison turned and said,

"Don't forget Mr. Enfield you are bound by the OSA. I trust your family won't get to know about this visit quite yet – better leave everything unsaid I would suggest."

His wistful look must have conveyed to Rennison all that needed to be said about his history and personal circumstances. Rennison held his gaze for a second or two and then, slightly embarrassed, turned on his heel and walked quickly towards a black Mercedes C Class saloon parked neatly halfway between the house entrance and the gate. It confirmed one thing – Rennison might well be with the SIS, but it was clear he had made little or no effort to research a certain Peter Enfield's background. As the thought came to him, so too did the suggestion that he should be thankful for small mercies.

18

It was nearly a month since he had bid Rennison goodbye and the passage of time had somewhat diminished his sense of anticipation as the enigmatic story behind the Ferguson's and the Odessa messages had begun to fade.

Nothing more had transpired in the way of unexpected visits, or any further contact with Rennison. On the one hand it was not to be expected. What he had contributed, if anything that was, was likely to be a very small part of a very involved and extensive investigation, and his limited intervention might well be at best a drop in the ocean – at worst, utterly insignificant.

On the other hand, he was intrigued by what the outcome might be, and felt entitled to some consideration. Even so, his pragmatic side realised that the chances he would see Rennison again if he were passive and remained in the background were slim, and being such a minor factor in the investigation his significance would be close to nil. Not, that is, without him contacting Rennison directly and trying to pry out the state, progress and direction of the enquiry.

However, that enquiry he suspected would be far from welcome.

As such, he had no option but to treat the event as an interesting but abnormal experience and to hope that one-day – perhaps – he would learn all of the dark, illicit details of the case and what eventually transpired.

As it was, he had other distractions. His periodic date with the lovely Catherine was imminent and with the Odessa girl now a forlorn and unapproachable dream, he was no longer faced with a decision that constituted a dilemma. Catherine was definitely not 'second best' and she had a considerable advantage; she was real – a very attractive flesh and blood woman who had no need to communicate through a website! He decided that his best option was to woo Catherine with as much power and passion as he could muster and not allowing it to lapse or fade. He was at risk of giving her the impression that his interest was purely platonic. Better to arrange their meetings more frequently so as to allow the relationship to blossom. She was now too valuable to lose. He envisaged Catherine and himself scooting down to some remote seaside town in Ella, and booking in to a double room. That picture was immensely pleasurable – all he had to do was contrive it!

He had taken care to shower, shave and dress well, and prior to his dressing had ensured that Ella was clean, polished and pristine. He was still prone to the odd spasm from the scar tissue around his right leg and back, but the dermal cream in general, and the analgesics when it really tightened, had quieted the discomfort considerably. He remained hopeful that in the end the spasms would abate permanently.

All things considered, he felt moderately optimistic as he brought the Jag's engine to life and exited the drive. He drifted up to the 'T' junction and with a slight squeal from the rear tyres allowed the 3.8 litre to deliver part of its potential power. The weather was good, the surface dry and the Lidmouth road virtually empty of other vehicles. Holding on to second gear and changing up at five thousand rpm he made sixty in a fraction over seven seconds. The exhaust note was thrilling. He took the wide black ribbon of road that took him the four miles to Catherine's home cruising at an enthralling eighty-five mph. The open top ran buffeting streams of air over the front windshield, and he began to feel the elation that a combination of speed, exhaust note and adrenaline created. The roadside woodland and vegetation began to flash by, visually smeared into variegated greens and browns by the speed. He became submerged in exhilaration and personal pride as his foot irresistibly depressed the accelerator downward, and the Jaguars full power came in, pressing him back into the driver's seat.

He continued to enjoy an open road; there was very little in the way of oncoming traffic to impart any curb to his speed or driving style. Bright sunlight, only fading to slight shadow from overhead foliage, meant the road remained well illuminated and there was certainly nothing in the way of traffic on his side of the road to either slow his progress, or risk an irate driver reporting him. He started to take bends under added power, letting the car drive itself through the curves. It was as he came back onto a straighter section, and he briefly checked his instruments, that he realised he was now well exceeding ninety-five miles per hour.

For a moment he was reluctant to listen to the note of caution popping up into his head but, as good sense overrode his excitement, he recalled how it came to be that he was ultimately able to enjoy this moment as he did. Betty, Bobby, the district nurse and an interminable period in hospital was a high price to pay for the privilege of wrapping oneself around a tree at ninety-five plus miles per hour. Not only that, he thought, as he slowed the car back to fifty, it had dawned on him with some amusement that Catherine would be less than pleased if he arrived at their meeting in a coffin!

As the thought came to mind, and the trace of an amused smile appeared on his lips, he glanced into his rear view mirror and was immediately gripped by what he saw. A black spec was on the road some distance behind him, and whatever it was, it was closing fast – very fast!

There were no blue lights and no sirens, so it was not a standard police cruiser.

He considered the possibilities.

It might be an unmarked police traffic car that had 'clocked' him during his moment of elation at ninety plus or, alternatively, it was some clown trying to prove he was faster than the E Type – just in case, he was obliged to hold his speed and eliminate the chance of being convicted of speeding.

It was no more than the time it took to take a deep breath before the car was close behind him. A black Mercedes – and as he glanced into his rear view mirror he tried to recognise the driver. Three times he switched his attention from the road to the mirror. There was still some doubt – the driver looked familiar – it could be Rennison but the black car's windscreen reflection was deceiving and made identifying the driver difficult.

He began to brake, and as he looked for a roadside parking area, the car behind started to flash its lights. There was no doubt now, the car behind was there for a reason, he was being flagged down.

It was another quarter mile before a parking lay-by appeared and he was able to slip off the road and pull up. The Mercedes followed suit, as if glued to his rear, and they both came to a halt only a metre apart.

It certainly wasn't Rennison in the Mercedes – but whoever he was, he was out of his car as if reversing the start of the Le Mans 24 hour race. The man was youngish, in his late twenties and well dressed. His natural, deep blonde hair was styled and he had a flawless, clean-shaven face.

As the man came up to the Jag's door he turned in the car seat towards him with some apprehension. Still sitting in an open car, as he was, meant he was vulnerable to an attack, and he wished he had reacted more quickly to the strangers rapid arrival. However, though looking down from an imposing height, the stranger remained standing, so positioned as not to appear directly intimidating, but close enough to be heard clearly.

"Are you Mr. Enfield, Peter Enfield? Apologies for interrupting your journey - a necessary intrusion I'm afraid."

It was a laboured courtesy; a slightly audacious and false apology, trotted out before expressing any justification for a nerve-racking chase.

He nodded in confirmation, held his dignity and waited for the man to give the apparently vital and overwhelming reason he had been flagged down.

"I have a message from my boss, Emanuel Rennison, he wants you to return to the house."

The query created no little resentment - so, Rennison had at last appeared again - but at entirely the wrong time! If he conceded to Rennison's demand he was definitely going to miss his appointment and annoy Catherine. If he refused he could miss, disrupt or damage something important. It was Hobson's choice then.

He pulled out his mobile and opened the caller list. In town he could use the phone routinely but he gave a gasp of frustration when it now told him that, just like his rural retreat at the house, there was still no available signal.

He didn't want the return to Rennison to take too long - but it might. The sensible course was to return to the house, phone

Catherine on the land line and either postpone their meeting to a later time today, or cry off with abject apologies and ask for another date.

He paused long enough to imply that he was not simply Rennison's puppet, and that though weighing up the importance of what he was being told, he could still ignore the summons. But the decision was made.

Instantly he engaged first gear and then with a quick glance at both of the road lanes he brought the Jag round in a tight circle onto the return side of the road. Out of the corner of his eye he saw the young man flinch as small stones were thrown up from the Jag's wheel spin. The man turned in astonishment at the manoeuvre and stood transfixed as the Jaguar suddenly appeared in the return lane of the road. He looked even more stunned as under full power the car accelerated away and left him behind.

It was wonderful – he had always wanted an excuse to push the Jag to the limit and now Rennison had given him one. He didn't care – at 110 mph, and eating up the miles back to the house, his sense of delight and accomplishment knew no bounds. When it came to Ella, any excuse would do and to hell with the speed limits –the security services would get a bill for any car repairs, fines he might attract and, if necessary, for the re-instatement of his license!

He came into the drive rather more rapidly than was safe. He had to brake hard, pulling the car to a halt with shingle splashing out from the skidding tyres; each locked wheel cleaving through the surface and leaving deep furrows in their wake. He exited the car awkwardly with no thought to his back and a sharp spasm reminded him of his infirmity. He ignored it as best he could, making a mental note to ensure Rennison knew he had a debt to settle for insisting he return to the house.

As he entered through the front door it became clear no one was actually in the house. He quickly searched the ground floors and it was only as he looked into the kitchen and saw the pool house door open that he guessed where his erstwhile guest was lurking.

He found the back door locked, which meant Rennison had used the side gate again to gain entry. Unlocking the kitchen door he made his way towards the pool house looking for Rennison's familiar profile. It was only as he entered the pool house that Rennison appeared, walking out of the hidden room and waiting on the pool walkway for him to arrive.

"Glad to see you Enfield – where's Fawly?"

"If you mean the man who flagged me down on my way to a very important appointment and issued your instructions, he's a good way back. *A propo* that, before you say anything Rennison, I have to make a phone call."

Rennison gave a curt nod and then said "Before you do, have you seen anyone skulking around the house since we last met?"

There was only one answer and Rennison should have known what it was – had he seen anyone suspicious he would have contacted Rennison immediately.

"My only visitors were the council refuse men on their usual Wednesday routine. I watched them like a hawk as they came and emptied the bins, and I was still watching them as they went. Now you must excuse me – the back door is open. You and your compardre – should he ever arrive – are welcome to a coffee."

Refusing to linger any longer and at risk of Rennison holding him back, he turned on his heel and returned back towards the pool door.

Just as he pulled at the door handle he heard Rennison lift his voice. It echoed and reverberated across the pool auditorium, bouncing off the surface of the water, the numerous glass walls and the roof glazing.

"Someone has cannibalised the PC – or so it seems. Try not to take too long, we need to talk."

19

He froze in his tracks for a good few seconds as he heard Rennison blurt out the news. There was a strong temptation to turn about and investigate what it was Rennison was talking about, but he was also persuaded that he really needed to take care of other priorities.

With his mind made up, he threw Rennison a terse "Back soon." and made his way towards the house.

As he opened the kitchen door he saw movement to his right and saw Fawly appear, pacing his way along the side gate pathway towards the pool house.

He decided to ignore everything for the moment and to try to salvage Catherine's feelings for him – if she would listen to him that was! He picked up the landline phone and dialled her mobile number with mounting apprehension.

"Catherine, hello, this is Peter – I'm sorry I didn't call for you when I said I would, something came up – Ella developed a slow puncture and it wasn't safe to continue. I'm having it fixed now – it has taken longer to find a matching tyre to the other one. I should be with you in about forty to fifty minutes. I'll make it up to you I prom…"

She didn't wait for him to finish "Don't worry – get here when you can, we still have plenty of time. Just be careful, I know you and I know the spell Ella has on you. No speeding to get here, do you promise?"

Her response left him grateful and obliged. "Of course not – I won't put myself or Ella at risk – I do promise. I'll see you soon." He had started to drop the handset when he caught the feeble sound of Catherine still speaking.

"Peter – where are you at the..."

He continued to replace the handset back into its cradle as he heard Catherine start her question, a question he didn't want to answer because it meant another lie, and for fear it could eventually expose his deceit. What Catherine didn't know wouldn't hurt her, and though he knew the maxim 'be sure your sins will find you out' was axiomatic, it was a fair bet she would never learn the truth.

So now it was time to see what Rennison was twittering on about. He intended to cut this current encounter with Rennison short – after all, whatever was going on was not, at this moment in time, top of his priority list, and not directly his problem.

He returned to the pool house to find Rennison and Fawly silently standing by the hidden room's door. As he skirted around the pool walkway and approached the two men waiting for him, Rennison stepped forward to meet him.

"Problem solved?" he queried.

"For the moment – but I have no time to waste. Show me what you were talking about earlier."

Rennison said nothing but turned towards the open door of the hidden room and gestured towards it – inviting him to go first.

Fawly, stiff and with a slightly resentful air, gave way to Rennison and then followed him into the hidden room.

As he took the lead, feeling Rennison close behind him, he entered the computer room to find chaos. He immediately saw what Rennison had been talking about. The computer had definitely been 'cannibalised' – in short, someone had started to disassemble all the internal circuitry of the computer. The side panels lay scattered across the floor by the back wall, while the chassis was now lying on its side in the middle of the floor. All plugs and cables to the screen, printer and audio unit had been disconnected and most hung like jungle creepers from the back of the desk. Inside the PC the motherboard had been ripped away and memory and interface cards now lay beside the computer chassis. Even the power supply unit had been unscrewed and left like an orphan on the floor.

It was not the vandalism that shocked; it was the fact that he had no conception of when or how this could have happened. Christ, he had been so careful to lock everything at night, had never left the house without ensuring the same security, and had watched hawk-like when any strangers were around.

"Well?" he heard Rennison say, but was unable to offer a reply.

He scanned the room again; everything appeared to be as it was. Besides the PC nothing else appeared to have been moved or broken.

Still aghast at the damage, and lost for any explanation, he shrugged his shoulders and started to turn away.

"No ideas on when or how this might have happened?" Rennison said.

"Not a bloody clue." he replied, still trying to work out how it was possible for someone to have the time to get in to the grounds, get into the pool and then complete the ruination of the PC. Then a thought occurred.

"I suspect the objective here wasn't just destructive – I never opened the access panels to the computer, so I have no idea what was inside it. Isn't it possible that the intention wasn't to destroy the thing, it was to retrieve something."

As he expressed his thoughts he realised yet another point.

"Tell me Rennison, how did you and Fawly get into the pool house without breaking in? I locked everything before I left the house this afternoon."

He turned to look at both men – each looking somewhat tense.

Then Fawly replied, almost as if he had been cued to do so.

"The two outer doors were slightly ajar when we arrived, I saw them just as we heard your car's exhaust note in the far distance and I gave chase."

Fawly's explanation did at least ring true – it meant that between the evening lock up the night before and his departure to meet Catherine late morning today, someone had found there way into the grounds. More to the point, they were able to unlock, or pick the locks, on the pool house doors.

Rennison gave wry look. "So it's a mystery again Mr. Enfield – but if we were to guess who it might have been, I suspect we would both come up with the same name."

The implication came as a surprise.

"Ferguson – but which one? I thought your people were on his tail, ready to nail him the moment he stuck his head above the parapet."

"No, we've lost the live one – he went underground three days ago and we have no idea of his location. He seems well able to loose a tail and not leave a detectable trail. By the way – it is Charles Ferguson we are chasing; the body we found in the hotel had a port-wine birthmark on his leg. We are still unable to get any background on the man – he doesn't appear to have any history. I reserve judgement on who killed him, though there is only one likely person in the picture. My guess is Charles Ferguson has been here in the pool house for a very good reason and, as you imply, not simply to destroy the computer and break contact with the web page messages. And yet, what we don't understand is that for all our contacts in Odessa, no UK agency has an ongoing operation down there. Oh, its true the arms shipment is missing, but how and why it disappeared has simply made this whole mystery into an even bigger enigma. As to your suggestion about the PC it rings true - simply destroying it would make no difference to what we know -only to what might be forthcoming. However, we know the messages have remained unchanged for some time, so it's a reasonable bet that Ferguson was after something that would provide a link between him and whoever is operating in Odessa. Okay, I'm afraid we have to leave now but given Charles Ferguson's record up to now I urge you to take precautions - I can't guarantee your security, so be on your guard."

He glumly nodded in agreement. "Alright, but in view of all the running around I have had to do on your behalf I've a mind to send you the bill for all the additional physiotherapy I'm going to need. I'm still not one hundred percent fit after all the hospital time I've had to endure. Let's face it, it's the least SIS can do."

Rennison looked blank for a moment and then sullenly acquiesced with a dip of the head and a forced smile. He then nodded to Fawly and both men turned and made their way back to the pool house doors. They exchanged a few remarks as they exited the pool house and then he watched them walk briskly to the side gate - it seemed it was their preferred method of entry and departure.

It was only having been alone amongst the disassembled and scattered PC for a good few minutes that he realised that neither Rennison nor Fawly had voiced a particular reason for their visit.

How had they come to be here at this time? How had it happened that they had timed their arrival for the exact time he had left? Perhaps it was coincidence - perhaps not. Whatever the situation he was now convinced there were too many unknowns for him to feel safe. With Charles Ferguson, an apparent killer, on the loose, and with him tied in to a thoroughly sorry mess, it created an almost palpable sense of apprehension.

But that said, what more would Ferguson want – if he had retrieved something from the PC then he had what he wanted – how on earth could he, Peter Enfield, still be important to Ferguson's plans. It didn't seem plausible.

As he stood bemused, letting time slip by, he suddenly realised he had a promise to keep. Catherine was waiting and he had no intention of delaying their meeting any longer. He stepped forward and kicked at the remains of the PC chassis in disgust – he was now obliged to buy a new PC and start from scratch. Even though his computer usage was very low, he had no intention of being without one.

As his foot struck the old PC chassis and the impact displaced part of the wire imprisoned motherboard, a small gold-black object jumped out from behind the motherboard and landed to the front.

Curious to see what the component was, he bent down and picked it up. It was an integrated circuit, but not one he expected to find – it had a quartz window overlaying the chip – this, he immediately realised, was an EPROM – an Erasable Programmable Read Only Memory. As he bent down and examined the motherboard he identified an on-board EPROM chip, but this one had been soldered in and was intact. What he had in his hand was not to do with the normal PC electronics – it had come out of something else, and whatever that something else was, it was now absent a crucial part. EPROM's were often used to store a computer BIOS, a Basic Instruction Operating System, in order to initiate the main software systems when switched on. If he didn't know better, the now shattered PC in front of him had not been simply one PC, but probably two in parallel. If not that, then tandem electronics, implying some kind of specialist operation. There was no doubt about it, there was more to this than either he or Rennison expected.

Pocketing the EPROM he gave the computer parts in the hidden room one last look before turning about and heading for the house. Harbouring a slight sense of foreboding, he rapidly locked up all the doors behind him as he moved from pool house to house. He did for the front door what he had done for all the others, making a strenuous effort to ensure the doors were fully shut, well fastened and secure.

As the front door latched tight, he ran for Ella and was moving out of the drive a split second after getting in; spraying out as much shingle from the rear wheels as he had on his arrival. As he passed through the gates and the adjoining lane came into sight, he made a mental note to rake the drive on his return; otherwise he would be left with a furrow-ridden drive and an eyesore.

The car sprinted out of the drive turning left onto the short section of lane from East Linkin leading to the Lidmouth main road. He had just started to apply the brakes prior to meeting the junction, when a figure burst out from bushes along the side of the lane. Whoever it was immediately occupied the middle of the narrow lane and started to wave him down with arms to the fore and palms upward, gesturing him to stop. The body stayed resolutely in front of the car and he had no choice but to instantly swing the car away from the maniac and brake hard. He stopped some five yards beyond the man, diagonally across the road and invading the oncoming side of the lane. As overwhelming relief for what had been a very narrow escape overcame him, he glanced back over his shoulder to see if the body in question was still upright. To his astonishment, the scruffy figure – unshaven, bedraggled and hardly recognisable, was none other than Charles Ferguson!

20

He had no time even to express surprise - Ferguson stepped forward and leaned down, resting his hands on the passenger's side door. His face was haggard and drawn, his clothes creased and soiled; the rings under his eyes and the grey tinged and scruffy beard all testified to a recent ordeal.

"Mr. Enfield, please don't be alarmed, whatever you may think, or have been told, I'm not any of these things - please believe me. I need help and you are the only one I can turn to or trust!"

For a moment that seemed like an age, he found it hard to determine what his reaction should be. Here was a man, a very unlikable man, if his previous experience was anything to go by, appealing for help. There was no reason why he should offer to help - not least that he might be talking to a career criminal and a murderer.

He slipped Ella into first gear with his foot depressing the clutch. If push came to shove, he was ready to accelerate away if Ferguson became hostile.

"They tell me you killed your brother - that you are the mastermind behind an arms shipment being diverted for criminal or terrorist purposes. More than that, you may have been responsible for the death of your sister and her children in a contrived air crash. All things considered, why should I trust you."

Ferguson shook his head in exasperation letting out a grunt of denial.

"Crap - no such thing - none of it true. They killed my nephew - not my brother. Before that, they blew my sister and her family out of the sky and they wanted me out of the way too. Christ Enfield - it's a long story and one you need to hear before you make any judgement. I know I was tight lipped when we last met but I had no choice. I'm not a threat to you, please give me an hour of your time and you will understand."

For reasons he couldn't define, he was inclined to listen to Ferguson's side of the story; but certainly not at that moment. Looking at Ferguson again he realised that the exhausted man he saw by his car was unlikely to be an immediate threat, and in no physical condition to be left at his present location. Yet he was a hindrance. Ferguson definitely wasn't wanted on his voyage to be with Catherine, and that priority, above everything, had his prime attention. Moreover, he had no intention of offering Ferguson his house as refuge even though it had once been a 'safe house' - that was too much of a risk.

"Have you any money Ferguson?"

"Ferguson looked stunned.

"What - money? Why?"

"Because you can't stay here, you need shelter and I can't talk to you this instant. I have other priorities. I need to park you somewhere safe for a short while before we can talk about all this."

Ferguson shook his head.

"Do you think I'm like this out of choice? I can't get money, the SIS have blocked most of my cards and are monitoring all ATM's and bank cash outlets in the hope of tracing me. I ran out of what little cash I had some time ago. I have nowhere to go and no one else to turn to." Ferguson snorted in disgust at his predicament. It was what he expected looking at Ferguson.

"Right – I don't know why but I'm going to help you, but as you say, it's a matter of trust. I will take you into town, put you up in a B and B and for the interim let you get cleaned up and get some food inside you. I have an appointment right now – it transcends everything – so you will have to wait until it's over before I can return to you and we can talk. Agreed?"

Ferguson hesitated and then, as acknowledgement of his acceptance, opened the Jaguar's passenger door and dropped into the seat.

As he fastened the seat belt he turned slightly and in a nearly inaudible whisper said "Thank you."

Ferguson stayed virtually silent for the four miles into town and simply nodded his thanks as they stopped outside a Bed and Breakfast in one of Lidmouth's more remote back streets. It was an early Victorian two up, two down middle of terrace. Apart from some re-pointed mortar, the odd reinstated brick and four brilliant white windowsills, it was virtually identical to all the other houses in the long terrace chain that made up the street. Except for the fluorescent sign in the window advertising 'B&B Vacancies' and 'Evening Meals – Surcharge' it was clearly anonymous and unexceptional. All to the good!

As Ferguson alighted from the car he pulled out his trouser pockets indicating his financial state.

He didn't need reminding and finding his wallet he pulled out two twenties and a ten pound note. "If the landlady insists on you paying up front, make sure you tell her you want a substantial evening meal. I'll be back here about six this evening – if I happen to be later than that don't panic, don't leave here and don't go out. You are safer if you keep your movements well hidden."

For the first time he saw Ferguson smile, "Yes, that's how I operate - why do you think I have managed to stay one step ahead of Rennison and his bunch. But thanks anyway, I'll see you later?"

"Yes you will. I hope it will be worth it."

He waited until he saw Ferguson admitted by a smiling, neatly dressed middle-aged landlady, and had a distant but vague recollection of starched pillowcases, crisp white bed sheets and the smell of Lavender water. He shrugged off what must have been a childhood memory and then depressed the accelerator well down, gunning Ella along the comparatively narrow, car infested, road. As he did so he was conscious of the fact that he was close to leaving a wing mirror or two behind as he negotiated his way back to the main road. His destination was the *Lidmouth Garden Restaurant* where he and Catherine were to meet. But now he was close to breaking his promise about caring for Ella, and the pleasure he anticipated in meeting Catherine had waned in the wake of Ferguson's appearance.

It was uppermost in his mind that he should forget the early afternoon's experience with Ferguson. This was particularly true for his forthcoming contact with Catherine; otherwise he was sure he would seem preoccupied and inattentive to her.

'Hell', he thought, 'it never rains but it pours and then it bloody well floods'. Today was the day he was due to dispense as much charm as he possibly could in order to get closer to Catherine. Yet should he appear preoccupied, he was as likely to distance himself from her as to create the rapport he wanted.

Inwardly cursing, he felt fate weighing in on him again; he appeared to be slipping back into the same inescapable entrapments his old life had flung at him.

Yet, whatever hassle might have assailed him in the past, he did what he always tried to do with Betty, stoically assuming the bright persona of the man he had hoped to be that day and hoping his lovely wife would not see through it. This time it was going to be a pretence again, but he dare not allow it to be a transparent pretence – there was too much at stake to let it slip.

He carefully turned Ella into the restaurant car park and cautiously manoeuvred her into a parking bay. He chose a parking bay on the fringes of the park – some distance from the restaurant and free from any other cars. Too often in the past his cars had served as punch bags for huge mud covered Land Rovers or battered, worn out and crash dented rust buckets, all of whom would somehow squeeze into the tightest space next to his. Then, with him absent, and with hardly any room to spare, they would hammer their doors against his car in an effort to allow their driver to squeeze their way out. Of course, usually the drivers had returned and driven away before he came back to retrieve his car – only to find one, or both of his doors scratched, dented or streaked with the paint of the departed car. He was not going to let Ella be the next victim of mindless, irresponsible, and sometimes jealous, idiots.

He locked the car and removed the under dash plug which disabled the car – a facility that Catherine's husband had installed. It rendered the ignition system entirely inoperative and was a nightmare to defeat; an indispensable security feature for what was a very valuable and otherwise very stealable car. When done he strode hesitantly through the parking lot into the restaurant entrance, pushing his way through the glass fronted swing doors into the foyer. The area was warm, plush and subdued. It was filled with the sound of hushed staff activity and a low background murmur of customer's conversation occasionally interrupted by the clink of cutlery and china.

As he looked through each adjoining archway into the serving area, he caught sight of Catherine already at their reserved table. He took a deep breath and made his way in. As Catherine saw him approaching she offered a broad smile – one of welcome and one of relief. He was massively relieved too; it was clear she was delighted to see him and at once most of his reservations about the forthcoming encounter receded.

As he sat down across the table from her she reached out and touched his hand.

"So glad you could make it – did you manage to sort out the tyre problem?"

For a brief moment he had forgotten his excuse for being late but then responded quickly.

"Finally – with some difficulty – tread pattern was the problem. Any number of makes of the right size but matching the one needing replacement was tricky. It was either that or replace both the old tyres with new ones and that was likely to be very expensive."

She gave him a quizzical look, "And you telling me that no expense would be spared in maintaining Ella! Shame on you!"

He bowed his head in mock disgrace and smiled as he looked at her again.

"*Mia Culpa* and you are right, but I didn't tell you that the problem of getting two tyres of the right size had its own problems – but all is now well. I would prefer to move the conversation along a bit and to ask..."

He suddenly realised that he had almost blown it. Catherine's obvious pleasure at seeing him had encouraged him to try to establish if she was happy to take their relationship further – but it was premature wasn't it? His enthusiasm had to be kept in check or...!

"What do you want to ask me Peter?"

"Only something minor Catherine – a query for after we have eaten – and to tell the truth I'm starving after dealing with Ella. Have you looked at the menu? Are they still serving by the way?"

She smiled "Yes to both questions, that's why we are here, they serve all day."

"Well done Catherine – I had visions of you and I surviving on ham sandwiches for the duration."

She shook her head "God no – if it came to that I would have taken us home and headed for the kitchen."

Her remark was an opportunity to test whether she felt he could be trusted – from trust there might be more, more than simple affection that is.

"In that case we could have gone to mine – you are welcome to explore it anytime."

"She presented another beaming smile coupled to an expression which seemed to convey eventual success and appreciation.

"Well, thank you Peter, I was wondering when I was going to see where you live, and to get a swim in this pool you keep talking about. Just for a while I was starting to think all that you had told me was imaginary."

His happiness following her remark soared, but he had no time to reply as a smartly outfitted waitress appeared. He could do no more than grin his agreement and leaned forward to pick up a second menu.

The meal and the small talk turned out to be extremely pleasant – he lost all feelings of anxiety and found it easy to talk to Catherine. Some of his jokes, even the more risqué ones, had her laughing freely and spontaneously. The enjoyment for both of them seemed to outweigh everything else. It was only when he caught sight of a wall clock, whose hands had apparently advanced three hours in what seemed only three minutes, that he was suddenly reminded of his appointment with Ferguson. It must have showed on his face and body language – Catherine noticed.

"Something wrong Peter?" she turned to gaze in the same direction she had seen him look, and saw the clock.

"Goodness, we've been here for hours. I'm sorry Peter, I do cackle on at times, have you something to do?"

He offered a glum and apologetic look. "Yes, I'm sorry Catherine – I forgot I was the reason we started late and I have yet to see someone to sort out some business. I'll get you home and go on to my appointment. Please believe me when I tell you how much I was enjoying today and being with you – I'm so disappointed. Don't worry, I will make it up to you I promise."

She bent down to pick up her handbag that leaned to the left side of her chair.

"Right Peter Enfield – I'll hold you to that and golly, I get a ride in Ella again."

He stood, searching for his wallet. As he did so his car keys slipped from his right hand pocket and as Catherine had moved towards him to exit the table, she retrieved the keys off the floor.

"Better still," she grinned, "I get to drive!"

He looked at her, knowing it was impossible to refuse someone he was now besotted with.

"Give me a kiss and you've got yourself a deal."

She didn't hesitate and he felt her melt into his arms. He felt her, smelled her and delighted in her, and for the first time in so many years, he really felt alive again.

"Dear me," she said as their lips came apart, "Had I known you were such a good kisser I would have given Ella to you for nothing."

"And had I known how good you were, I would have paid three times as much."

As they exited the Restaurant she took his hand "Three times as much? Is that all?"

They both smiled at one another and then broke into laughter.
***

Still gripped with amusement, Catherine looked around the parking lot and gave a shrug of her shoulders.

"Where is she Peter?"

He pointed to the far end of the lot.

"In a place all of her own, I try to make sure she isn't clouted by the doors of other cars. Come on, I know where she is."

She took his arm as they made their way through all the still crowded parking bays and very soon the back of the E Type came into view.

"Oh, she's really spick and span Peter – I can't wait to take her onto the road. Oh, by the way, I looked for the article about the plane crash and the er' Fergusons – no sign of it I'm afraid. You might have to visit the library in town and see if they have a back copy."

He shook his head. It's okay – I'm not in the least concerned, it's a long way down on my priority list and I'll catch up with it some time soon. But at the moment I'm interested only in the lovely lady that told me about the article, the one who is now about to have the thrill of driving Ella."

He smiled inwardly to himself, wondering whether he dare play the trick he was tempted to play."

"Okay, ready when you are." he said slipping in to the passenger seat.

She took the drivers seat and put her handbag down on the floor between her legs and the seat. He watched as she pulled the seat belt around and fastened it into the lock.

She checked for neutral on the gears and turned the ignition key – as he expected, nothing happened.

"Peter, what's wrong, she won't start – oh, of course!"

He gave a gentle chuckle. Holding up the security plug he said, "Your husband was a clever man. But, it will cost you another kiss to get her going!"

He had been right, the B&B smelled distinctly of Lavender coupled to a slight odour that was vaguely akin to scented bleach. The landlady was a throwback to another era, only in her fifties, yet having all the appearance and behaviour of a landlady from a 1930's seaside boarding house. Her dark blue, polka dot dress fell modestly to her ankles, which in turn showed a hint of thick tan stockings. On her feet was a pair of dainty, single strap patent shoes with a discreet silver buckle. Her greying hair was beautifully wound into two buns, one above each ear, and the simple pearl necklace she wore around her neck complimented her pale, unblemished facial skin. Only her lips had a blush of colour.

"Mr. Ferguson is in the garden – he's just eaten and I let him have his coffee in the open. He does seem to be a little reserved – has he been unwell? His clothes were terrible – I've given him some of my late husband's clothing while his are being washed. I'm so glad I didn't throw all my husband's clothes away!" She was well spoken, a gentle, softly modulated voice with a hint of having at one time been coached in an elocution class.

"Very sorry to hear of your loss. As for Mr. Ferguson, he has been through a difficult time of late – don't be concerned, if you've fed him he's definitely on the way to being restored."

She smiled, and with an outstretched hand pointed the way.

They passed through a drab but airy sitting room, which from its early décor had been unchanged for decades; then on through open French doors and into a large and spacious conservatory. The conservatory was modern, a vast contrast to the sitting room. The conservatory in turn stepped down onto a surprisingly long and well-tended garden. As he espied Ferguson, the landlady turned and retraced her steps into the conservatory.

Ferguson sat at a wide, radial-spoked hard wood patio table shaded by a large gaudy parasol. It was set back within a ring of variegated shrubs and small ornamental trees. He sat nursing a coffee cup, clearly replenished by the coffee service in front of him. The whole of the white porcelain coffee set was mounted on a gleaming silver tray.

"I see you are being well treated Mr. Ferguson."

It was clear Ferguson had not heard him arrive and for a moment he appeared distracted and at a loss.

"Oh, Mr. Enfield - glad to see you. Please sit down."

Ferguson waved a hand at an adjacent chair.

"Can I offer you a coffee - least I can do given that you are paying for it!"

Ferguson smiled, the colour had returned to his cheeks and he appeared much more animated. The clothes he wore were slightly too big for him; a check shirt and grey twill trousers, but all very clean and emanating a 'just washed' look and smell.

"Thanks, I will - two sugars please."

Ferguson leaned forward and began to pour from the elegant porcelain coffee pot. He dropped two sugar lumps in and held up the milk jug enquiringly.

"Yes - milk please - very white."

"Say when." Ferguson said as he began to pour.

"That's it - many thanks."

He took the proffered cup and saucer and took a sip - it was superbly aromatic and clearly very high quality and expensive.

"Thanks – well, now I'm here we had best get to the point – I still can't be sure why I gave you the benefit of the doubt. Convince me!"

Ferguson gave a short droop of the head and then looked up, his eyes locking with his.

"No doubt you believe that Rennison and Fawly are genuinely security agents – and you would be right. What they haven't told you is that I was in the same job as them for a long time...field agent, working on external threats to the UK. My sister was in a similar job but mainly on admin'. Your house, which at the time was a safe house, was her home because she also acted as housekeeper when it was periodically needed for a range of security operations."

He nodded as Ferguson confirmed what he already knew. "Yes, I know all that – other than the fact that Rennison speaks of you as a criminal and makes no mention of your security agency background. What I don't understand is what's at the root of all this business surrounding the PC, the mail order bride messages, and why is it that Rennison and his bunch are now treating you as a threat to national security. What's all this about an arms shipment being diverted? Not only that, if you are, or were, in the same agency as Rennison and Fawly why are you on the run – is what Rennison telling me true? To any observer it's bewildering – nothing seems to make sense!"

Ferguson bowed his head in acknowledgement.

"Listen Mr. Enfield, I don't know all of what you have been told, but here's my side. Almost a year and a half ago I had been suspended from my section – why isn't relevant at the moment – and I was staying at the safe house with my sister and her children. Just after I arrived, and to my amazement, she introduced me to a man whom she claimed was my half brother. My sister and I were both adopted by the same family but, according to my sister, not long after we were adopted, our biological mother re-married and quite quickly had another child. After reaching adulthood and discovering he had a half-brother and sister, he eventually identified and located my sister and I and decided to make contact. What neither of us knew was that Malcolm, that was his name incidentally, was an opportunist and a bad egg. He intercepted, or somehow got sight of, a confidential communiqué regarding the delivery of an arms shipment. Only my sister should have known about it, since she was handling the logistics from the UK to Estonia where the arms were destined. However, Malcolm saw a chance to make a great deal of money. I don't know how he did it yet, but he arranged for the shipment to be illegally diverted to another destination. Not only that, he made it seem that the whole process had been initiated by my sister and myself, even to the point of creating a plausible but phantom agent in Odessa who sent us coded messages using agency codes and cryptics; these we assume he had uncovered in a code book in the hidden room. Just as I was starting to unravel what was going on, my sister and I became aware of the fact that we were under investigation by our own internal security people – clearly they had been notified about the arms shipment and we were the prime suspects. I decided it was virtually impossible to extricate ourselves from the mire, so I arranged for my sister, her kids and myself to take a vacation – to Canada first and then to the US. You should understand that by this time Malcolm had fled the nest, and we were unable to pin down the very person who knew what had happened and why. We were well and truly exposed – escape was the only option, after all, who in the agency would believe in the existence and culpability of the mysterious

Malcolm. And even if they did, not only had my sister permitted an un-vetted individual to have access to highly confidential material, I was equally to blame for not insisting he be barred from the house."

Ferguson paused, taking another sip of his coffee. It was the opportunity to interpose.

"Okay - much of what you say I am aware of, but surely you must know that your movements and behaviour were bound to arouse suspicion - look at what happened at the airport when you boarded the plane with your sister and her kids. The CCTV footage clearly shows you supposedly getting on the plane and then departing - leaving your sister and her family isolated. Okay you told me all this when we met before but surely some one with security training would have realised it looked incredibly suspicious"

Ferguson suddenly looked surprised.

"How the hell did you know about the CCTV footage...? Oh, of course, Rennison! Well, as I boarded the plane I was still fuming about our situation, so I said to my sister that I was determined to nail Malcolm for the mess he had made for us, and I was going after him again. She wanted me to stay with her, but I decided locating Malcolm was the only way we were going to be exonerated from any charges against us. As the passengers travelling on our aircraft were still coming aboard the plane, I left my seat and slipped back through the oncoming queue and then through the check-in, telling them I had left a package in the departure lounge and that I would return in good time. I still had my boarding pass but, as you now know, I did not intend to return."

"And what about the air crash - what did you think when you heard the plane had crashed with no survivors?"

Ferguson stared ahead for a few long seconds, grief rolling

across his face. Then he threw his head back in exasperation.

"What did I think? I thought I knew exactly why the plane had crashed, and I didn't believe it was accidental. Malcolm, had a hand in it somehow, and regardless of whether I was right or wrong, I was going after him."

"It appears you finally caught up with him."

"Two or three times, but he was bloody elusive – each time I was on his tail he slipped away. Christ knows where he is now, and I'm running out of time."

"No...what I mean is, I know you caught up with him because Rennison told me."

Ferguson became rigidly attentive. "Rennison told you...what?"

"That this half brother of yours is dead – they found him in a London hotel room – he'd been poisoned."

Ferguson immediately looked aghast and turned his head away. For a short time he simply stared at the table, cloaking himself in silence and apparently in shock. The seconds passed and after a slight shudder he looked back.

"No – I don't credit what you are telling me. Rennison told you that I'm sure. But if Malcolm is dead, which I doubt, it's down to Rennison and his cronies."

"Why would he bother to lie about it – he's supposedly looking for you, and he knows you are still on the loose. He claims he has no idea who Malcolm was, or his supposed role in this matter. Personally, my feeling is that your crusade is now futile."

Ferguson stood up, stretching to his full height and pushing his chair back with a scrape.

"Listen – I know Rennison far better than you and he has a complete picture about Malcolm. Rennison was always faithful to one thing – Rennison. He manipulated, trapped or neutralised anyone that had an adverse influence on his investigations or career. I had years of seniority over him but Rennison was too ambitious. He wanted me out of his way because I had priority in terms of promotion – but that's not the half of it. I was a particular target of his because he had suspicions I had caught him with his hand in the till – I came to believe he was selling sensitive intelligence to anyone that would buy it. Truth was, at first, I couldn't prove it – he was very slippery and covered his tracks well. Then I convinced my chief that things were looking black as regards some of our operations and voiced my suspicions about Rennison. Reluctantly my chief agreed an investigation and I arranged for an intercept on Rennison's desk telephone. In one particular call he mentioned the 'safe house caretaker'. It was my sister he was referring to – she was processing information he wanted – information about an arms shipment. It was less than an indictment, but enough for me to ask for further surveillance. I persuaded my sister to move her work area to somewhere less accessible – hence the hidden room in the pool house. What I didn't know was that Rennison had pre-empted me – he had filed a carefully fabricated report under a 'need to know' basis with the section director and I was implicated as being reckless with confidential information. My own investigation was deemed a smokescreen and though I protested strongly I was suspended pending an enquiry; so I moved in with my sister temporarily. Almost immediately, she introduced me to Malcolm...told me his story, and told me he was taking a room in the house for a short while. Given my situation, I had misgivings about this but as things stood, I had very little sway in the way of options or objections. He had been given an unambiguous caveat regarding his stay – no prying into anything my sister was doing. He appeared to honour the stipulation and over the summer weeks I began to think I had misjudged him; he was affable and obliging and I became less suspicious of his motives in finding us – his long lost siblings. He even contributed to the domestic bills and arranged the odd jolly for my sister and myself. Nevertheless, it was inevitable that he would come to learn about the hidden room and on one occasion, as I was taking my sister's children to playschool, one of them asked why Uncle Malcolm spent so long swimming in the pool; why he always came out with his hair dry, and why was it he always locked the pool door and swam alone. I could only offer one answer but I kept it to myself. Thereafter I suspected his reason for visiting the pool was to get into the hidden room and scrutinise my sister's correspondence and documents. In that surmise, I was only partially correct. The truth was, as I now know, he had also spent time modifying my sisters computer. My doubts about Malcolm were confirmed when my sister confided in me that an unknown website had been uploaded on to her computer and she could not delete it. Not only that, it appeared to be a mail order bridal site originating either in Russia or the Ukraine. Worse still, it was delivering messages that implied we were connected to an outlaw organisation. When messages from central SIS, confirming the diverting of an arms shipment also appeared, we knew we had been deliberately compromised. We decided to confront Malcolm about what was happening but Malcolm had timed it right – the bastard had vanished."

For a moment Ferguson appeared to be intent on continuing his invective but then he froze, took breath, licked his lips, and slowly collapsed back into his chair, searching weakly for his coffee cup.

As he sat listening to Ferguson, the viewpoint from each of the roles in the impossibly fantastic interplay now reduced to a confusion of different perspectives and claims.

Who could he believe?

How had the simple act of buying a house led him into such a web of unwanted and irresolvable circumstances? Part of him furiously resented the unwanted participation he had once again become immersed in. His decision to keep out of the potentially damaging game Rennison, Ferguson and others were playing had been thwarted by Ferguson's re-appearance, and having heard Ferguson's story he more and more wanted out of it. He remembered the old adage, *'if the rules say you can't win, don't play the game'*, and he was now convinced that any further involvement would result in him being the looser. His earlier determination to absent himself from any of the adversaries machinations was once again forfeit. However, just one thing needed clarification.

"I take it that it was you who disassembled my computer – what were you looking for?"

Ferguson turned back after another sip of his coffee.

"Yeah, sorry...I had a feeling that I could find something that would confirm my suspicions about Malcolm tampering with the computer, and thereby disprove our participation in the arms shipment allegation we were facing. But there was nothing obvious – though I'm far from being a computer expert and had very limited time. Just in case you think it's all down to me, I have a feeling Rennison and his crew tried to get into the computer too. Just before you and I met for the first time, I'm damned sure I saw Fawly in the vicinity of your house on his way back to a black car."

He sat looking at Ferguson utterly perplexed, now even more baffled by all the conflicting views than before. Interrogating Ferguson was not going to illuminate the situation any further – there was no way of telling who was being entirely truthful.

He changed tack.

"What do you intend to do now – and please don't look at me for more direct help. I don't want any further engagement with this situation and I'm closing my doors to all and sundry. I'm the innocent party in all this, and I'm becoming fed up being constantly dragged into it and having my privacy abused. All I am prepared to do now is to give you a little additional money and then you are free to go, as you will. And please, whatever the outcome of your investigations, or your quarrel with Rennison, I don't want to know. I will report everything – that is, everything vague and incredible as it might be to the police if either you – or Rennison come to that – appear at my front door again. You and Rennison might see this as a game, I don't. I'm the one having to pick up pieces that should never have been broken in the first place."

Ferguson looked thoughtful and then gave a short nod of his head.

"So, you don't believe me...okay. It's no game by the way – far from it. Still, I'm grateful for your help so far. I'll take it from here, thank you."

He winced, "It's not a question of whether I believe you or not – it's my reluctance to get immersed in something I don't understand; and something that could likely undermine, or reverse, all I've gone through to be where I am now. I'm sure you have no idea what I'm talking about and I have no intention of explaining it all to you – but if you were me, I'm sure you would see my point of view."

Ferguson stayed impassive and then held out his hand.

"Mr. Enfield, you don't need an extraordinary reason to stay out of it. Were I you, I'd be of the same mind – again, my thanks and I'm sorry about the computer."

He shook Ferguson's hand warmly, chastened by the fact that

for all his previous enmity for the man, he had now revised his opinion to some extent. Ferguson's earlier aggressive demeanour had vanished, to be replaced to all appearances by a civil, sincere and dignified manner. It was not the same man, though he was cynical enough to accept that this might be what Ferguson wanted him to think; but if Ferguson was playing false, he had done it very well.

Then, he remembered his promise.

"Here, it's not much, forty five pounds, but it's all I have at the moment. I hope it helps. I take it you have paid your landlady."

Ferguson nodded in agreement; they both stood up and shook hands once again. There was nothing more to say and it was only as he walked back through the conservatory and said a courteous goodbye to a silent, and seemingly disapproving landlady, that it occurred to him that his conversation with Ferguson must have been overheard. He considered the possible consequences but foresaw none that could be a major threat. As his thoughts ran on, he suddenly remembered the Eprom. Too late – but possibly it was to his advantage.

22

Maybe it was the latent stress arising out of the meeting with Ferguson, or perhaps just the anxiety he'd felt before meeting Catherine, but as he steered Ella into the driveway his lower back, already uncomfortable, became intensely painful. It had been a long and fraught day and he guessed that tense and tired muscles were now adding to more scar tissue contraction. Whatever the case, he needed to get into a hot bath and quickly. He drew Ella up as close to the front door step-way as possible and with only a few feet clearance left her marooned like a four-wheeled barrier to the main access of the house. He had no qualms - it was his house after all.

He made straight for the kitchen and had the kettle boiling for a cup of coffee while he searched the medical box for his emergency anti-inflammatory tablets. He prevented the kettle from completing its heating and made the coffee with water 'off the boil'. The coffee was immediately drinkable and he downed three anti-inflammatory tablets and a pair of painkillers to accelerate the relief. There were more upstairs in the en-suite wall cabinet if he failed to get any respite.

He limped upstairs and made for the bathroom. He heard the boiler fire up as he started to run water into the bath and as his head came up his eyes automatically scanned across the large frosted pane of window glass that served to illuminate the bathroom. The window faced the garden, and although insufficiently transparent for objects and garden buildings to be well defined, the frosting was reasonably shallow and it was able to convey a general shape or colour. Now, down in the garden, he saw a body shape and movement. For some reason, he wasn't surprised – again his thoughts turned to yet another of Rennison's unannounced visit's.

What was utterly unexpected, and froze him into a clutching, morbid fear was the sudden blackout of the window as a hood was forced over his head and powerful arms pinned him into immobility. Even worse, was the sudden sharp soreness of a hypodermic needle driven into his left buttock. As this happened, fear turned to panic, but panic rapidly subsided as his mind sank away and he sought refuge inside his head with his old friend the voice of sanctuary, a voice that told him it was time to sleep.

When he surfaced, he came back to a hazy consciousness, trailing the little voice from the deep darkness where it lived and which kept repeating something almost unintelligible, but sounded like *'No-more-sleepy-sleepyhead-wakey-wakey - sleepy-head - wakey-wakey'*.

But waking up brought him into a world of intense and un-remitting pain, and as he tried to open his eyes he was obliged to keep them closed. Tears instantly flooded out in response to the excruciating sensation of torture coming from his wrists, his lower legs and his back. For a moment he slipped back into oblivion and then with fearful reluctance re-surfaced, desperately attempting to struggle away from what was causing all the pain – but movement only made it worse. Above all the torment he had to endure the freezing cold – still naked, he was already badly chilled by the dank surroundings and it was getting colder. As his mind tried to override the upsurge of terror, he realised that he was bound to a chair, and it was the bindings around his wrists and ankles, strangling each limb with thick, immensely tight cable ties that was the seat of most of the pain.

The pain in his back he recognised – it had been there before he'd blacked out and some of the rest appeared to be cramp, but whatever the source he found it impossible to ignore. He attempted to relieve some of it by straining forward and back and tensing the muscles in his body, but nothing came close to any relief – if anything it was worse.

As he tried to move he grunted and gasped, or let out a "Dear Christ" through gritted teeth as each spasm of pain reasserted itself. How he had come to be where he was had no immediate answer – all he knew was that it was terrifying, nearly to the level of abject panic.

He was so consumed with his predicament that he was hardly aware of his surroundings, but two things did register; first, the incoming light was limited to an oval weather and insect stained glass window built into the facing wall above his head. Second, it appeared he had been positioned in the middle of a forbidding grey-stone room that had moisture seeping from the walls – the sheen of the moisture, and the weeping algae outgrowth glistened grey-green in the sombre window light. Added to this was the smell; a dank, pungent, all pervading odour, which was very much akin to rotting vegetation.

As the chair tottered with his efforts, he had the idea that if he were to tip over, the impact might break the chair and allow him to escape. It was worth a try, and he began to make exaggerated movements to destabilise the chair. It was excruciatingly painful and he began to gasp again with the pain and effort from each shift of his body, only persevering because at last the chair legs began to lift from the floor.

Awash with pain, he threw his weight sideways to gain momen–

tum and the chair started to follow all his movements. He sensed it required only one last contraction of his tortured limbs for it to topple. As everything became severely unbalanced, and the chair started to creak as three, two and then one lone leg was left in support, something suddenly applied a downward force and snapped the chair back onto four legs.

For a moment, he was at a loss to understand how all his exhausting effort had been wasted. Then a voice close to his left ear said, "Now, now Mr. Enfield I should stop that if I were you - you might hurt yourself!"

He froze in shock - now caught in a subjective expansion of time, and for the first time detecting ice-cold sweat rivulets creeping slowly down his face. He tried to twist his head around to see who was speaking, but it was impossible. Whoever it was had retreated further away from the back of the chair and remained out of sight.

Then the voice came again - a little distant this time.

"Better you and I remain unknown to one another Mr. Enfield - I assure you that seeing me will have no influence on your future, or our negotiations."

The voice had an edge of familiarity but he couldn't place it. The voice spoke as if he had total insight and confidence, as though it was always in command.

Still breathless and now drenched in cold sweat, he shifted in the chair still trying to alleviate some of the pain - through gritted teeth he gasped out the obvious question.

"Negotiate...what exactly?"

From the sound of sharp footsteps behind him, unmistakably caused by leather soles and metal heels on hard flagstones, the unseen individual appeared to step further forward and gave a slight snigger of irritation.

"Come, come Mr. Enfield - we know the PC in your pool house was vandalised. We also know that whoever did it was looking for something. It's that something that is important to us, and we think you have it."

His befuddled pain racked mind hardly registered as the man spoke. All he wanted was for the pain to end - he might just give everything he had for that to happen.

"Christ, whatever it is you can have it - just what are you looking for?"

His remark was followed by yet another sniff of polite indignation.

"Surely you know Mr. Enfield - it's Peter isn't it? You see Peter, neither Rennison nor Ferguson has stopped visiting you. They still appear to be searching for something to do with the computer in your 'er 'office', and whatever it is seems to be of paramount importance to both of them. Now, my information is that the PC was recently vandalised, and for good reason one would think. That reason - I'm tempted to propose - was to recover something inside the computer. Since neither of the two wandering minstrels I have just referred to appear to have been successful, I can only conclude that either their search was pointless – that is, there never was anything to recover in the first place - or it was found by someone else. Am I clear so far?"

Now it was obvious why he had been kidnapped, and he knew full well where the unknown speaker was taking his argument. If he was to escape from the present agonising situation he had to think fast - he had to divert the man's focus from him to someone else.

"Loosen these damn bindings, I'm losing circulation in every limb, it's bloody painful - everything is going numb, if you don't release me soon I'm going to get some serious problems."

There was a brief silence.

"Well Peter, perhaps we can come to an arrangement – you get your freedom from that chair and I get what I want...and I think you know what I am talking about."

It was doubtful if he had any option, but it was worth a try. Raising his voice he let his tone reflect anger and resentment.

"You may think I've got something you want, but you should not eliminate Rennison – I wasn't the one that discovered the vandalised computer, he did – well, it was Fawly and Rennison. Fawly caught up with me a mile or so from my house and on Rennison's instructions called me back. I have no idea what Rennison was doing while I was away and he was alone in the pool house. Listen, would Rennison tell me if he had found something? Would he tell me if it was he who was responsible for sabotaging the computer in the first place? No, he definitely wouldn't! Whatever you're chasing it's a fair bet Rennison has it, certainly Charles Ferguson hasn't got anything to support his cause, otherwise he would have slipped away by now and begun his promised vendetta against Rennison to clear his name."

His retort seemed to have some effect. The silence that followed his outburst was heavy and intimidating, but the man interrogating him had obviously heard something that interested him.

"So, from what you say I surmise that you and Ferguson have had an interesting *tête-à-tête* – I didn't know that. Seems we have been remiss. That aside, why should I believe you Peter, knowing Rennison as I do he can be very persuasive at times. Bribery and coercion go hand in hand with his *modus operandi* – and you could be one of his converts."

It was too much, and he said so.

"Don't be bloody daft, I'm not interested in this bloody stupid business. I got dragged in because I was unlucky enough to become the owner of one particular house. All I wanted was a quiet life and I don't give a damn about Rennison or Ferguson or anything to do with either of them. My last involvement with Ferguson was to take pity on him. My only involvement with Rennison and his crew was to attract their attention by having the bloody computer in my pool house. Whatever their collective interests, Rennison or Ferguson, I've washed my hands of all of them. I don't know who you are, or what it is you are chasing, but you're wasting your time with me - I'm not part of the bloody scheme."

It was all he had - his head lolled to the side and he felt utterly spent, The pain in his hands and feet was beginning to fade - it was a very bad sign, the circulation had stopped and he was in danger of total atrophy in every limb. Only the painkillers and the anti-inflammatories he had taken before his abduction was holding the agony at bay. Nevertheless, unless he was released soon, he would be crippled for life.

He held on - somehow he clung on to the belief that he was hard to kill - that having survived before, he could do it again.

Time passed and slowly his stoicism began to fade and he came to believe he had been abandoned - left to die.

Then he heard what appeared to be a whispered conversation; short pauses broke in as though body language or hand motion and signs were occasionally taking the place of words. It was clear there were at least two individuals behind him.

Now came a long silence, nothing else seemed to be happening.

Nothing penetrated his half conscious state other than the sound of a rising wind buffeting the outside walls. As the wind lifted he heard heavy rain striking a distant metal roof like a machine gun.

A decision had to be made. He tried to speak but his physical condition was wretched – nothing came out. He was close to giving up, and had he been able to speak he would have volunteered possession of the Eprom. Enough was enough – he wanted to live but not as a cripple. Now, as cold bit deeper into his body, he began convulsive, unstoppable shivering that shook him further into physical and mental exhaustion. He lapsed into a sense of hopelessness – for all his determination to survive the willing spirit had been defeated by the unwilling body. Soon he would not even have the reserves of energy to shiver; after which was certain death.

Then the sallow window light vanished, and the world went black, as the opaque hood he had been forced into in the bathroom was refitted over his head. This sudden covering was rapidly followed by another hypodermic injection, this time in his arm. In a way, he was deeply grateful for not being forced to witness his own oncoming death. Indeed, it was a mercy to be permitted to drift away into oblivion once again – deep into another pain-free world.

It was a good world, an amusing world. A world where he was a big soft sausage wobbling on the shoulders of two strong men walking one behind the other, but out of step, so that the front of the sausage was constantly out of phase with the back. It only stopped when the big men found a large frying pan and dropped him in. For a while, the pan was cold, and the world fairly pleasant. But then it started to heat up and he felt the fat begin to drip out of him. It was too much, and he tried desperately for a way out; but all that happened was that he kept sliding back down the inclined sides of the pan every time he attempted to crawl up. The more he slid back the more he started to panic, as each return made him hotter and hotter until he was resigned to burning up.

Then his friend, the little voice, began to scold him for being so incompetent, and told him that since he couldn't get out of the frying pan the fun was over and it was time to return to wakefulness. As it spoke, he began to rise, leaving the pan behind. He began to become aware of another world – this one was far from distinct but it made his eyes light up behind his lids and sent messages of pain to him. Now increasingly sentient and aware of a racking universal torment in all his limbs, he tried to wriggle away from an even greater one in his back.

Suddenly the light in his eyes gave him distinct pictures; blue-grey here, white fluffy things there – all interspersed by smaller lumps of deep grey cotton wool. Now his naked body added to his senses as a slightly warm flood of air, flowing over his skin, conveyed gentle warmth.

He finally came too lying over the front passenger and drivers seat of Ella, and as he moved his head to see over the car's window trim he saw the front door of his house. Realising, thankfully, that for the moment he had somehow escaped the torture and was still alive, he gave thanks to his guardian angel, mentally kissing her smiling lips in gratitude. Nevertheless, the pain began to overwhelm him again, not least the red-hot poker that was forced point first into his back. Added to all this was an inability to see well, his sight was telescoped and bleary and he saw his feet and hands through eyes that refused to focus properly. Even so, he was horrified by the deeply indented and swollen purple-red blobs at the end of his arms and legs. Again, he wriggled, trying to remove whatever it was pressing so painfully into his lumber region – a he moved, awareness filtered in to his mind – it was the car's gear stick. With a supreme effort, he shifted his position and slipped away from it, relieving some of the torment.

Slowly surveying his hazy surroundings, he appeared to be alone; no matter his poor vision, there was no one else near him. Regardless of his condition, he was now condemned to trying to get into the house on his own, and began the clumsy, feeble movements that would get him to rest and safety. He needed painkillers desperately, and it was no more than three yards, taking in part of the hallway and a flight of stairs, to the bathroom's analgesics stock. Thereafter, with the pain mitigated he yearned for his bed and the hope of sleep. He used the still numb heel of his left foot to repeatedly attack Ella's passenger door lock and eventually succeeded, sliding out of the car feet first and on to the front door step-way. He twisted over to his front and on all fours inched towards the door, praying he would find it open.

It took all of five minutes to crawl the three yards to the door and each movement increased the torture. Reaching up he tried to push against the door but there was no movement at all, it was soundly locked. As he berated himself for stupidly expecting an open door, or to find some keys left in the lock - something that could not in this instance be the case - it was clear to him that his only option now was to take the side gate access to the kitchen door and try to break in. With a brief cry of frustration and disappointment, he rolled to his side, drawing his legs up into a foetal position and hoping for a reduction in the pain and renewal of strength. For the moment he tried to wait for some of the ever-increasing agony in his limbs to abate as pins and needles began to signal a return of circulation. As the torment started again, tears of wretchedness, humiliation and dejectedness started to roll down his face and he began to sob. All his previous traumatic episodes had seen him taken to the limit of his endurance, but at this moment he was well beyond it.

As the tears began to flow he flinched back as he heard the door lock operate.

To his astonishment, the door swung open and as he craned his neck to look up, he found himself staring into the face of Charles Ferguson.

23

He woke to find himself in his bed and alone in the bedroom. As he listened to the silence in the house he concluded that there was no one else with him. He imagined Ferguson had put him to bed and from the dressings around his feet and wrists had carried out some basic doctoring. If so, he was immensely grateful; he tested movement in his wrists, hands, ankles and feet, finding that most of the pain had subsided into a dull ache though he was having to contend with massive swelling and engorged blue green tissue marking ruptured blood vessels. As he pulled back each dressing there were still deep-set, indented, and distinctly angry looking weals around each ankle and wrist where the cable ties had bit in. Some of the skin was sloughing off and behind it blood was seeping out. He guessed that the only thing keeping the pain down were the analgesics and anti-inflammatories.

He slipped around the bed, bouncing on the mattress unsteadily and pulling the bedclothes away. His stomach was gurgling with hunger and it needing to be satisfied - food was a definite priority. He was unsure of his legs and tried to experiment in standing by sitting on the edge of the bed and planting both feet on the ground. As he did so, he heard a noise - someone was coming up the stairs.

He had no time to react, as half a body appeared, rising up at the top of the staircase and slowly emerging to full height on the landing. It was Charles Ferguson, carrying a wide tray with bowls and plates stacked upon it. Carefully balancing the top-heavy tray against tipping, his tall and wide shouldered figure shuffled gingerly into the bedroom.

"Hello Enfield, glad to see you back in the land of the living. Thought I might get some food down you – after your ordeal my guess is you could do with it."

Ferguson smiled, pulling back the bed covers more fully while holding the tray with one unsteady hand; then he carefully placed the tray at the end of the bed.

"Are you telepathic – how did you know I was up and how are you still here?"

"Heard you move – your body moving the bed – the kitchen is directly below, your bedroom floor here is the kitchen ceiling, and given my situation I'm tuned to any noise in the house however slight. Anyway, I was getting a snack so I thought of you. Here, have some soup; better you have soup first...you shouldn't eat too much too soon – your guts may rebel."

Ferguson handed him a bowl of what appeared to be tomato and vegetable soup – one of 'back of the cupboard' emergency 'cuppa' soups. Whatever its status, it smelled and tasted delicious.

As he wolfed down the soup he was struck by the incongruous situation. He was in effect being nursed by someone who by rights should not be here, someone who should have vanished from his life, never to be seen again. Why was Ferguson back in the house?

As the final spoonful of soup and the last crushed crouton glided down his throat, he gave a nod of thanks to Ferguson who had now picked up a plate from the tray and was about to exchange it for the empty soup bowl.

"Toast and cheese – take it easy, don't throw it down, chew it properly."

He paused as he held out the soup bowl for Ferguson to take in exchange for the plate.

He was now ravenous, the soup having stimulated his appetite. But he held off biting into the toast and cheddar cheese to pose a question.

"How is it I waved goodbye to you yesterday and here I am saying hello to you again today. How is it you were in my house when I arrived back?"

Ferguson smiled – an indulgent smile tinged with what may have been regret – and replaced the soup bowl on the tray.

"We said our goodbyes five days ago – I have been nursing you for the last three!"

He was caught in mid bite and turned to see if Ferguson was joking. From Ferguson's now grim expression, he clearly wasn't.

He put down the plate on the bedside table, his appetite arrested for the moment.

"Five days? Christ, say that again!"

"I came back to give you some news the day after we last met – I arrived here early morning and found the house wide open and deserted. The front door was ajar so I immediately had my suspicions. I decided that if what I had discovered here was innocent, then at some point you would return – but, of course, you didn't. However, I decided that my being here was safer for the while, since I doubted Rennison and his crew would need to come back. I also decided to wait for forty-eight hours – before reporting you missing; after all I had little inkling of your situation. I hesitate to admit it, but staying here was very much to my convenience too. That said, I had no idea at all about you until you were dumped outside the door on the second day. I was in the hallway when I noticed movement behind the glazing on the front door. It was you trying to get in – and you were in one hell of a mess. I got you up here into bed, stuffed tablets from your bathroom cabinet down your throat and hoped for the best. I had no chance of getting you into hospital or contacting the police and emergency services without exposing myself again; so I kept watch over you and prayed you would recover. You were unconscious for almost 60 hours – whatever they pumped into you must have been a massive dose of some long–lived hypnotic. You were in one hell of another world for a long time. There were times when I thought you would surface as a complete psychotic. Maybe that was the idea, I don't know. What I do know is that whoever did this to you was probably part of the game you and I are aware of. I can only assume they believe you have, or might know the whereabouts of, what I was looking for in the computer. Like Rennison and company they want to prevent anyone else getting at whatever they see as the smoking gun. I thought the last message on the Odessa website you told me about was the key to finding the originator, but clearly it wasn't. Since you got sucked in to this sorry mess simply by accident, I'm really sorry you had to endure what you have – my fault really. Do they have any reason to think you know more than you say you do?"

Ferguson's revelation and the query left him cold – three days had disappeared and he had only a hazy recollection of any of it. Even the memory of the ordeal in the old stone building, wherever it was, seemed like a past dream.

He turned to Ferguson, noting again the man's impressive physique. He could see how he easily he was lifted up the stairs and put to bed.

"I never saw them you know – I was getting ready for a bath. Without warning, a hood went over my head and I got a hypodermic in me. Next thing, I'm in this grimy, derelict, stone built barn of some sort, tied into a chair by incredibly tight cable ties and being questioned by a figure that always stayed directly behind me and out of sight. I came out of it lying across the front of the car – and the next thing I see is you! Christ – I can tell you, I don't want any of that again."

Ferguson sniggered. "Thanks, I didn't think I was that ugly!"

He ignored the joke – it didn't register.

"No – not you. But here's something that will cheer you up and answers your question – though this admission comes with an apology. I did find what I think you were looking for – a semiconductor chip, an Eprom, which I'm sure was part of the computer. I didn't tell you when we met at the boarding house – I felt I needed a bargaining chip – sorry for the pun. I'm sorry too if you were compromised even further, but now you know about it, I'm happy for you to have it. It cost me what I have just gone through – and incidentally, I never made known to my kidnappers that I'd found it. I imagine the Eprom is important – if so, it could help you expose who it was planted the information about the Odessa arms diversion."

Ferguson eyes widened and he shook his head in disbelief.

"My God – an Eprom? Why the hell didn't I notice it when...?"

"Easy to miss something like that – it was pure luck that I found it. It's in the glove compartment of the Jag – Ella's been keeping an eye on it for you."

Ferguson looked puzzled "Ella?"

"Sorry – name of the car – my E Type – why don't you check it out, I'm going to try to make the bathroom and remove this stubble on my face; then I'll see if I can get dressed. Hope you don't mind but I prefer to struggle in private."

Ferguson gave a nod of his head and stood up from the bed.

"When you are decent there's a development you might be interested in, I'll talk to you when you are ready."

24

Ferguson remained downstairs a he gingerly stepped into underwear, socks, shirt and jeans. Painful spasms greeted his attempts as his wrists and feet were asked to carry out tasks beyond their state of repair. Simply pulling underwear from draws, and extracting clothes out of wardrobes that seemed a mile away had him panting and almost exhausted. He had overestimated his recovery and strength.

Two or three times he sat back onto the bed to wait for a particularly painful moment to pass. He twice had to pause while shaving – even holding and manipulating a lightweight electric razor around his face with bruised and swollen balloon like hands had sapped his reserves. It took another five minutes to extract more medication from the blister packs and with distended and uncooperative fingers convey them to his mouth.

After managing a limping descent to the ground floor and on into the kitchen – fighting further fatigue and increasing spasms of pain – he brewed two mugs of coffee. He then carefully steered himself and his two trophies into the lounge. Ferguson was already seated, and watched in admiring silence at the infinite care with which his host guided himself and his injured limbs about, nodding his thanks as a coffee mug was placed delicately on the table in front of him.

Having completed this chore, and deeply thankful it was over, he stretched slowly back to the vertical again taking care not to incite more stabs of intense pain from his hands and feet. He then turned, and sank gratefully into the adjacent settee. As he collapsed into the soft upholstery he realised he should have taken more analgesics with him; but too late, the kitchen supply was depleted and the others were upstairs in his bathroom cabinet.

"Well done – I didn't think you would carry it off".

He turned to see Ferguson smiling in admiration.

"Nor did I, but I'm damned if I'm going to let those bastards who tortured me win this round too. Christ, I'd love to get my hands around the neck of the shit who interrogated me, I'd repay all this agony with interest."

Ferguson gave a smile of agreement.

"Now that's something we might well pursue with success. I said I had something to tell you and it's an interesting development. Are you up to it?"

He nodded grimly. Ferguson took breath.

"While I had the safety of the boarding house you took me too, I had no one else to talk to except my landlady. I'm sure it wasn't inadvertent, but she was privy to a large part of our garden discussion, and as we conversed it was clear she had more insight than I – or anyone else for that matter – might have expected from someone like her. I discovered that she was a retired special branch case analyst having married a colleague in the same service. When he died she retired to open a Bed and Breakfast – to supplement, so she claimed, her widow's and personal pensions. However, my guess is that it was simply to have the occasional chinwag with guests – she certainly didn't need the money! My God, the meals were wondrous and she simply couldn't stop being generous with clothing and anything else I needed. She hardly appeared interested in my paying her for my room; sheer luxury by the way, and as it went, I half expected her to pay me for agreeing to be a guest! Anyway, she and I had an interesting exchange of ideas – and yes, I glossed over the events you and I know about. I gave her some of my background after I heard about hers. I felt she could be trusted and, in a way, that trust has borne fruit. Not that she made a direct contribution, just an observation. She said in that her experience it wasn't what you could see that was crucial – it was what was yet to be seen that made the difference. In short, don't presume you have the whole picture – events are often moulded by invisible hands so look outside the main picture and eliminate any external influence before focusing too much on the obvious. That made me think – maybe Rennison, my half brother Malcolm, and indirectly yourself, were not the only ones manipulating, influencing or taking part in the game. The Odessa debacle was probably much more than we estimated. While I was waiting for you, I considered my landladies advice. Recalling all recent events, I asked myself, what information I was relying on as valid and what were the bounds of the issue. For some reason I kept harping back to the day my sister introduced me to my supposed half brother. Why I asked myself did I take her word about him as credible? She, I remember, appeared to have no doubts about him, and as things stood at the time, I had no inclination to question everything – I was too immersed in my own troubles to be dubious or distrustful. Anyway, while I was here on my own, that is before you were dumped back here, I phoned an old associate of mine to do some checking for me. He contacted me during the time you were abducted. What I was told turned out to be a revelation. My biological mother, and of course that of my sister, did remarry after we were adopted, and Malcolm, our half brother, was born very soon after my sister and I had our second and third birthdays. What we didn't know was that our mother had yet another child two years later – another son. He was named Meredith, and Meredith turned out little better than his brother Malcolm. Both were pathologically bad. In fact, Meredith served two prison sentences for extortion and armed robbery; the only crimes for which he was actually convicted, but not for which he was responsible. He has an arrest sheet as long as your arm – some of it for Internet scams. He'd picked up some 'techy' training from somewhere. It seems our biological mother married into a criminal family called Bennet. Like father like sons it appears. It's conjecture I know, but I am inclined to the idea that Malcolm and Meridith got wind of my problems and using the excuse of a family reunion, thought I could be of use to them – not surprisingly since I was in such a weak position. It must have been heaven sent for Malcolm to find he had walked into a haven of secrets with my sister handling SIS documents. I believe that Malcolm found out about the arms shipment and, in collusion with Meredith, switched the destination. He was clever enough to make it seem that my sister and I were the culprits – the smoking gun was the Eprom – sourced I suspect from Meredith and generating plausible fake messages; all supposedly coming from a female contact in Odessa. However, I can't pin the plane crash on either one of them as yet, and there is no doubt that since only Meredith is supposedly alive, only he is able to say more on that matter. Once I can download what's on the Eprom, Rennison will have his proof and he can follow it up – more importantly I can get out of Rennison's way and chase Meredith. He'll pay for what he has done to you and me. "

As he listened to Ferguson he saw the logic of the statement. Yet, the appearance of this Meredith Bennet so late in the game came as a surprise. Why would Meredith Bennet not be long gone by now? If the story held water, the arms shipment was now money in his hands, and he had no reason to want to come out from the dark. Not only that, if Meredith was the one who had put him through so much pain, why was the Eprom still so important?"

As his hosts only response was silence, Ferguson gave a patient and expectant look.

"You find it all hard to believe?"

No he didn't, he said – not all of it, but if it was credible, he was unsure how to handle the implications.

"Truth to tell I've had too much of this business – as I told you before, I'm only interested in extricating myself from the whole bloody mess. I care not one bit that this Meridith Bennet has appeared as a player, nor that he and his crew have succeeded in hijacking an arms shipment and have apparently disposed of his own brother and half sister in the process...and I can only sympathise with you that he most probably had a hand in the death of your sister – but where I really do care is that it's a danger to my well-being and my future. I care even more that they made me suffer, and that they might do it again. If I had any sense I'd report this bloody business to the police – that is, if it wasn't for the fact that the resulting investigation would create an upheaval far worse than things are now. More likely, the police would take the view it wasn't their jurisdiction and pull in SIS. Rennison and his bloody department would simply get it passed back to them. It would be futile – a full vicious circle, of events."

Ferguson nodded in agreement.

"I understand – and I have no intention of trying to dragoon you into taking any more risks – I know what it's like to be on the receiving end of unwanted interest. I think it better I go on my way and do what has to be done. I found the Eprom by the way, I feel a little more confident now. That said, you may not be in the best state to fend off any pressure, do you want me to ask your GP to drop in – from the look of things you could do with a little TLC."

He gave a gasp of disgust.

"All I need is rest, some time for recovery and some more bloody pain killers. Before you go could you nip upstairs and dig out my prescription tablets in the bathroom cabinet. They are intended for the scar tissue on my back and legs but they will definitely help my wrists and ankles."

Ferguson gave a brief nod of his head, stood up and left the room.

He instinctively looked above him at the ceiling as he listened to Ferguson's methodical footsteps climbing the stairs; then the tread softened as movement was muffled by the thicker carpet on the landing, bedroom and on-suite bathroom. He mentally urged Ferguson to make haste. Regardless of the risks in over-dosing, the need for more of his medication was becoming crucial. Now he was upright his hands and feet were becoming more blotched and swollen, and though both feet had a similar purplish hue, the left foot was much darker and was beginning to refuse any movement. Added to it all was an ever persistent throbbing overlaid with pins and needles in all his limbs. He decided that once he had suppressed some of the pain and swelling, and Ferguson had left the house, he was going to soak both his hands and feet in as much hot water as he could stand to encourage circulation. After that, he was going to pray.

Again he heard footsteps on the stairway and Ferguson appeared carrying blister packs and a glass of water.

"What dose do you...?"

As Ferguson came close he reached up and tried to grab the

two blister packs but only managed to hold them between the palms of his hands. He dropped the blister packs onto his lap. The tablets were lined up like so many regimented pimples and he quickly estimated that even with largish doses he could get by for at least four days. He looked up at Ferguson. "I need three of each – can you help?

Ferguson reached down and ripped open three blisters on each pack. He then walked to the kitchen and came back with a glass of water. Using his cupped hand Ferguson rested the side of his hand against his mouth and funnelled the tablets in. He thankfully swallowed the six capsules and half the water.

Ferguson stood by with a frown on his face. "You're not too good old son – you sure about a doctor?"

"No – I don't want to draw attention to myself and the easiest way for that to happen would be to have a doctor call and for me to end up in hospital – which I'm certain would follow. As far as Meredith Bennet is concerned I'm actually safer here by myself – I'll pretend no one's at home.

Ferguson gave a non-committal shrug.

"Okay – your decision – I'll be on my way."

Even though the pain was still distracting him, two important issues came to mind.

"Listen, you will need money – take all you can find from my wallet in the right hand bedside cabinet...assuming it is still there of course – and since you are five miles from civilisation there is nowhere you can go without transport; the rural bus service is abysmal and a taxi would leave a trail – so that's out! I never thought I would ever say this, but I am going to lend you my E Type... and by Christ, you had better take care of her or else. The keys are on top of the cake tin on the left work surface as you go into the kitchen. You can't miss them. Now...please, leave me to repair and recuperate and don't forget my warning – you pay for any damage to Ella."

From his stance and stunned facial expression, Ferguson stood not only astonished but also overwhelmed by the generous offer. He whispered a "Thanks – understood – I owe you...I will repay you." and made for the bedroom and kitchen. As he entered the hallway he called back "I have some experience with an E Type – don't worry, I'll be careful."

By the time Ferguson reappeared, holding keys in his hand, some of the overall pain and the areas of pins and needles had noticeably abated, and he was deeply thankful that the medication had kicked in so quickly. He nodded a curt acknowledgment as Ferguson indicated he was about to leave and turned his head to concentrate on fighting his injuries. Only a few seconds seem to pass before he heard the front door being pulled shut followed some seconds later by the low exhaust note from Ella announcing the firing of the engine. Then he heard Ferguson give a short lift of the engine revs after which came the familiar but quickly receding burble of the tuned exhaust system as the car drove away.

He gave up a short prayer that fate was on the side of Ferguson, Ella and of course himself – someone who had just broken a definite, uncompromising promise to both Catherine and himself. It was difficult to rationalise his reckless generosity to Ferguson, even though deep down he knew he would have made the same decision again. Nevertheless, coupled to anxiety for the safety of the car and an abiding sense of guilt; for all that he felt a sense of relief as the sound of Ella died away – all he had to do now, besides keeping his fingers crossed about Ella – was to be kind to himself and demonstrate stoic patience while his injuries resolved. At worst, the promised bath was a looming ordeal but it could also be therapeutic – and so, pain or no pain, a bath he would have.

First, however, he needed another coffee and once it was made, he could treat drinking it as a distraction; a diversion from any discomfort or pain while soaking in the warm bath water. He tested the reaction of his feet and ankles to standing, and though he found it far less painful than he expected, the swelling made his walking unsteady. Another round of pills and there was a good chance he would be able to make it upstairs to the master bedroom en-suite and there wallow in comfort.

Getting to the kitchen was less stressful than envisaged, and as he took a sip of his newly made coffee, the oncoming climb up the stairway appeared feasible.

Rounding the doorway of the kitchen, he caught sight of the front door and was startled to see movement behind it. A shadowy figure, backlit by the bright sunlight, appeared to be searching around the door, and as he watched the strange activity the door chimes rang out.

He was reluctant to answer it, but realised that it was unlikely that Meredith Bennet, or anyone like him would bother to ring the door chimes unless they were sure to be seen as innocent callers. Even so, it was an outside bet.

He limped the twenty paces to the door slowly and carefully, trying not to risk a fall. The individual behind the door now stood motionless, as if in expectation of a response. But as he made it to the door, using his right elbow to awkwardly turn and disengage the locks, the chimes rang out again.

The caller, it seemed, was less than patient.

As all the locks finally disengaged and the door came open, he was faced with a tall, olive skinned male with jet black hair and a broad smile which as it broadened exposed gleaming white teeth.

Christ! It was Isaac!

25

"Well, I can feel a pulse in the injured tissue in all your lower limbs and because they are all equally warm it makes me think you have no serious vascular damage. I believe you will recover in time – but you have a lot of damaged tissue and some necrosis where the ties bit in. Given the subcutaneous haemorrhaging, I would prefer to see you in hospital for observation – you are going to need a great deal of patience and probably some physio'. I can't believe this is the result of deliberate torture. How did you get into this mess?"

Isaac had completed his examination with him lying on the longer of the lounge settees. He recalled that as the front door opened he had attempted to step aside as Isaac entered. Instead his swollen feet had rolled slightly and he lost balance; Isaac had the quickness of mind to see what was happening and managed to prevent him from collapsing onto the floor.

Now he had all kinds of queries to answer from Isaac's not so subtle interrogation, not least why he had been so stupid not to seek medical help, and how had he become entangled in a criminal operation.

"It's essentially what I told you earlier, when you came in; it started when I first occupied the house, with me finding a hidden room in the pool house with a PC installed. I saw a web page for mail order brides and messages supposedly from one particular woman. To any reasonable observer, they were intended for whoever used the PC last. I subsequently found out that the messages were fake; someone had used them to implicate innocent parties, the Ferguson's that is, in the diversion of an arms shipment to Odessa in the Ukraine. The rest you know about - in outline at least - Charles Ferguson, the death of his sister and her children, Rennison, the two Bennet brothers and so on."

He tried to condense the whole history into one sound bite but it felt inadequate. Isaac looked doubtful.

"And you are convinced that your injuries were caused by this Meredith Bennet - that he kidnapped you and wanted you to reveal what had been found in the vandalised computer."

He nodded agreement.

"Yes, but that was it - I had found what the bastard was looking for as I kicked over the remnants of the PC, an Eprom, and I gave it to Ferguson to enable him to prove he was not involved in the arms diversion."

Isaac gave a shrug.

"Okay, I'm beginning to see the whole picture. From one point of view you've been lucky, from another your luck never did recover - remember, I know your history."

Isaac smiled; his sympathy was genuine but it was a laboured courtesy.

Now that Isaac had given him a reasonably positive prognosis, he felt a little more optimistic. But what was Isaac doing here in the first place?

"I can't say I'm not pleased to see you Isaac, but what made you decide to visit me today - how did you find me?"

Isaac's eyes twinkled "Pleased to see me Peter? I would have thought you would have said that my timing was impeccable - and how grateful you are that I made the effort to follow up your enquiry about my whereabouts during your last hospital appointment. Look at me, I'm a doctor – it was easy to find you. You're a patient with well-documented hospital records. Your contact details, including your post-code, were at the top of the first page of your records. Now given that, isn't it amazing what a Satnav can do?"

Isaac's sarcastic comment stung a little but he knew it was tinged with good humour as well, and he had no reason not to thank his lucky stars and his guardian angel that Isaac had turned up when he did.

"I'm sorry, don't misunderstand – it is really good to see you and you know I'm eternally grateful for all your present and past support... and of course your friendship. Tell me, what do you propose to do now. You're patient, that is me, yours truly etc, is currently sprawled over the settee and somewhat under the weather. He's hoping you might stay a little longer and have dinner. Yes?"

It was a ploy, and Isaac knew it. There was no way a meal could be arranged given his patient's physical condition. Instead Isaac, with weary compliance, stood up and disappeared into the kitchen returning forty minutes later with omelettes, fried potatoes and salad.

Now his gratitude to his friend reached mountainous heights – he had no idea how famished he was until he smelled the food; and regardless of the way his feet complained by having to contact the floor as he sat up, he devoured the meal like a ravenous wolf.

He wielded his knife and fork vertically, each hand holding the handles inside a fist. It was clumsy and frantically done – he tore and stabbed at his food until he finally carried some into his mouth. Like his feet, his swollen, still throbbing hands were ignored – he had moved into survival mode.

Isaac watched as the plate he had just delivered was scoured for the last morsel of food. He had hardly enjoyed a mouthful of his own, and yet half of all the food he had just delivered had swiftly vanished down his patient's gullet.

"Slow down Peter. When did you eat last? God, I suspect I may have to treat you for gross indigestion quite soon."

He grinned at Isaac – knowing that he had embarrassed himself, and yet suddenly felling invigorated by the comfortable presence of a stomach full of food. It really made a difference to his spirits, and for inexplicable reasons the torture in his feet and hands had abated.

"Phew, sorry Isaac, I didn't realise how hungry I was. That was delicious – I could eat it all again."

Isaac stared at his own plate for a few seconds and then pushed it away from him towards the now empty plate of his apparently revived patient.

"No – it's okay, I won't deprive you of yours Isaac!"

Isaac pressed on, "I insist, I had a good breakfast, you didn't."

There was no hesitation, and as the plate came onto his lap he demolished the remaining food without comment.

By the time he had finished, Isaac was on his feet with his car keys in hand.

"Are you off already? I was hoping..."

"I'm on duty in forty minutes – you may not believe this Peter but I have lots of other patients besides you. Now I can't promise to see you every day, and regarding your medical treatment, I have ethical considerations – your GP would not be best pleased if he or she were excluded from your treatment. I am going to contact..."

He raised a blotched hand.

"No, sorry Isaac, you can't – I never registered locally with a GP and I have no wish to have a local GP report my injuries to the police. You've seen my records. All my current medical records were started just prior to the time we first met – when I moved here I was in a different catchment area and my old GP took me off his register – as of this moment, you are my GP!"

Isaac shook his head, his dark complexion and jet-black hair emphasising his reaction.

"Okay – okay. It's not altogether ethical but I hear what you say. I will return each evening to see how you're getting on. Between 7and 8pm I should think. Now, don't you dare over-dose on your medication, particularly the Tramadol, you'll do more harm than good. I will notify your consultant and get you another prescription in a couple of days. I hope I don't regret this – really you should be in hospital, but I can see I'm wasting my time on that score. I'll try to bring you a meal, a take-away that is, and some bread, milk and eggs when I visit tomorrow. In the meantime, you will have to do the best you can with what's in the fridge. Can you cope?"

He nodded and gave as cheerful an acknowledgement as he could muster. Isaac in turn lifted a parting hand and left.

He heard the front door close and a little later the sound of a car driving away.

He was tempted to try to get into the kitchen and clean everything up. However, he realised that standing on his feet and using his almost useless hands was not going to accelerate his recovery. Instead, he managed to get the TV on and settled back to distract himself from his injuries by immersing himself in two hours of classic motor racing. He could not but notice the inclusion of two racing E Types on the track. He suddenly remembered his extravagance with Ferguson, and instantly regretted it!

26

It turned out to be a long and boring day not helped by the fact that he felt tired, listless and fed up with battling the periodic resumption of severe throbbing and pins and needles in his limbs. He'd slept badly, the settee made a good bed but lying in the dark with nothing to distract the severe discomfort from his hands and feet became a nightmare, and he was far too groggy to make it to the kitchen more than twice and get warm milk.

He was tempted to ignore Isaac's warnings about his prescription and when, in despair, he found himself stumbling, crawling and generally dragging himself around at three in the morning, he doubled the dose.

It had no discernible effect on his aching limbs though he had a moment of ironic amusement when he realised that his back, which the medication was aimed at, had given him no trouble at all for some time!

Isaac appeared on cue around 7.30 pm that evening. The television was turned up and he hardly noticed him standing by trying to attract his attention. He reached for the remote control and gingerly squashed the appropriate nipple to mute the sound.

Isaac pursed his lips in exasperation.

"You are a fool Peter – I walked into a completely open house. You had no idea I was here – I could have been anyone. If the story you told me is true you were very much at risk!"

He nodded glumly. As things stood he was far too depressed to take the warning seriously – he was tempted to quibble but hadn't the strength.

"Yeah, hello Isaac, thanks for your appearance. I'm afraid I'm not up to much. Had a lousy night and the medication isn't helping much. Is that a curry I can smell – I could eat a horse. "

Isaac gave a look of professional concern and carefully deposited the white plastic carrier bag he was holding on the floor.

"What do you expect, a miracle? You have a lot of tissue damage around your extremities and I warned you that you would have to be patient. Now lets have a look at how you are progressing."

He watched Isaac move around the front of the settee and felt his legs being lifted onto the coffee table. Isaac bent down to examine his feet. He 'tut tutted' a few times but said nothing intelligible. Then he extracted a needle probe from his shirt pocket and began to poke various parts of his foot. He could feel it dig in and he winced every time it penetrated. After his sixth yelp Isaac grunted again and repeated the exercise on both his hands. Again he distinctly felt the probe indent the blotched flesh on his swollen hands and reacted accordingly.

"Well," Isaac said as he stood up, "you are not going to lose your hands and feet unless you decide to be stupid and mistreat them. I have carried out the necessary diplomacy and deception with your consultant – at some risk I might add – and you now have a new prescription, one to increase blood flow, a powerful anti-inflammatory and some analgesics. Again, I warn you not to over-medicate – you will pay for it if you do. I would guess that most of your over-sized appendages will be back to normal in fourteen to twenty one days on condition you get enough rest, nutrition and medication. Now, your are right, I've brought a curry for us to..."

They both reacted to the sound, turning their heads to look in the direction of its source.

There were two of them, one tall and with the elegant, formally dressed appearance of a London lawyer, the other smaller and smartly outfitted in a light grey striped suite illuminated by a pink shirt and silver grey tie. Each seemed opposites – the smaller one being blond and having a light complexion, the other with jet black, perfectly groomed hair and an olive tinge to his skin.

"Fawly?"

It was all he could say – he recognised the one but not the other.

"Yes indeed Mr. Enfield, and we're very pleased to find you at home"

Fawly then sniggered, and smiled as his companion gave a sardonic nod of his head.

Isaac had stood impassive as the short exchange took place. Now he spoke with a voice Peter had only heard once before in a hospital van, a long time back – a voice cold and menacing.

"And who is your friend – Mr. Fawly is it? Did I hear my patient correctly? Will you introduce us?"

Fawly looked at Isaac and then at the settee, giving some time to studying the swollen feet propped up on the coffee table.

"My friend, Doctor, or whoever you are, is..."

"I am Meredith Bennet and I can speak..."

The smaller man spoke loudly and insistently, but was himself interrupted as Fawly lifted his voice to drown out what Bennet was saying.

"Yes, allow me to introduce Mr. Meredith Bennet – my business partner."

He was poorly positioned, with his feet on the coffee table and his head craned around, to view the two new arrivals. Moreover, he felt decidedly at risk as things stood and needed to at least try to face any oncoming threat. With a slight exclamation of effort he pulled his legs down and turned his seat towards the two men facing him and Isaac. Strangely, his preoccupation with the two men markedly reduced the discomfort from his legs as his feet contacted the ground. He had already surmised that Fawly and Bennet were a rogue team and were not in his house for a pleasant, social evening. It was perhaps better to feign ignorance.

"I take it this is official Fawly – are we to expect your chief, Rennison?"

Again, Fawly sniggered, as did Bennet, a mocking grin appearing on his face.

Then Fawly's expression changed instantly, reverting to a face that was threatening and dangerous.

"You can forget any thoughts about Rennison – his interest in this affair has, I think, terminated."

Shocked by Fawly's statement he was lost for words – seconds passed as he groped for a response.

"He's dead?"

Fawly features gave way to a weak smile and he leaned his head back, as though composing an adequate reply.

"No Mr. Enfield, not at all – but when you get your fingers trapped in a car door and each one is so badly crushed they have to be amputated, it does tend to incapacitate you – a little!"

Isaac turned to look down at him – they both caught each other's expression and each conveyed alarm. As he caught Isaac's expression he decided that stupidity was now a better ploy than ignorance.

"So, that being the case what are you doing here, is SIS still chasing Ferguson? If so, you can see I am somewhat compromised myself, I doubt I can help you."

This time it was Bennet who was first to speak.

"My half brother has a lot to answer for, the bastard double crossed us and we want to know where he is. Not only that, we think you know why it is we want to find him. Our last conversation was terminated too early – you fooled us then, but you won't do it again."

So it was definite – Meredith Bennet and undoubtedly Fawly were the two obscure figures behind him during the torture session.

"You bastards! So it was you two – and I fooled you, with me half dead? I have nothing to give you except my disgust, contempt and a deep and abiding loathing for people like you. If I could I –"

He hardly saw the movement – certainly the two newcomers didn't. Isaac suddenly bent down and dipped his hand into the carrier bag containing the curry.

As he withdrew his hand it held an automatic pistol. He straightened and pointed it at the two men. The gun never wavered; it was rock steady.

Fawly and Bennet froze momentarily and then Bennet gave a short, slightly strangled laugh.

"Oh-ee – looks like the doctor ain't the doctor, and my guess is the gun's a fake and he can't use it!"

Isaac stayed a he was except for a slight step forward.

"Wrong – I am a doctor and this is a real weapon – Browning 9mm if you want to know, and the proof of the pudding can be had. Just refuse to do as I tell you and you will learn that you are terribly mistaken on both counts."

Now the situation had become deadly and he suddenly realised that he was dangerously close to Isaac; any exchange of fire would mean he was in the firing line. He didn't know for sure if Fawly and Bennet were armed, but it was a reasonable bet. With his still

175

useless feet and hands there was nothing he could do to change his position or alleviate the situation.

However, he knew Isaac's background – they didn't. To defuse the likelihood of violence he tried to convince them of their very real peril.

"Don't think he won't do it," he said, his voice slightly tremulous, "the doctor has a previous record of eradicating people like you – I suggest you do as he says."

Fawly and Bennet gave a fleeting look to one another and then faced Isaac with contemptuous expressions, each apparently sneering at the odds. As if a silent starting pistol had been fired, they suddenly broke into violent movement.

They dived away from each other, instantly clawing inside their jackets for weapons. Isaac simply watched, making no change in his stance until he saw first Fawly and then Bennet pull out handguns.

The next moment shots rang out and each of the targets squirmed and writhed under the onslaught of impacting bullets. Both men hit the ground, still vainly trying to avoid the fire. In the ensuing reverberation of the gunshots the two lay wholly helpless, their arrogance vaporised by each bullet that had ripped into them. For all their confidence and bluster they were now reduced to impotence – no longer capable of mounting a threat.

For Bennet there came all consuming dread, he was still conscious and fighting to survive. Horror, anguish and adrenaline energised him and etched his face with agony as he tried to stifle the blood pumping out of an artery on his lower left leg while still attempting to escape the suffering of a gunshot wound high up on his right thigh. Fawly however remained motionless, flat on his back, with blood leaking from several wounds.

The shots had been deafening, and the events evolved as blurred slow motion. For him, time stretched out to an unbelievable length. He didn't even have the good sense to duck as Isaac had opened fire, instead, frozen to the spot, he'd sucked in breath as the side blast from the Browning caught him, and simply stared open mouthed as the two targets were gunned down.

"Dear Christ, of all the stupid..."

Isaac turned, put the gun down gently on the coffee table and ran forward to the two downed accomplices.

Bennet was crying, a whimpering moan that bespoke agony and panic.

And then, as Isaac applied pressure to the pumping blood coming from Bennet's leg, a figure with his left arm in a makeshift sling, and carrying a heavy automatic pistol, appeared from the side recess of the hallway arch.

27

He sat dumbstruck by the appearance of the grim faced newcomer. There was no doubt about it, it was Rennison and he had a murderous look on his face.

"Let him bleed."

It was said in a harsh, forbidding tone, reinforced by the way Rennison's pistol was pointing at Isaac.

Isaac looked up. He seemed not to be surprised.

"So it was you – I only got two shots off. Who are you?"

"None of your bloody business – I told you not to attend to these two rats – leave them or you go the same way."

Isaac gave an almost inaudible 'huh' but made no move to obey. He continued to apply pressure to Bennet's leg.

"Are you bloody deaf or stupid – I'll give you one more chance, leave the bastard."

Isaac looked up at Rennison again.

"I'm a doctor – I never intended to terminate these men, only incapacitate them. I don't know why you are here but I suspect it's for revenge. You fired the other shots, I will remind you my friend that revenge is a cold dish."

Rennison looked round and caught sight of him sitting on the settee with both hands and feet bloated, discoloured and encircled with the indentations from the cable ties.

He shook his head and addressed Isaac again.

"Not as far as I am concerned doctor. If I'm right your patient

Mr. Enfield over there, and I, have suffered badly at the hands of these two. I only just salvaged my fingers after these shits finished with me. Add to that the most extreme betrayal by one of them, and the murder of a brother by the other, and I tell you truthfully, revenge is sweet. Don't you dare try to appeal to my better nature – don't you bloody dare."

For a moment Isaac remained kneeling by Bennet, but as the piteous sounds subsided into silence he took hold of Bennets wrist with his one free hand and ignoring Rennison entirely bent his head in concentration. He remained still for some seconds and then slowly stood up. As his hand came away from Bennets leg the arterial bleeding had stopped. Isaac's hands were drenched in blood and he looked shattered. He made no move to shake off the blood but looked up, locking his eyes with Rennison.

"You have your wish – this one is dead, cardiac failure from blood loss and shock."

Rennison smiled.

"Good – now I will deal with Fawly there – payback for extreme betrayal and my damned fingers."

Isaac looked down at the prostrate Fawly.

"You're wasting your time – he's dead too. I assumed it was all leg injuries – but you shot to kill. "

Rennison stared hard at the body of Fawly. It was clear to both observers that he was not breathing.

"Well, well, isn't that good news. And yes, I did. Two birds with five shots – oh, I'm sorry doctor, two rounds from you makes seven. So much for your Hippocratic oath – what is it? Oh I remember, '*first, do no harm*'! You certainly did some harm here, and as far as I can tell you intended it. What are you doing carrying a weapon around with you – what kind of doctor are you?"

He had listened to the two antagonists with bated breath,

praying that Rennison was bluffing when he threatened Isaac. Now it was time he tried to defuse the situation. Not only that, what had just transpired had created a bloody mess (literally) in his home. How in God's name he was going to extricate himself from involvement in two killings was anyone's guess.

"I would remind both of you that this happened in my house, I have no idea…"

Rennison almost snarled as he spat back at the interjection.

"Shut your mouth Enfield – I have my doubts about you as well so don't push your damn luck!"

He suddenly realised that for reasons he could not fathom immediately he had become an enemy of Rennison, viewed as equally obnoxious as the two men now dead on the floor. With all that had happened to create the sheer injustice of his present situation – he was suddenly overcome by an upsurge of furious resentment. Without a single qualm or misgiving, he ignored his lack of dexterity and using both hands as cups lifted Isaac's Browning automatic off of the coffee table.

He fumbled for a second but managed to get his swollen right forefinger into the trigger guard – for all its difficulty and unfamiliarity, he rapidly had the gun aimed directly at Rennison.

"Fuck you Rennison…swing that gun in my direction and I swear by all that's holy I will blow you to kingdom come. At this range I can't miss. I want some answers from you and you had better make them good because given what's happened here this evening, I don't think one more body will make a lot of difference to my future or the future of my friend over there. I'm sick of this bloody merry go round of you, Ferguson, the scum over there and all the other secretive characters circling me and my house. Now what the hell is going on, what has Ferguson said to you – where is he and where is the Eprom? How did you know these two were coming here and why did they want you out of the way? Why is it that this business hasn't been resolved or stifled? Surely the arms shipment has been traced."

He watched as Rennison absorbed the questions and as he fired them at Rennison, Isaac slowly bent over Fawly's body and putting his ear to Fawly's chest confirmed his demise. He then lifted the head, and as it turned a large patch of blood and matted hair indicated where a bullet had penetrated the skull.

Isaac then stood up and turned, looking down at the barrel of the Browning, his body in effect now blocking the line of fire.

"No more deaths Peter – and I'm not sure you would be particularly accurate with that gun. Please put it down, I'm sure Mr. Rennison here has no real wish to add to his tally, so you're not under threat. Let's terminate this predicament now and try to sort things out."

He looked at Isaac standing before him and realised that he had no chance of targeting Rennison. But should Rennison use Isaac as a shield, and open fire from behind him, he was an easy target.

"Get out of the way Isaac – if what he said to me was sincere I have every reason to keep the gun."

Rennison suddenly stepped away from behind Isaac and held up his automatic. He then carefully shifted his sling and placed the automatic on the floor.

"I apologise Peter...really. What I said was out of order. It was said in the heat of the moment and I'm sorry. For a time back there I wanted everyone to pay for the pain and treachery I have experienced from Fawly and his cronies. You can't believe how much. That said – have you got any pain killers – my last dose is wearing off."

Isaac nodded, as if agreeing with the change in Rennison's attitude and indicating that the levelled gun was no longer necessary.

Reluctantly he allowed the gun to drop. In a way he was grateful, his injured hands were complaining severely about his determination to hold and steady it.

"Okay, but I still want an explanation Mr. Rennison. I have two dead bodies in my house and without a guarantee of a way out I'm likely to be the poor sod lumbered with a murder charge. So, answers please – or I pick up the gun again!"

Rennison ducked sideways so as to be fully visible at Isaac's side.

"Look – I know I've blundered – yes, I got Ferguson's role in this matter completely wrong. I discovered it when I found that Fawly was in touch with Merdith Bennet. It was a fluke accident – he accidentally left his mobile on my desk after we had a meeting to discuss progress. Having the mobile I casually checked his calls. I was horrified to find what I did. I decided to confront Fawly and try to find out his involvement in the arms shipment debacle. He denied any part in diverting the arms shipment and told me to prove my suspicions 'whatever they were!'. Even Meredith Bennet's number on his phone was of no consequence he said, Meredith Bennet was merely a potential route to Ferguson and the late Malcolm Bennet – a quest we were officially tasked to do. I then added it all up and realised that every move I made was because Fawly had deliberately seeded the ground with false clues and intimation. I was led by the nose to the conviction that Charles Ferguson was not the culprit in the arms diversion. I decided at that moment that Fawly was manipulating everything and had probably been central to the arms diversion. That's as far as I got before I was waylaid in the multi storey car park and they tried to amputate my fingers. They were masked but I heard a single expletive; a voice which I recognised – Fawly's. That of course sealed it as far as my suspicions were concerned. What they had not seen was me fixing a radiotracer to Fawly's Mercedes twenty minutes before they ambushed me. That's how I came to be here. As to your question about Charles Ferguson, I have not seen him since he was suspended and I have no notion about what you call the Eprom. I could be wrong about Ferguson– if so, and if necessary, I hope to make amends. I believe the arms shipment is still concealed somewhere – probably the Ukraine. Had these two not played gangster they might still be alive to tell us about it. Though there is one thing I am now becoming sure of, they were not the masterminds of the operation, just well paid stooges. There is someone else behind all this – whoever it is they are pulling strings to smokescreen everything. Now, please, please tell me about this – what was it you called it – an Eprom?"

Rennison slowly walked forward and sat on the settee alongside him. Now close up he could see the drawn, ashen face of someone exhausted from enormous pain. He very quickly empathised and leaned forward to scoop forward the analgesic blister packs on the coffee table. Isaac came forward and dropping three tablets into Rennison's right hand he leaned forward and offered the remaining water in the glass.

Rennison mumbled an almost inaudible 'Thank you' and just after swallowing a mouthful of water and six capsules, leaned back into the settee backrest and fainted.

28

Isaac slowly and carefully unwrapped the dressings on Rennison's left hand. They revealed a horrifying set of swollen and blackened digits. Since Rennison was still unconscious the examination was in the absence of any objection or protest.

As he tested each finger Isaac became less and less concerned that the injury would require immediate surgical intervention. He had just completed redressing the hand as Rennison slowly regained his senses and as Rennison became fully conscious and aware of what Isaac was doing, he snatched back his hand in panic.

"Your okay Mr. Rennison – I was just having a look at your fingers. You're lucky – none of them are broken, just some severe bruising. They are going to keep you awake at night for a while, but with care and treatment you should have your hand back in a couple of weeks."

Rennison offered a weak smile, his voice now reflecting his condition.

"Ah, thank you. So you are treating Mr. Enfield too. More to the point, where did that automatic pistol come from? I would never believe a doctor would carry firearms, or does it belong to your patient sitting next to me?"

Isaac stood up from his kneeling position and looked down at his two patients. For a moment he appeared to be in thought.

"Seems I have taken on a real problem. Neither of you two

are fit to help me and I can't decide whether this mess gets settled by removing the two bodies over there and concealing them, which on my own I can't do, or I simply call the police and we try to extricate ourselves from this by fabricating a simple but plausible story about two armed burglars. As to your question Mr. Rennison, my history and my involvement with firearms would astound you."

He had watched and listened with ever increasing dread. He felt vulnerable, not only because he was physically incapacitated, but also because too often in his life he had moved from what was bad to even worse.

As he often reminded himself, all he had to do was stay in one spot, trouble no one, and the world pissed on him.

The present situation felt as though urine was coming in buckets full, and he knew he would grasp at any plan that offered a way out. Certainly, what Isaac was saying summed up the dilemma.

Rennison, still obviously suffering, and who now began talking in a low whisper, then offered a solution that removed the greater part of his anxiety.

"I think I can get a clean up crew in here...SIS still has the facility. They remove and dispose of bodies, the 'aftermath' they call it, and do what is necessary to eradicate forensic traces and markers. Only problem is, I will have a lot of explaining to do and I suspect I will be suspended pending an inquiry. I suppose it's the lesser of the evils. All things considered, I'm confident I can talk my way out of any investigation...after all, Fawly's close association with Bennet and the trail to Odessa would justify what has happened. You of course doctor had no part in it – you never had a gun and you never opened fire. I did it all."

As he listened to Rennison's strategy he was left with a definite sense of renewed hope. If it could be contrived, as Rennison said, then there was a fair chance the whole situation might result in closure.

He yearned for an end to it all and what Rennison was proposing would absolve Isaac and himself, leaving only Ferguson as the one person still operating as though the original *status quo* continued. If Rennison and Ferguson could compare notes the chances were that it would clear the air and re-focus the whole investigation into the arms shipment diversion. What was on the Eprom, still in Ferguson's possession, could clarify everything.

He spoke up.

"I think what is being proposed is our only alternative – what do you think Isaac?"

Isaac and Rennison looked at him with thankful expressions. Isaac, apparently not wanting objections to arise against Rennison's plan, gave vent to his feelings.

"If you can swing it Mr. Rennison, I can see it solving a lot of problems – my only concern is that you are hardly fit to handle any unexpected or unnecessary stress – as for Peter, he needs extensive rest and recuperation too, probably far longer than you. Having to contend with the hassle that will ensue if we don't succeed in what you are proposing is not something I personally want for myself, or for you two, to endure. However, I make no strenuous objections – it appears to me to be not only Hobson's choice, but the only practicable option. Okay that said, we do nothing until tomorrow – you both very much need rest. I'll cover the bodies and we will try to recharge our batteries by sharing the curry I brought earlier. Good that I bought more than enough for the three of us. After we have all had some food, I suggest everyone tries to sleep or rest – tomorrow I suspect is going to be busy."

29

Looking back it had taken on all the signs of a surreal event. The morning had found him and Rennison groggy from heavy does of painkillers and anti-inflamatories. Isaac had woken early and prepared a small breakfast of toast, butter and tea. As he nibbled at the toast, pre-cut into strips so he could handle it, Rennison had settled for two cups of strong tea and had then gone off to the downstairs toilet, apparently for morning ablutions and some privacy. When Rennison was asked if he wanted some help he had returned a grim smile and politely declined.

Later they had learned that Rennison had used the landline to contact his office and call up the 'aftermath' squad.

When Rennison returned he announced that he had reported the situation and that when his people arrived we were both, 'on pain of really fucking things up', to say absolutely nothing regarding the situation. Isaac and he had nodded vigorously in agreement at the warning; not wanting to encounter any part of the 'pain' Rennison was referring to.

As time dragged there was little to do, so Isaac gave Rennison a condensed history of his early life. All the exhausted Rennison could say was "Christ – no wonder you hung on to a gun – I wonder you can trust anyone now. I consider myself lucky you didn't send a round in my direction!"

By eleven a.m. two large transit vans arrived and six men dressed in white anti-contamination suits uncovered the bodies and zipped them into body bags.

It was a slow silent ritual as they moved each bag out of the house and into the back of one of the vans. Then they fitted respirators and politely asked that the sitting room be vacated. When it was noted that he was injured and effectively immobile, they simply picked him up and gently deposited him onto blankets laid over the kitchen floor. With him out of the way, they started to 'scrub' the area of carpet where the pools of congealed blood were concentrated. Each unit sprayed out blood protein denaturing enzymes and then washed, brushed and vacuumed the residue, similar in operation to a domestic carpet cleaner. Then came the bleach cleaner followed by the sight test for blood splatters on the walls and fabrics. Finally residual traces of blood iron were tested with sprays of Luminol and anything found was cleaned away until it was undetectable.

At the end they reported to Rennison that the area was entirely free from any forensic trail and left the house as quietly and as smoothly as they has arrived. As the two vans drove away Isaac stood with Rennison at the doorway watching the departure. He himself was still stuck in the kitchen, but just managed to hear the conversation of the two men as the vans left the drive.

"Well doctor, I trust you will take care of Mr. Enfield – I hope his recovery is swift. I suspect I won't see you or him again for some time so I wish you good fortune. Thank you for taking care of my fingers, I'm grateful for the favourable diagnosis."

Isaac appeared to be absent-mindedly checking Rennison's sling and dressings and then, as he appeared to finish, said his farewell.

"I hope all goes well with any inquiry, I can only be thankful you were able to remedy the situation. I take it you will do the sensible thing and have your GP check your fingers over the next few days. If you start to lose sensation in any one of your fingers, or the colour changes -.''

As he spoke a black car drew into the drive and turned so that the passenger side was facing the house front door.

Stepping out onto the front door walkway Rennison turned, looked at the grey sky, and then smiled at Isaac.

"Lousy day for a major career change Doctor. Don't be concerned about my fingers, I will have the medics keep an eye on things. Say goodbye to Mr....I mean Peter, for me. Tell him I'm sorry for all the trouble you've both suffered. Perhaps I might one day compensate each of you. Goodbye."

As he realised that Rennison was not going to come and personally say his goodbyes he tried to shout out his own, but his voice was lost – all that came back was the heavy sound of Rennison's feet on the gravel and almost instantly a car door slam. Then he heard the engine rev up and the car wheels began to crunch into the drive as it moved away. He was left with an eerie silence that reminded him of how strange fate was.

Isaac came into the kitchen a few minutes later, stared at him sitting on the blankets with his back propped up against a kitchen unit, and gave a wry smile

"How do you feel?"

"Feel? I hurt like hell everywhere and I feel pissed. Why didn't Rennison see me before he went?"

Isaac frowned. "I don't know, and I must admit it didn't occur to me that he was being deliberately discourteous. Perhaps he felt too guilty about things – he knew how damaged you were."

Yes, he was damaged, but as far as Rennison was concerned the SIS man wasn't directly responsible for what had happened. As usual, it was fate pissing on him.

"Well, I hope he survives. He certainly rescued us out of what could have been a real mess. What about you Isaac, are you going to be able to put all this behind you?"

Isaac shrugged and sat down on the blanket beside him.

"Like all bad things, I rely on time being a healer. Like my past events, I'm not going to let what happened sour the rest of my life. And on that note I suggest that you see this moment as the back edge of a passing phase in your life. You should look forward to recovery and for everything to settle down and become routine."

He gave Isaac a quizzical look.

"Surely you jest – without your help I've got weeks of stumbling around trying to survive and even then I can see a good few hurdles to jump over before things settle down and become routine as you put it."

"Isaac stood up and looked down. "I'm going to arrange for and agency nurse to see you periodically and I will call in too, to make sure you are on the mend. You will get your prescriptions though the nurse and any eventual physiotherapy you need will be at the hospital. You will have meals delivered so all in all you will only have to worry about recovering, which I assure you will come about."

He looked up at Isaac wide-eyed and in shock.

"How on earth can I afford – ."

"You can because it's going to be worth every penny – believe me, the alternative is not worth thinking about. If you really do get stretched I can help. Now, no more protests, I need to get another dose of your prescription down you and to get you into bed. I can't stay much longer, I'm already in trouble for missing a duty shift in A&E. So I have a lot of explaining to do. Come on!"

He was lifted bodily by Isaac into a standing position and with his arm about his neck shuffled out of the kitchen and took the stairs one by one up to his bedroom. He collapsed into his bed thankful that the limited load on his feet had not caused excessive pain. Isaac had returned a little later with his blister packs and some water.

"I will do my best to arrange everything so that you are not left alone for too long but your help won't arrive immediately. Use your bedside landline if anything goes wrong, or if nothing transpires by tomorrow mid-day. Phone me and I will try to expedite matters. Are you comfortable? If so I will see you later."

He gave a wave of acknowledgement and watched as Isaac turned on his heel and walked towards the landing. He heard nothing more from him as he descended the stairs and picked up his effects in the lounge.

As Isaac slammed the front door shut, he hoped that the bloody incident he had recently witnessed in his house turned out to be a non-event – that it had never happened and neither he, Rennison nor Isaac paid a price for the rewriting of that particular piece of history. The one disappointment he felt about the incident was that regardless of how it had actually happened, he imagined himself with Isaac's automatic, firing continually at Fawly and Bennet and feeling the satisfaction of paying them back for all the pain, misery and humiliation they had conferred on him.

It was as he imagined that very satisfying scene, he began to drift off – untroubled by moral conflicts or the potential consequences of recent events.

30

Catherine had accepted his story about being struck down by a form of Phlebitis and he had persuaded Martina, his Philippine nurse, not to say otherwise.

It was a good deception, one suggested by Isaac during an earlier visit, and Catherine had no reason to think otherwise.

At first she become very tearful on seeing the state of his feet and hands, and at first he, and afterwards Isaac, had found it difficult to convince her it was not going to be a permanent disability. For some reason she didn't notice the now rapidly fading weals where the cable ties had dug in and subsequently no difficult questions arose. After composing herself she had decided that she should remain in the house to nurse him, but he had persuaded her otherwise. He trotted out all the plausible reasons Isaac had coached him in; like she would have to watch helplessly as he shed necrotic tissue from every limb, the physio' was going to be painful and distressing (just walking again with swollen feet and atrophied muscles would require a stoic approach) her own commitments would become subordinate to his, and there was the matter of a conflict between the prognosis and her own expectations – she might be too hopeful of a rapid recovery and it was not going to be. All in all, it was not the ideal basis for becoming a mother hen.

However, Catherine reluctantly accepted her role as pseudo nurse, wife and lover without the promise of consummating either of the last two. But this he found very frustrating – had she agreed to jump into bed with him instead of reading to him, or spooning food into him, he would have been the happiest and swiftest of recovering patients. It was however a catch 22 situation, and he could not have the one without the other. However, he had a daydream and it only required Martina to be out of the house on a walk, his hands and feet to be partially healed, and Catherine to be in the bedroom close to the bed and within reach. It was a nice dream, a lovely distraction, and something he hoped might transpire.

However, at the back of his mind was a small concern. So far Catherine had said nothing about the absence of Ella. It was out of the question that while on her first visit to the house, and exploring it, she would fail to realise that the car was missing. Yet she had said nothing about it. This was either because of repressed anger and refusing to discuss it's absence, or afraid that bad news might hinder his recovery. Possibly she didn't know if he was aware the car was missing. By broaching the subject he would certainly know, and it could hurt him. Nevertheless, her apparent discretion created a tension and apprehension in him – that she knew more than she was disclosing, and he awaited the fateful day when she would confront him with a "Peter, where is Ella." Or "Why did you... ." and a possible "What happened after... ." and so on.

However, it failed to materialise and he was only alerted to the reason why it failed when without prompting Catherine said, "I see Ella is well covered outside. You must have got the rain-covers on her when it was fine – she's as dry as a bone underneath though a bit close to the house. Perhaps we can go for a drive again soon – when you've recovered and fit that is. I'll drive!"

He hoped that her tucking in the bedclothes was enough to

hide the sudden body jerk of surprise he exhibited as she spoke. Martina had said nothing about the appearance of the car, but her taciturn way, limited English and apparent disinterest in the household business explained her silence on the subject.

So Ferguson had come back – just a he promised. Obviously he had found the cover in the boot. Not only had he returned, but supposedly unable to access the garages had left the car near the house and had used the cover for protection.

But why had he then vanished without making contact?

Was he still on the run? Surely not!

Supposedly he intended to disclose what was on the Eprom to Rennison as soon as he could, and thereby remove the suspicion surrounding him and his sister. By now he should have become a free agent, exonerated from the arms diversion and in no way implicated in what Fawly and Bennet had been doing.

As he lay cocooned in Catherine's version of a well-made bed (hospital corners even) he pondered on the four-wheeled enigma now parked outside the house and covered in weatherproof sheeting.

If Ferguson had secretly come and furtively gone, why hadn't he heard Ella arrive?

The car's exhaust note was distinctive. If he hadn't heard it then he, and everyone else in the house, was most probably asleep; so Ferguson had most likely arrived in the early hours. But then, if he drove Ella in and parked her, how did he leave? He was dying to get down and look at the car in the hope it might render a clue or two to the puzzle. But it was out of the question for the moment – he had a good few weeks worth of bed rest and physiotherapy to contend with before he stood a chance of standing and walking completely unaided. But it would come – the moment he was able to, he was determined to inspect Ella. He smiled to himself as an amusing thought came to him – envisaging pulling back the weather sheet on Ella and finding Charles Ferguson still in the driver's seat and fast asleep!

31

It took longer than he hoped, even with the professional administrations of Martina and Isaac coupled with Catherine's encouragement. True, the pain from his feet and hands had virtually gone, and his right hand had nearly returned to normal so that he was almost able to close a fist and grip a comb or a knife. Isaac had said it was akin to recovering from frostbite, but that was no consolation and he had no intention of sticking his hands into a freezer to confirm Isaac's opinion.

Most of the blotchy capillary bleeding had faded and he had been spared any significant necrosis. But his walking was still a tad dubious, a combination of slow healing, too much bed rest and muscle atrophy exacerbated by his weak right leg. In the beginning his progress had been excruciatingly slow and he often stumbled or tripped, but he accepted the discomfort and embarrassment, simply persevering and refusing on principle to call Martina or Catherine for help.

Still, he was hobbling around. The more he was able to increase the number of steps before resting, the more he saw himself one day walking out of the front door and pulling the covers back off of Ella. They let him into the garden on dry, sunny days and the more he exercised, and the better he performed, the less he saw of Isaac.

He still felt under the microscope though. Catherine and Martina kept him under observation from the kitchen window.

He occasionally wobbled to a halt and bowed to them as he arrived back close to the kitchen on his cautious, circuitous garden amble. As he limped past, they were usually sipping coffee, both side by side peering out of the window at him. They tended to smile their congratulations and lift their mugs in salute every time he completed a circuit and came abreast of them. Martina was reporting his progress to Isaac who now had no reason to maintain close surveillance of his patient's progress, and so was seen less frequently.

On all the good weather days he continued to exercise around the gardens, meandering through the many neglected pathways and flower beds (another task he had to attend to when fully fit) slowly working his feet into remembering how to control his balance and movement.

He was certainly improving, physically and psychologically. Nevertheless, to bury bad karma he always skirted the pool house and the hidden room, not wanting in his vulnerable state to tempt fate.

As one day blended into another he ran his mind over past events – always trying to identify and compare the factors that had triggered each incident that had so often blighted and overwhelmed his life.

And yet, for all his misgivings, he felt more resilient than he ever had.

Isaac had always been his role model – *'what doesn't kill you makes you stronger'* he had intimated. True it was, but he was learning that for some it also changes everything – your whole character. Adversity knocks chunks off your confidence and any trust in a benevolent God – *'if God loved you Peter why did he confer on you such a litany of misery and pain'?* Nevertheless, Isaac had defended him at risk of his own life, as though put in place yet again by divine intervention to rescue him from complete and utter disaster.

It was hard to reconcile his feelings; what or who could he rely on?

Yes, he had reason to regret and to distrust, but these feelings stung less then they had. The appalling memory of his family's funeral was now a sad link to bittersweet reminiscences, a few of which occasionally came to mind. Some were truly of happier moments; Bobby as a baby, Betty on their wedding day, the odd respite as they all enjoyed a summer's day by the seaside; all moments whose recall was once obscured by darker events which did not now reduce him to waves of grief.

Now, as before, he saw a future, not an unrealistic fairyland or one approaching Utopia – he was now far too cynical for that and too scarred by past events – but maybe one where the problems thrown up in life were resolvable; in short, no different than those of the average person.

If Catherine consented, it might just come to pass.

Earlier in his recovery Catherine had intimated that she could, and maybe would, move in with him as a trial – to see if they were completely compatible. Whatever that took, he was determined to make it work. With her he could develop a happier existence – none of the previous factors that had marred his life were now prevalent. Chances were he could aspire to a normal life, and if so Catherine might be the catalyst.

Once more he prayed that all the horrendous episodes he had experienced were history and not to be repeated, that now there really was no valid reason for feeling guilty or maudlin – after all, he had survived and it was possible he had been spared for a purpose. This was the third time he had needed to reconstitute his spirit and reconcile the bitterness and the blessings in his life

– it was, he hoped, the last time – and yes, he had reason to feel hopeful. Catherine, for example, in a moment of pure empathy, had succumbed to his pleading for a 'cuddle', and one thing had led to another. Even better was the fact that she confessed to have enjoyed the experience and, she added, there was no need for him to appeal in quite the same way again. Martina had been astonished the first morning she had found them together, but her smile of approval removed any sense of condemnation.

And yet, underneath it all, he was troubled.

Isaac had said very little about the incident when Fawly, Bennet and then Rennison had appeared. Not to understate it, he had been more than reticent about it.

Isaac had expressed not a word regarding the episode, and even when just the two of them were together, he was unable to prompt him into discussing it. Isaac had remained tight lipped over the whole of his recovery period; it was somewhat ominous and it occurred to him that Isaac might be hiding something. If so, what?

He had tried to flush the concern from his mind but it kept reappearing. It was definitely a source of unease and started to become irritating. Apart from Ella and the gardens, it was another task he promised himself – to get to the bottom of Isaacs secret – if there was one.

It was a warm, bright, windless morning when he opened the front door and peered once again at Ella now cloaked in her silver grey weatherproof cover. Now was the moment he had patiently anticipated; weeks of coveting the moment when he was fully functional, and the reward for his long suffering was the promise of being able to drive Ella again. He had long dismissed the silly idea that Ferguson might still be in the car, indeed all negative considerations and recent events paled against common sense and the thought of actually being mobile and resuming a normal life.

He sensed Catherine standing behind him as he stared at Ella, savouring the moment he was about to experience.

"She's still there Peter – you covered her well, I hope she hasn't been harmed in any way."

He half turned towards Catherine, earnestly hoping his expression didn't betray the fact that it wasn't he who had left the car covered, and that his promise to her had been broken. But if Ella was fully intact it was a harmless white lie; no one would be the wiser. He prayed that Ferguson had done nothing to leave clues that someone else had used the car.

"It seems an age since I drove her Cath' – not since I was...not since the Phlebitis came on. If I can get her to start we'll have a spin this afternoon."

She smiled. "Fingers crossed then – want a coffee?"

He nodded appreciatively and she turned back towards the kitchen.

"I'll get the cover off and we will see."

He stepped onto the pathway and covered the few yards to Ella at a normal pace, resisting the urge to hurry. Had he wished, he could have made a stab at running; the healing was almost complete – but running? Well, that for the moment he sensibly resisted.

He stepped around the shrouded vehicle unsure which was the front of the car or the back. He decided that Ferguson would have used the conventional access to the house; left of drive in, right of drive out. That being the case, he lifted the cover to his left and at once saw the chromium spokes of the nearside front wheel. In seconds he had the cover removed entirely and rolled up. Only then did he give the car a full inspection, and as his eyes scanned over the bodywork and the cockpit his spirits lifted.

Apart from some slight fungal growth over the seats and a few spots on the dashboard, nothing else in the cockpit indicated abuse or misuse. He circled again, no – nothing. No rain incursion, no sign of any damage, not a thing untoward. She still gleamed as though recently polished and there was no sign of condensation in the instruments.

Deeply relieved he took the ignition key from his jacket pocket and leaned into the driver's side in order to insert it for an engine test. As he did so his eye caught sight of a white sheet, half hidden under the driver's seat.

Leaning in he pulled at the corner of the sheet and revealed an A4 sheet of paper folded in two. He came upright, already in the process of unfolding the paper. It was likely it had been blown off the seat as he had removed the cover – he had no recollection of leaving anything in the car before Ferguson's departure.

As the two faces of the paper were exposed he saw handwriting.

Hello Peter – trust you have recovered well without complications. The car was a real tonic, haven't enjoyed myself so much for ages and she goes exceptionally well. Wasn't able to get anything sensible out of the Eprom directly – some kind of encryption. Man I know with experience in decrypt is working on it. I will stay out of sight until I have all that can be gleaned from the chip. Rennison AWOL for reasons unknown. Will get to him asap. Will contact you as soon as I have something to report.

Charles.

There was no date on the note but given the time Catherine had mentioned the car being parked outside the house, the note had been penned some five or six weeks ago.

So it was possible that by now whatever was on the Eprom had been deciphered. But if that was true why no word from Ferguson? Not only that, it implied that Rennison had gone walkabout days before the episode with Fawly and Bennet. It was a puzzle, but not one he wanted to grapple with there and then. He was due for a jolly - a wholly deserved jolly and he was not going to let the residue of recent past events mar it.

32

They took a long and enjoyable drive in the country, passing through East Linkin and on to villages he'd heard of but had never visited. Finally, passing a thatched country pub they decided to stop for a drink and investigate the menu.

He actually overshot the car park entrance and was forced to back up a hundred yards or so. As he turned in, Ella received admiring glances from all the patrons taking their drinks outside the tavern. It was a rare traditional sight with the greater number being agricultural workers having their lunch break; all sitting around rough hewn tables and benches shaded by brewery emblazoned parasols.

He parked in a parking bay remote from all the other cars, as was his usual habit in protecting Ella from other careless or jealous drivers. The sun was out in a clear blue sky so he wasn't tempting fate by leaving Ella with her hood down.

The driving had stimulated both his feet so that he had a slight sensation of pins and needles in his toes, particularly the right – 'clutchitis' he named it, but he knew he still carried the long term consequences of the day he met Fawly and Bennet.

He held Catherine's hand, and made his steps to the pub's entrance careful and measured, not wanting to allow over-confidence in his walking to bring about a fall. Inside the pub the mid day patrons were noisy and cheerful and too many to allow migration to the dining area an easy option. In they end they had a fifteen minute wait before they were shown to a table but eventually they were enjoying a well-cooked meal and excellent service. Even the wines they chose were thoroughly palatable and as the contents of each bottle were despatched he suddenly realised that he could well be above the legal limit.

"I'm not going to have any more," he told Catherine as she proffered the bottle once more "I still have to drive us home and I would like us to get there in one piece and without me facing a drink-driving charge"

She smiled approvingly, withdrawing the bottle and leaving it where it had been originally placed.

"Of course Peter – my fault, we were enjoying our time so much I didn't think."

He nodded. "Not did I – but I have a solution, we drink the place dry – everything on the wine list – and then book in for a nights recovery here in the pub. There's no rush – we don't need to get back home for any pressing reason – let's enjoy it while we can."

Catherine gave him a blissful smile.

"Are you sure – I mean can we get a room?"

He had no intention of not getting a room – alone with Catherine in the same bed, in any location, promised paradise.

"I'll check, have another drink or have a look at the desserts on offer. I'll be back."

Catherine gave him a serious look.

"Careful – watch your step!"

He made his way to the public bar; still awash with throngs of patrons cheerfully emptying the Pub's stock of whatever was drinkable.

He stood at a space opened up between the bar stools, and studied the bar staff working with measured speed as orders came in. He wondered if any of them had visions of a future that did not involve constantly fulfilling the alcoholic needs of permanently inebriated locals and all the transients like him and Catherine. Just for a moment he really felt able to count his blessings. Not for him any more the daily grind; with the fear of dismissal hovering over his head resulting in his not being able to pay the mortgage or the utility bills. He had suffered too much – but the final outcome definitely had its benefits. He had achieved his ambitions as regards house and car, he was still solvent and Catherine was talking about selling her house and moving in – he in turn was thinking about them getting married.

Yes, now he could count his blessings.

As the thought arose, a moustachioed man wearing a white shirt and a polka dot tie suddenly confronted him on the other side of the bar.

"Yes sir, can I help?"

"Yes you can, is it possible to hire a room for the night, a double room. My, er, wife and I have just enjoyed a lunch here and we rather like the look of your evening menu. I can't really enjoy it if I have to drive back home – if you see what I mean"

The man smiled appreciatively.

"Of course sir, you prefer to keep your license rather than having to surrender it to the courts. I understand completely. Bear with me, I'll just find the register."

He waited patiently as the moustachioed body disappeared around the bar access and the cheerful patrons kept up their well-lubricated chatter.

He looked back to view the dining area but Catherine and his table was obscured by a narrow arch and the short step-way that led to it.

As he turned back the man and the polka-dot tie had reappeared.

The register was already facing him and the man had a ballpoint pen on offer.

"If you would care to sign in sir, we have two guest rooms and one is still free. It's forty-five pounds per night for a double room but that includes breakfast. We ask our guests to settle prior to taking a room - I trust you won't object."

He reached for his wallet. "Plastic okay?"

"Indeed sir, no problem. Sign there if you will."

The man's finger pointed to a pre-printed box on the register underneath one already filled in.

He took the pen and started to write next to the titles 'Name' 'Address' and 'Date'. As he did so he looked up at the previous guests details. It was a name unknown to him but the address was in the United States.

"I see you get visitors from all over - given how far off the beaten track you are your reputation must have travelled internationally."

"True sir, but we get a good many foreigners from the language school at the old manor up the road. In fact most of the people you see here today are staff from the school celebrating the end of their courses. The rest are locals."

As he finished writing his address and dating the entry in the register, he handed back the pen.

"I imagine the students and staff keep your business buoyant. You certainly keep the quality of your menu and wine list at optimum."

Moustachioed man smiled in gratitude.

"Thank you sir, I assure you that your stay here, and the food, will be to your complete satisfaction. However, in answer to your view on the language school's students, they are usually conspicuous by their absence - that is, hardly ever to be seen.

Their courses are crammed into them I hear, they are simply too tired at the end of the day to do anything else but sleep. In any case, have you ever tried to order a beer in Arabic? Don't laugh, they very seldom try out their new English language skills in this place!"

He was amused for the moment and then it passed as he felt a sudden revelation.

It was something Isaac had said before he left.

"I get many different patients you know – many more these days that don't speak any English. I seem to be speaking more Arabic than English lately. It's good that I'm getting the practice, I'm going to need it."

He thought that Isaac was simply referring to his more numerous Arabic speaking patients, but with him being tight lipped about his discussions with Rennison, what he had said at the time now seemed to take on an ominous significance. Isaac's remark may well have been the perfect ambiguity, but as he considered past events, it suddenly caused a chill to run down his spine.

When he rejoined Catherine and confirmed the booking, she suggested a post-lunch constitutional walk to explore the area around the pub and to work up an appetite for the evening meal. He had no objections and they slipped out of the joyous atmosphere of the pub and rapidly found a signed footpath that started at the rear of the pub's garden. Just before they followed the path he was able to check Ella – she was alone and just as they had left her. For the moment he had no need to worry about her, nor his concerns about Isaac. Both slipped from his mind.

The pathway ran on for only a short distance before it opened up into a deserted riverside picnic area with a scattering of weathered picnic tables and cross benches. A few ducks and wild fowl scoured the quietly flowing river for food and the riverbanks were well populated with scurrying voles and water rats. The area was so idyllic and pleasant that they were tempted to remain there for the afternoon. However, the pathway beyond the area beckoned and so he decided to take a chance with his feet and take their exploration a little further.

As they slowly meandered along the pathway, still tied to the riverside, he watched Catherine pleased in every respect with her and appreciative of the way she had blossomed since they had become a couple. He felt this was an ideal opportunity – it certainly had all the right vibes.

"Catherine!"

He turned to look back at her.

"Isn't this beautiful?" she said, and did a small pirouette expressing her joy.

"Yes, only the damn pebbles and my feet make it hard to go down on one knee."

She suddenly halted her movement.

"What Peter?"

It was spontaneous – he hadn't planned to say it but it seemed the right time.

"Catherine, I love you. Will you marry me? Even though I'm asking you standing up and it's not as romantic as it should be."

All he could hear was the rustle of wind in the saplings skirting one side of the pathway, and the odd lapping of water from the river. It was as thought time had stopped still and for a second or two he sensed too much hesitation from her. For an instant he despaired, that she might be composing a gentle rejection.

Then came the beaming smile, the droop of the head and the open arms that expressed delight and bliss.

As they embraced she had her head on his shoulder with her lips close to his ear.

He was expecting a 'Oh Peter, yes of course I'm so happy' or perhaps "Darling – I never thought I could be the one."

Instead she whispered gleefully "I will have to sell my house you know." and nibbled his ear.

"Is that a yes or a no?" he asked.

The days had flown by. There was no need for a church wedding they decided, and so the banns had been called at the local registry office in Lidmouth. A handful of Catherine's friends were invited but as the invitations were sent, his lack of close relatives and with no direct link to his now deceased family, meant he could only invite a very few. He sent an invitation to Isaac, and to Janet his old physio', but disappointingly neither RSVP'd and neither eventually came to the ceremony. Nevertheless, he refused to let it spoil things and he excused their absence as pressure of work.

After the registration they enjoyed a small reception in a local pub and then drove to Southampton to take ship.

The honeymoon was booked for an extensive cruise around Europe and the Mediterranean. It had the advantage of not putting too much stress on his recovering feet or his occasional creaking back. Catherine appeared perfectly happy with every one of the arrangements. He detected not a hint of sadness when they put her house in the hands of an estate agent practising close to her address. She continued to beam with excitement as everything came to fruition. And yet he didn't want her to forget; he wanted her to retain at least some memorial to her late husband. A man he understood who had treated her with love and respect. He raised the subject just the once and experienced a slight moment of embarrassment and shame when she replied, "Peter darling, you would have to rip out my heart to take away the memories of John enshrined in it. I will never forget that gentle, endearing man whom I loved. Now I am happy again with another man whom I love, and John would never begrudge me that."

For a moment he saw a tear well up in her eye but it quickly vanished and her wonderful smile reappeared.

The honeymoon turned out to be virtually idyllic – there were a number of middle aged couples on board the ship who were enamoured with the news that they were recently married and ensured they were seldom lonely – though in truth they sometimes did crave a little more privacy. Yet their new acquaintances were never demanding or intimidating and they enjoyed some delightful sightseeing and memorable moments with them, experiences never to be forgotten.

The ten days at sea turned out to be marvellously therapeutic and not only did his ailments and past injuries seem less debilitating, but by the end of the cruise he had widened his waistline and regained almost complete functioning of all his previously crippled limbs. Catherine conceded that he was now operating very well in every respect!

Arriving back in Southampton they picked up Ella from a secure car park near the docks and drove back northward in a constant chatter about what they had done, the people they had met and the sights they had seen. Catherine talked about doing it all again when the money from the sale of her house went through. It seemed like a good idea to both of them.

On arrival at the house it seemed as though they had been away for months and although they missed the shipboard conviviality, they were glad to be home.

Catherine wanted to move her effects from the second bedroom, where she had originally slept when he was in recovery, into the main bedroom so that everything would be conveniently at hand. In any case, she said, she had far more to transport from her old house and the second bedroom would be needed as the overspill for everything that would not immediately fit into the main bedroom. At first he thought it improbable; that she was teasing him – but then his past experience with women and their worldly baggage gave the lie to his doubts so he started to re-organise.

Both the bedside cabinets in the main bedroom were full of the detritus that those with a magpie disposition collect, and he was the perfect example. Having to move everything from the left-side cabinet to the right meant first of all going through every old supermarket receipt, incomprehensible operating instructions for the bedside clocks, anonymous telephone numbers, plastic boxes of unknown origin (and assorted orphaned socks) to determine what to keep.

It was as he sat on the bed with the cabinet draw to his side, laboriously picking out items and discarding the rubbish, that he picked up a stiff cardboard calling card which had only a single name and a telephone number printed on it.

It was as he remembered it – a plain white card with the name 'Emanuel Rennison' followed by a telephone number.

He had been submerged in too much trauma for far too long for him to recall that Rennison had given him the card at their first meeting. The card had been dumped into the bedside cabinet on the basis that he was never likely to need it, or would want to need it. Given all that had followed he now realised it was the naïve assumption of a simpleton.

Now he had Rennison's contact number, it provided a route to satisfying his curiosity. Now he could ask Rennison what had happened to Ferguson, and perhaps at the same time settle his unease about Isaac. The latter was on his list as a priority, not having seen Isaac at the wedding had been hurtful and saddening; he wanted to know why. The hospital had said Isaac was on a sabbatical – but (they claimed) they knew no more than that.

Standing in the hallway he picked up the phone three times, only to replace it in its cradle the same number of times.

He was unsure of what he was going to ask, and less than secure about the possible consequences. What he didn't want was to somehow be sucked back into the bloody business surrounding the Odessa Bride, if indeed it was still active. What he wanted was good news; that Ferguson was now exonerated, that Rennison had wound up the arms shipment debacle, and that Isaac was on a well deserved sabbatical somewhere overseas where it was idyllic and sunny. Any information bordering on that would be a massive relief.

Yet somehow he had a premonition that it was not to be.

At the fourth attempt he decided that not knowing was as bad as finding out all the things he didn't want to hear. In the end he accepted the inevitability of what he was attempting to do. To know or not to know, either way he would be risking a troubled conscience. Gripping the handset with a slightly unsteady hand, he dialled the number on the card and waited to hear the dialling tone.

The ringing continued for what seemed an interminable period. He was just about to give up and replace the receiver when the dialling tone abruptly ended and a distant voice said "Yes."

"I'm Peter Enfield – is this Mr. Rennison's contact number?"

There was a pause and then came the reply,

"Wait."

For a moment the line went dead and then he heard some kind of re-connection taking place after which another voice said "Caller, please identify yourself."

For a second he felt frustration but then remembered whom he might be dealing with. SIS, if indeed the call had been routed to SIS - were bound to be cagey.

"My name is Peter Enfield - I am known to Emanuel Rennison - he will confirm it."

There was no reply, just another silence, but then he heard a receiver at the other end being picked up and a voice responded.

"Peter, this is Rennison - I trust you have recovered."

He felt a wave of relief go through him as he heard Rennison's query. At first there was nothing in his tone to imply or indicate anything dubious.

"I'm virtually back to normal thank you. It's been a very long time since the events at my house. I suppose you have weathered the storm?"

Rennison hesitated; clearly he was weighing his reply.

"Yes, it's...history."

"Right, may I ask you - have you seen Charles Ferguson recently. I know he was attempting to contact you - supposedly with some important information."

Again, Rennison was slow to answer.

"You need not worry about that Peter. Everything is in hand."

"So he has seen you then - I assume you are further on with the Odessa situation."

Again, there was a long pause, with the telephone line offering only a hissy silence interspersed by the odd crackle.

At last Rennison replied.

"You have no need to enquire Peter. As I said, everything is in hand."

Suddenly, there seemed no future for the conversation; Rennison was giving nothing away. In short, it was going to be pointless and discouraging.

"Can't you...all I need to know is if everything has resolved and if you have by any chance news about Isaac – remember he..."

Rennison suddenly cut in.

"Sorry Peter, at the moment I can't help you. Give me some time and I may be able to update you. Bear with me please. I'll be in touch."

With that the line went dead.

He held the receiver tight to his ear in the hope that Rennison might still be at the other end, but after a few more seconds he was clearly listening to an open line with only faint static as company. Left with a sense of acute disappointment he dropped the handset back into the cradle and turned away.

Catherine had come downstairs and had stood a few steps up listening to the conversation.

"What was that love? You look quite distressed, is there a problem?"

He turned to her with a forced smile on his face.

"Nothing sweetie, I was hoping we could get an early booking for the other med' cruise we were told about but it's fully booked at the moment – we might get a cancellation though – fingers crossed."

Her response was neutral.

"Never mind – I'm sure there are others, it's no big deal. Anyway, my house money hasn't come through yet so it's a touch premature. Want something to eat? I'm famished."

He nodded enthusiastically, though mentally he was still struggling with the outcome of the exchange with Rennison. He would have to bide his time to get the answers he wanted, but get them he would.

33

Having quietly fumed for a few days after Rennison's stone walling he decided to try another route.

He phoned the hospital once more but Isaac was not to be found. Personnel said he was signed up for a sabbatical and an official refresher course, but declined to give details since it was subject to hospital security rules and the Data Protection Act. He grunted an acknowledgement as the personnel officer finished her trite reply, hardly convinced of what she had told him.

With his last hope stymied, he had no more contact details and he had run out of anyone he could appeal to. It remained true that only Rennison had an overview of the current situation, and that direction appeared futile.

Though he pondered at length on what options he now had, the conclusion was always the same – none! He had no access to the information he wanted – not unless Rennison relented, or he could find either Ferguson or Isaac, and both of them had vanished off the face of the earth.

It was heartbreaking as well as deeply irritating. For the moment he had to bite his lip and accept the impasse. He knew full well that just because a door was closed now it did not mean it might not open at some time in the future. Unfortunately, patience was a virtue he had hardly mastered, but if it was all he could depend on, then Amen. Time would tell.

It was four days later that the front door chimes sounded and Catherine responded.

He had just finished talking to the pool maintenance technician and had shown him out by the nearer of the side gates. Catherine had decided she wanted the pool to be available and not to be drained.

He had a hankering for a coffee and had returned to the house by the kitchen door, ready to switch on the kettle. As he did so, he heard voices coming from the front door, voices which drifted into the kitchen. At first he only recognised Catherine's voice, enquiring after the identity of the visitor. As the male voice replied he froze with astonishment; he instantly recognised it – Rennison was back!

He decided that he was in no mood to appear welcoming to Rennison. He took three mugs and started to deposit coffee granules into each, as he did so he heard footsteps coming down the hallway and Catherine came into the kitchen.

"There's a Mr. Rennison from the Legal and General insurance company just arrived, he would like to see you about your settlement."

It almost caused him to laugh but he suppressed it and smiled back at Catherine.

"Coffee?"

"Oh yes please – shall I ask Mr. Rennison to wait in the lounge? I can make the coffee if you wish – I'll ask Mr. Rennison if he wants one"

It was a good suggestion – some privacy was going to be needed.

"Okay darling – I've met him before so I know his taste in coffee. Ask him to wait for a moment and don't worry, I'll finish the coffee's."

"Oh good, when you are ready, I'll take mine to the pool."

He found Rennison sitting on the settee his arms folded.

"Good to see you Emanuel, I see your fingers are better – coffee?"

Rennison grunted approval and reached up to take the mug.

"As I remember you take it as it comes – its milk and one sugar this time."

Again Rennison simply grunted.

He took the seat opposite the settee and taking a sip from his coffee he studied the man in front of him. Rennison was holding his mug with both hands, his fingers wrapped around the outside of the mug. The previously injured set of digits still showed the remnants of the bruising and some slight signs of scarring from the injuries.

"I see you are fully mobile again Peter and your hands have returned to normal. I'm glad for you. Glad also to meet your new wife – a lovely woman."

He smiled inwardly, what he had been looking at in Rennison, Rennison had been considering in him.

"Yeah, both of us close to fully functional – I suppose we are lucky, unless of course in your case the consequences did not end when they should have."

Rennison looked towards the hallway, clearly not wanting to be overheard.

"It's okay Emanuel, you can talk, my wife is in the pool, she enjoys a daily swim."

Rennison nodded his thanks.

"I'm sorry I appeared tight lipped when you phoned me – these days I don't even trust a secure line coming in to my office. After the incident with Fawly and Bennet here I had to assume that the arms diversion was not entirely of their doing. You'll remember I said something to that effect before I left – they were stooges acting for someone or something else. I had a very difficult time getting my superiors to believe that what happened here could not be avoided – they conceded in the end, grudgingly of course, but gave the assignment a much lower priority, meaning I was allowed to continue the investigation but without the higher classification that warranted any more resource. Since I was very lucky not to be suspended I had to swallow the decision. In short, I was on my own. But that said, I still had an unerring sense that I was dealing with someone close, intent on spoiling my investigation, and that I could deter too much surveillance and interference by appearing not to chase the case too vigorously. However, a one-man band is at a disadvantage as you might guess. Now, Fawly was the key Peter, how he, a well experienced SIS agent became involved in the other sides operations was central to finding out who was behind the arms diversion. I was damn sure that the Ferguson connection had something more important to do with it than I had at first suspected. And yet all I did have was suspicion – I dug into Fawly's background as deep as I could go and it revealed nothing of direct significance. All I can say is that I suspect he was the source of the agency codes used on the Odessa web page. GIFT – *Got Identity – found target*, and GIFTI2 – that is *Group Identification Finalised – Tactical Intervention Imminent* was intended to convince us that our agency was actually involved – of course it was a cold joke to confuse and delay everything.

I then checked again on the brother and sister team, the Ferguson's records – again nothing, other than he was running businesses on the side and had been suspended from operations for that and because he had argued with a very senior officer. Apart from telling the man he was pathologically stupid, Ferguson threatened to punch his lights out. It seems at the time the man was his sister's supervisor and Ferguson felt she was being badly treated. You will recall Ferguson's size – there was no doubt he could do what he threatened to do. So, the short of it is I drew another blank at first – and then to my amazement Charles Ferguson showed up!"

As Rennison paused he confirmed "I know, Ferguson told me he was going to make contact with you the moment he had evidence about the Eprom."

Rennison nodded agreement and put down his mug. He dug into his inside jacket pocket and then withdrew a small plastic bag. He waved it theatrically, making it clear that the bag contained the Eprom.

"He told me the story about you finding this and allowing him to have it. He gave me the decryption of what was programmed onto the chip. It seems that it was a look up table which generated the false website back-page and updated messages within a random time frame every time the PC was activated. There was nothing in the programming to indicate the encryption origin so the decrypt was effectively futile. What wasn't obvious at first was the realisation that the micro-etched serial number on the chip gave provenance and destination. After checking with the US manufacturers it appears that this Eprom was part of a batch originally exported to Europe, a quantity of which ended up with a wholesaler in London. I then traced it to an electronics outlet operating through the web. They had only sold thirty of the Eproms since they had started to stock them. They kept records of all Internet sales and one of them was to a certain Malcolm Bennet...now thankfully deceased I might add. I believe that Malcolm Bennet got his brother Meredith into the arms shipment game after he disclosed what he had learned from Ferguson's sister's work. However, I guess, and it is only a guess, that either greed, or some other family dispute caused a rift and Malcolm Bennet became a threat to their plans – in short he was expendable; hence his murder. Knowing how evil Meredith Bennet was, it would not surprise me that he had carried out his brother's assassination himself. Certainly Meredith Bennet had the knowledge to programme the Eprom and install it in the PC in the hidden room."

Rennison paused and took a sip from his coffee.

"Lovely coffee Peter, very welcome – now...to continue.

There is a glaring question hanging over all this, why divert the arms shipment to Odessa. The assignment started with legitimate papers, sending it to the NATO exercises in Estonia, but somewhere along the line it was hijacked and then diverted. There is nothing to show that it actually got to Odessa, or for what purpose. One could argue that the Ukrainian government in its fight against Russian backed separatists would be very pleased to get their hands on it, but it is unlikely they are involved. If the shipment got diverted through Odessa, it didn't linger there for long. The trail peters out the moment it apparently landed at Odessa and thereafter everything goes cold. One can only conclude that it was either a ship to ship transfer before the main ship got to Odessa, the second ship then secretly unloading at Odessa, or the shipment was broken down prior to arrival, re-packed and then unloaded at the dock in innocent looking crates and moved by road in smaller lots. Either way, the only sniff we have is that Odessa was supposedly where it got diverted. It may be that it was not Charles Ferguson's doing – you could presume he was simply in the frame at the wrong time; part of the disinformation game the opposition are good at. When the ship that apparently loaded the arms shipment arrived in Odessa it was checked out and the ship's manifest identified the cargo from the container's ident' but neither the Captain nor any of the crew on the ship remember it being there – which makes everyone deeply suspicious. Likewise, the most pressing question is why did Fawly and Bennet give the game away by fabricating the web page with messages supposedly from Odessa – the very place the shipment was apparently unloaded. There's no rhyme or reason to it – in effect they told us where to look for it. I can only assume they thought they were being very clever by leading us by the nose straight into a complete dead end.

And that's practically it Peter – you are now up to date with the investigation except for one aspect of it, and I'm not sure you won't be taken aback by what I am about to say, so I will give it to you straight and without frills. Charles Ferguson is now in Odessa. Your friend Isaac is presently in Beirut. Both of them are working for me!"

He almost dropped his coffee. The jolt of amazement spilled some, but he managed to park his mug on the coffee table before he reacted again.

"What? Jesus, I thought Isaac was...well, being cagey. How did this come about?"

Rennison held a rigid expression, sombre and inscrutable.

"I was stuck – without departmental approval and full support for my investigation I had too little resource to do what I needed to do. The only contact I had in Odessa was the Kiev British embassy security officer, and he could only do so much given that he was on temporary secondment to the investigation. He travelled to Odessa but could only stay for a limited length of time. He carried out the dockside enquiry about the shipment and reported the confusion about the cargo disappearing from the ship the arms were supposedly on. However, he did come up with something more intriguing. He learned that one container unit was unloaded by non-dockside labour – very late at night. It had caused a degree of hostility from the usual stevedores because they were asked to work late and refused the bonus on offer. When they found out it had been unloaded under their noses so to speak there was a row. They were offered a larger payment to avoid further confrontation and that was the end of it. Now Charles Ferguson is following things up, in particular this mysterious nighttime unloading and who, if anyone, paid the stevedores for it to be kept quiet. Isaac...he never told me his family name by the way...agreed to go to Beirut to be poised to follow up another possibility, that the shipment was going to be routed to an Islamic State group. He's fluent in Arabic and seems fearless as regards the dangers he might face. I warned him, and told him I would understand if he declined my request, but he told me he detested what ISIL stood for and would do everything he could to help. If Ferguson comes back with the information I think he will obtain then Isaac will be in a position to intercept the shipment if, that is, it is still in the Ukraine and gets moved to the middle east. If I am right about where the arms are destined, I don't believe they have actually reached the Middle East yet. And if you ask me why I think so it's because the moment we knew the arms had been hijacked the Ukrainians agreed to start checking all road, rail and air shipments outgoing from Odessa, and as yet nothing has turned up."

He sat listening to Rennison with rising anger and resentment.

"So Isaac's all ready to provide a one man interception once he knows the arms are being shipped to somewhere close by is that it? Forgive the obvious statement but how the hell do you expect Isaac to work this miracle? If you've sent him on a suicide mission, and it sounds like it, you can get out of my house right now, and don't come back."

Rennison froze, a look of indignation on his face.

"Get off your soap box Peter, Isaac was under no compunction, he could have said no. If he had, that would have been the end of it. I asked him, I didn't pressure him. He knew full well what the risks were and was prepared to take them. The same goes for Charles Ferguson."

They sat looking at one another, and allowed the silence to calm the dispute.

"Okay, but you know how I feel. Isaac is my friend and salvation – without him you and I would have been much the poorer, if not probably dead. You have put at risk one of the noblest people I have ever met. I hope to God you realise how costly this scheme could be if it goes wrong."

Rennison nodded.

"Tell me about it – you might consider what I've done almost a forlorn hope. It depends on digging out the relevant intelligence and then being able to do something about it when it arrives, with little or no resource to act on it. However, although it isn't a contingency plan, what Ferguson and Isaac are doing may, even at worst, only draw out whoever is organising this sting at the other end. Which comes to my reason for being here. Like your friends, I don't expect you to agree, but you are the only person I have in the picture who I can ask. I want to ask you to shadow me for the next three weeks. In short, I want you to watch my back and report if you see anyone on my tail, or anyone preparing to do me some harm. If you can do it I can operate more effectively and we may get a way of finding out who or what we are in contention with here in the UK."

For a moment he was dumbfounded, left speechless by what at

first seemed an outrageous request. Seconds passed slowly, like a watched clock, before he was able to articulate his feelings.

"Don't be silly, I'm nowhere near one hundred percent fit, I have a new wife who would never agree to this and I'm simply not trained to dog your footsteps. I'd be spotted seconds after I started to follow you, and even if it wasn't seen on day one, after a short while I would be noticed and it would be clear you had a shadow."

"Yes, exactly, that's what I am hoping for – remember, you are watching me. What do you think the opposition will think when they learn I have a tail."

"I've no idea, other than the possibility that to get at you they might have to eliminate me!"

"Yes, but they could also assume that I was under surveillance by my own people, that I was still under suspicion. They could also decide that I was not to be touched, that my own team would keep me stuck below the surface and out of their way."

It was a dangerous assumption and he said so.

"Come on, this is 'might' and 'could'; what if your theory is diametrically wrong and they simply decide to get rid of both of us in one go?"

"Then you would have both severely miscalculated!"

The voice came from the hallway, and it was unmistakably Catherine.

She appeared clothed in a white bathrobe, a pink towel wrapped over her head and hair.

He was staggered; he had entirely forgotten his wife's swimming exercises.

"So, husband dear, what happened to my coffee? I waited only to be disappointed. I'm even more disappointed to find that your friend there has nothing to do with the Legal and General

Insurance Company. I only got to hear the last part of your conversation, but I suspect there is a lot I don't know about you Peter Enfield, or you Mr. Rennison."

He knew he was cornered, it was now impossible for Catherine not to demand the whole story, and that was going to be a seriously disruptive stain on his new marriage. God knew he didn't want to lose her but that was a distinct possibility.

He stood up, his facial expression and body language distinctly mortified by her discovery.

"Catherine, I'm so sorry…"

She raised a hand, waving away his attempt to placate her.

"As I said, I only heard the latter part of your conversation but before I hear the entire story I should like to suggest something. Instead of you, Peter, following this gentleman here, why don't you simply reverse the roles? It seems to me that if my less than truthful husband over there was the one under surveillance by you Mr. Rennison, it might appear to others that they had to know why it was happening. Let's face it, why would the individual most dangerous to their operation be following a complete stranger? I'm not well versed in these matters but I would be worried that there was something going on and to counter it, it would be necessary to clarify what it was. As such, you would still be the target Mr. Rennison but you have a better chance of drawing out whoever it is you want to expose. It's only my opinion you understand."

Rennison stood up and with the two of them standing side by side there followed a tense, embarrassed silence.

Finally, Rennison spoke up.

"I'm very sorry Mrs. Enfield, I cannot apologise enough for deceiving you and I'm sure your husband feels the same. But I am afraid Peter is under a strict confidentiality agreement having

225

signed the Official Secrets Act. He was not at liberty to disclose what he knew to anyone at all, even to you his wife. However, if I can invite you to sign the OSA everything will be revealed. Oh, and by the way, I think your suggestion has merit. I think it should be adopted."

Rennison looked at him, a quizzical look that said 'why not humour her?'.

He had no liking for any of it, but had a feeling that once Catherine understood the whole story, and even though she would not be as enthusiastic as before, she would still leave him with little alternative. It seemed that as usual all he had to do was sit quietly, mind his own business, and the world pissed on him.

"Well, Peter?"

Catherine clearly wanted him to speak up.

He felt the weight of her displeasure.

"I'll get you a coffee." was all he could say.

34

It was a miserable start to the exercise.

Storm clouds had drifted in on the day they had travelled up to London and the grey cast sky had delivered a deluge of water as they left Waterloo Station. The rain refused to stop for the next three days, making each sojourn from one location to another an ever more depressing process. What was worse was the fact that they had subsequently agreed that Catherine's proposal was flawed, in that Rennison was obliged to scurry in and out of SIS HQ frequently whereas he, the reluctant Peter Enfield, could not. The only sensible way was for him to tail Rennison and not the other way round, regardless of the likely risks in the arrangement. No doubt Catherine would be disappointed by their decision to keep to the original plan, but it was unavoidable. Not only that, he doubted she really understood the gamble they were taking, Rennison had been economical with the truth with Catherine when he had précised the story behind his appearance, and how the hidden room and its contents had sucked in both himself, Marie Ferguson, her brother and subsequently Peter. He carefully understated and glossed over much of the less palatable aspects of the story, so much so that she came to see all the events he described in neutral terms. He spared her the events leading to the deaths of Fawly and Bennet and made mention of hardly anything else that might upset her. He was so persuasive and disingenuous that she could make no connection between his reference to finger injuries or the Phlebitis her husband had supposedly suffered from. Neither was she exposed to the extent of the menace they were encountering – it seemed more of a mystery adventure than a dangerous mission. All in all, Rennison had done a superb job of making all that had happened, and had yet to be done, seem very routine. But it wasn't.

Yet what he was doing now was routine – to the point of being mind numbingly boring.

Rennison had been in 86 Albert Embankment, the SIS/MI6 building at Vauxhall Cross, for four hours and he was sick of either simply looking across the bridge, walking VauxhallGardens, or standing on the other side by the security entrance in an entirely similar position waiting for him to come out. He was in no way convinced that he didn't stand out like a sore thumb, and that anyone in the opposition, unless totally blind, would fail to notice him skulking about. Only in the evening, when he tailed Rennison from Vauxhall through the underground to his flat near CrystalPalace, did he become any less despondent.

It was the same procedure every time. After Rennison had walked from the underground and entered his home building he was careful to wait another interminable ten minutes outside the entrance to the 1950's three-story apartment block before going in to join Rennison. This tactic was to ensure no one was tagging the both of them before he made his own way up to see Rennison. It was Rennison's decision, but in his opinion it constituted a futile precaution – after all, anyone tailing him, who knew he was tailing Rennison, would simply keep out of sight.

The fourth night he came to a decision. He was hunched up close to Rennison's three bar electric fire trying to drive the cold and damp from his bones and he knew it could not go on.

"I'm sorry Emanuel but I've had enough. I'm constantly wet,

I constantly have to move position so as not to appear a fixture and I'm constantly hungry. Not just that, I'm still fighting old wounds and I'm not up to this kind of punishment. Add that to the fact that I can't see how you would fail to identify a tail if there was one. It's beyond me! I've watched you for four days now and other than the tube, which is far too crowded for any kidnapping, you are too much in the open for a snatch – the opposition would be stupid to try to get you if you continue as you do. Honestly, we are wasting out time!"

Rennison listened attentively, all the time sipping a large scotch.

"Okay Peter, I hear what you say. Are you hungry by the way?"

"I'm bloody starving. Are you aware that while you are enjoying lunch in your canteen I have to walk at least half a mile to find anywhere providing a decent, moderately priced meal. Okay, I know you are footing the bill but it's all becoming too much of an ordeal. I'm sorry, but we have to think again."

Rennison sank the last of his whisky in one swallow and put his glass down on a fireside table.

"I agree, and you will be pleased to know that you will only be on duty in the morning and in the evening from now on. I've been handed an admin job, part of a security analysis I'm familiar with. It means for at least the next week I'll be ensconced in SIS HQ. All you have to do is tail me in, return to this flat if you wish and then be there at SIS at say five thirty p.m. and tail me back home. Okay, it's four tube journeys a day, but you'll no longer have to endure what you've had to put up with over the last four days."

He listened attentively with some sense of relief. It was in effect a partial stay of execution but he would still be required to keep watch on Rennison and it still appeared a pointless exercise.

"I hear you – but I've already told you that I have serious doubts that my tagging you is in any way worthwhile. As I said, given the present circumstances you are not an easy target. All things considered, if anyone is, it's me!"

Rennison offered a grave smile.

"True, and I'm sorry Peter. But as far as I can judge the risk to both of us is justified. Sooner or later the opposition are going to have to make a move. When, and if, they learn that Ferguson is nosing about in Odessa, and if we are right about the arms not having moved very far beyond Odessa, they will conclude that we, or I, have not let the trail go cold – that we are still chasing them and that they need to do something to protect their investment. Please stick with it for at least another week. Tomorrow I'm hoping to change tactics, I'll let you know what it entails tomorrow evening."

He nodded his head, conceding the point and hoping that whatever the promised new tactics involved it would reduce his vulnerability.

He leaned back from the fire, listening to the rain now pelting the night black window of the room. He must have seemed a piteous sight, for Rennison took pity.

"I don't feel like cooking Peter – had I a wife I suspect we should be enjoying a prepared meal by now. However, I know a very good Indian not too far from here. Let's gorge ourselves and hope for better luck."

It sounded wonderful and he quickly confirmed his willingness to down a curry. Collecting their umbrellas, topcoats and gloves, he led the way but had to turn back quickly, leaving Rennison at the threshold of the front door.

"Forgotten something?"

"Yes, my prescription, the analgesics, I'm surviving on them at the moment. Scar tissue on my back, and my feet are not yet used to so much punishment – both get uncomfortable when I'm dogging you in cold and wet weather."

"Don't worry," Rennison said, "where we are going the curries are so hot your feet and back will glow from the heat."

It came as a welcome improvement. Rennison's change of tactics was to involve another man.

Alex Morton was an old hand from SIS that Rennison had extricated from a potential dismissal. Morton had disrupted an SIS investigation into international money laundering by staying too long at a race course to watch the second favourite, the horse he had backed, take first place. For Morton this distraction took precedence over him watching an individual central to the SIS investigation. As it turned out the blunder made very little difference to the final outcome of the investigation, but a disciplinary hearing took Morton's disregard for instructions very seriously. Rennison gave evidence on Morton's behalf, and coloured the instructions originally given to Morton so as to make them somewhat ambiguous. In the end Morton got the benefit of the doubt and was forever grateful to Rennison for his slightly untruthful support. However, Rennison now called in the favour and after arranging some annual leave from his department, Morton took up duty as the second watcher, keeping an eye on the two in front.

With Morton at his rear and the reduced duty cycle he felt very much more optimistic. He and Morton had most of the day off after chaperoning Rennison into SIS and then back again in the evening. Morton was a proficient shadow and he never once caught sight of him during the journey's they took unless they occasionally collided outside Rennison's flat in the evening. Even then, he usually jumped as the tall, unshaven Morton silently appeared to wish him a friendly good night. Rennison usually chuckled when he heard how ghost-like Morton was, saying that Morton had been trained in the old school and could track a soviet agent for weeks without ever being detected.

And so it continued, late into week two and without any apparent emergence of the opposition. He was beginning to feel more than sceptical about the possibility of uncovering anything tangible and his evenings with Rennison had taken on a somewhat tense relationship. He missed being with Catherine and yearned to have the business concluded so he could return to a more comfortable and predictable life. More than that, his dreams were becoming fixed on Catherine, and their lovemaking, and he was becoming daily more frustrated.

He suspected that even Rennison had his doubts but was reluctant to make the decision to call it a day. On the Monday, the first day of week three, they had returned home to begin the preparation of another of Rennison's frying pan meals. Rennison was chopping onions and he was laying out bacon, potato waffles and opening cans of baked beans when there was a knock on the front door. It was already late and dark outside – there was no reason to expect visitors and so the two of them immediately tensed.

Rennison looked at him and shook his head, picking up a tea towel and drying his hands. He waited as Rennison walked towards the short corridor leading into the flat and then he heard the door open. A muffled conversation followed and then Rennison, with his right hand trailing an automatic pistol, walked into the kitchen diner; behind him came Alex Morton.

"I trust you two have met." Rennison remarked placing the gun on the work surface beside his onions.

He eyed up Morton again, the tall figure was in his late forties, lithe but wide of shoulder, apparently one of those lucky ones inherently fit regardless of any excesses he might indulge in. His thick hair had greyed slightly but his face had hardly aged, it was relatively unlined and he now appeared to be clean-shaven even at this late hour. His eyes were a deep hazel and he carried the hint of a sardonic smile.

"Well Alex, it must be important otherwise you would have used the mobile number I gave you!"

Rennison's sarcastic tone was intended to reprimand Morton but he appeared unmoved.

"Yes, it is important, you two have picked up a stalker and a watcher. I had to be certain of both before I reported it. Better you know it from me before they twig who I am. I had to ensure that I could locate their address and that neither was still on the streets before I told you."

Morton's report came as a shock and a relief at the same time.

Rennison turned to Morton.

"When did you find out Alex."

"Over the last two days. Peter was behind the one trailing you yesterday and I only confirmed the same face today. I waited until you broke contact by entering SIS and then followed the tail back before following on again for the return journey this evening. Then later, I picked up another body outside the flat here – only stayed here for a short while but definitely some kind of surveillance."

Rennison glanced round to offer raised eyebrows – it was an affirmation of his theory that he would eventually become a target.

"Did you get an idea of whom we are dealing with Alex? Any ID at all? It would improve the chances of our next move if we could identify the men we are up against."

Morton hesitated and then spoke.

"It's a woman. Your particular tail is a woman. The person outside tonight was a man, but you are being stalked by a woman!"

He and Rennison froze.

"Say again!"

"It's a woman, for four journeys she's tailed you and then returned to a hotel near the park. She's close enough to ensure she can pick you – and us – up on our way into Vauxhall each day – though I doubt she has twigged that you have two guardians."

As Morton spoke he desperately tried to remember if anyone on the journey in that morning had become even slightly familiar. He racked his brain to recall anyone appearing suspicious, or had been close to Rennison in the tube too frequently over the past few days for it not to be coincidence. But too often people travelled in the same seat and in the same carriage for all their commuting simply because they got on the train at the right time and at the right station when it was nearly empty. To not see a familiar figure would be unlikely.

Rennison turned to him.

"Did you pick up anything Peter, anything ring a bell?"

He was suddenly flustered; for all his care surely he could not have missed a woman tailing Rennison.

"No, sorry – I detected nothing untoward, nothing or no one exactly the same two days running. Certainly no woman stood out."

Morton cleared his throat.

"That's because she was out of sight, she travelled in the next carriage to the one you and Emanuel were in. She stayed back behind both of you on the way to the underground and only stayed in the same carriage as you two on day one. Once she knew your destination and routine she only had to confirm it once again and then she had you tagged. My guess is that now she knows our travel habits she's working out the best way to nail you."

Rennison stood thoughtfully for a moment.

"So, any idea who we might be dealing with Alex, did you get any recognition from the faces you saw?"

Morton smiled – one that conveyed a measure of confidence.

"I wouldn't bet too much on it, though as you know I do like a bet with the odds in my favour. But I have to say the face I saw this morning did strike me as familiar. It was a very long time ago but I'm sure I came across her once. If I had to plump for where and when then I'd say she is, or was, SIS/MI6."

The comment by Morton came as a distinct shock for both of them.

"You think so Alex?"

Morton shrugged.

"Well, she has obvious training in surveillance or she's been taking professional lessons. She might be a bit rusty but she did everything by the book and I was fairly fortunate to notice her keeping tags on you Emanuel. Likewise, the moment you got near to SIS she broke off. She had no intention of getting too close. Makes me think she fears being recognised or has been instructed not to get too near whoever is running her."

Rennison simply gave a small whistle and whispered, "Bloody hell!"

For a long minute or two no one spoke. Morton looked longingly at the food on the workbenches and licked his lips. Rennison stood deep in thought and made no move.

He watched the two men, wondering what they would do in

the present situation. If Morton was right they were under investigation by their own people. It did not bode well regardless.

Then, as if revitalised, Rennison came to life.

"Looks bad doesn't it. It could be that we are being seen as going rogue by our own people. And yet I doubt that it could be official – if so, I would have got wind of it I'm sure, and so far nothing has filtered in to my office that makes me uneasy. It seems to me that we can either wait to see what develops, and risk becoming targets, or nip the whole thing in the bud. Instead of us being the targets, we go after those aiming for us. You say you have the address, er, the hotel, where this mysterious women is staying Alex?"

Morton nodded.

"Okay then, it's five forty five, we'll pay her a visit later. In the mean time we eat. Hungry Alex?"

Morton smiled and nodded again, this time far more enthusiastically.

35

Rennison left the black Mercedes parked around the corner from
the hotel. The Park Hotel was once an impressive Edwardian villa
but had over the years seen too much in the way of extensions
and redevelopment so that now the somewhat neglected façade
was all that was left to remind people of its heritage.

The entrance was approached across a broad pavement that led
up to a flight of ever widening stone steps. The light from the
electric bulbs in two converted gas street lamps illuminated the
glass revolving doors that spun guests in and out. More sensible
visitors used the glass side doors and entered the hotel less dizzy
than otherwise.

Inside, the three lost all sense of sound as the thick carpeting
muffled their footsteps and the veritable jungle of tall artificial
potted plants made the choice of direction confusing.

Rennison pressed on looking for the reception desk and with
a "Got it." walked to his left to be confronted by a long polished
desk overhung by a tall archway.

He followed Morton, letting the two professionals take the lead.
It was a situation he had reservations about, Rennison and Morton
knew what they were doing and he didn't.

Rennison gave the desk bell a sharp slap and it rung with a loud
dissonant chime. Seconds later a side door, leading from the area
behind the desk, opened and a young, dark haired, woman came
out. She smiled; a wide tooth-exposing smile that had the look

of a well practised 'perfect it in the mirror' smile.

"Good evening gentlemen – rooms for the night?"

Rennison shook his head and gave her a look at his SIS warrant card, as did Morton.

"We have reason to believe that one of your guests is involved in illegal activities and is now wanted for questioning. We are looking for a woman...Alex!"

Morton moved forward.

"She is tall, flaxen hair, light skin tones and last seen wearing a beige top coat. She may have left her room early this morning only to return about six this evening."

The girl behind the desk suddenly turned white and her hand, resting on the register, began a slight tremor.

"Oh dear, I...you – must mean Mrs. Donaldson. But she's gone, she booked out...almost an hour ago."

The ingratiating smile from the receptionist did nothing to reduce the collective disappointment that all three showed.

Rennison pressed on.

"Did she leave any forwarding address, what was her address when she booked in?"

The receptionist turned the register towards her.

"It says here 1 Strawberry Fields, London but that's all."

"Nothing else, no forwarding address?"

The girl cowered at Rennison's insistent tone.

"No – she never gave us one, not now and not before."

Morton suddenly spoke up.

"Do you mean she has stayed here before?"

The girl nodded.

"As I remember, twice over the last six months. Her husband stayed here too."

Rennison jumped in.

"Husband? What did he look like?"

"Tall, lovely complexion, very powerfully built. Fair hair like her. He had a lovely car, a Jaguar, red it was. I think he called it an E Type."

He almost choked as the receptionist blurted out the last sentence. "Christ!"

Rennison turned to face him.

"What's wrong Peter, something you can tell me?"

"I think so, some time back, when I gave Charles Ferguson the Eprom, I also lent him my car for a time. You've seen it, a red E Type Jaguar. It's too much of a coincidence don't you think?"

Rennison said nothing and simply looked at the ground for a short time. Morton moved forward.

"Tell me, do you remember, when this Mrs Donaldson left the hotel, if she was picked up...you know, by Taxi or a private car?"

The girl gave another beaming smile at Morton in payment for his less than forceful query.

"I saw the car, I helped with her luggage. It was a silver car, not a Taxi. It was a...BMW, yes, a BMW with a funny badge on the back and I remember the number plate started with the same letters. It was M5 something, oh...M50 OOO – yes, I think so."

Rennison turned to Morton.

Alex, get your contacts in the DVLA to trace that number plate – M50 OOO was it? If we can find the car I think we have her too. Likewise, from what we have just heard, I suspect we have Charles Ferguson as well! God knows, if he really is involved in this we've been well and truly suckered. He's meant to be in Odessa damn it! Alex, get back to SIS and put me down for sick leave for the next few days, oh, and while you are at it send out a recall to Ferguson, just in case. I'll give you the details in a moment. Let's see if he responds."

36

Alex Morton arrived with the DVLA data mid-morning the next day. Rennison was in the bathroom so he got to see the paperwork before Rennison came out. As he was shown the paperwork he saw that the BMW was registered to an address and a postcode that seemed familiar to him, and as he stared at it he gave a gasp of astonishment.

Rennison appeared at that moment dabbing his face with a towel.

"What's wrong?" Rennison asked.

He handed Rennison the typed sheet of paper Morton had delivered.

"Don't you recognise the address Emanuel, it's mine, the old safe house!"

Rennison stared at the type written text and simply handed it back to Morton.

"Bugger – they really are good at closing doors aren't they. Never thought Charles Ferguson and his accomplices were this clever. In everything they appear to have thought two steps ahead of us. We are now back to where we started and

I don't like it at all."

Alex Morton cleared his throat. "Not quite – my soggy brain has been working overtime since last evening and I think I know who we are dealing with. Nine years ago I was on refresher course for deep penetration agents – God only knows what it was all about, not a lot of what was said penetrated me. However, what I do remember was a blonde haired girl who vanished after the second week. I heard she had been taken off the course as unable to continue – she was pregnant. Her name, because I checked, was Marie Ferguson, the same girl I saw the other day."

It was too fantastic, and he said so.

"No Alex – can't be, Marie Ferguson is dead, she died on Flight 554, the one that crashed on the way to Vancouver. You can confirm that can't you Emanuel."

Rennison held up his hand to wave away any further comment.

"Hold on Peter, if Alex says he saw her then I trust his judgement. Listen, if Ferguson can play 'first you see me then you don't', I don't see why his sister would be any less able. I'm beginning to think we have been at the wrong end of this conspiracy all along. But be that as it may, knowing who we are chasing and why we are chasing them doesn't for one moment tell us where they are. The truth is we are stonewalled again – we have no bloody idea where they might have gone to earth and not a single lead to take us in the right direction. Come on boys, I'm receptive to any thoughts that might help."

Morton moved forward and waved another piece of paper at Rennison.

"I don't know for definite where they are now Emanuel, but I do know where they were a long time back. I checked Marie and Charles Ferguson's personnel file as far back as I could. Both originally hailed from an address near Winchester, an address in Twyford called *Clear Spring Farm*. It's a seven hundred acre dairy farm and according to land registry still owned by the Ferguson family. Now it proves nothing as regards the whereabouts of Marie and Charles Ferguson but as a betting man..."

Rennison slapped Alex Morton on the shoulder.

"Well done Alex, and of course it would be a long shot, not your cup of tea I know 'cos you only like the favourites don't you. But you know what they say; if you don't play you can't win. Let's see what *Clear Spring Farm* has to offer and who's offering it!"

The rain had just turned to drizzle as they drove slowly down a rutted half-mile track towards some farm buildings on the horizon. In the fields on each side of the track Friesian cattle munched grass contentedly with utter indifference to the passing car. The potholes and depressions in the track, half filled-in with broken bricks and gravel, made the going in the Mercedes very lumpy and by the time they reached a wide circular brick laid driveway they were deeply grateful.

Rennison turned the car so that it was broadside on to a large brick built Victorian farmhouse. It had been extended over many years and presented a whole range of different brick tones and sizes. The upper story had been added at some time after the first and had a brick and flint border separating the two levels. The windows were square, with the odd cracked windowpane and weather worn glazing bars – it was almost Georgian in style.

On the left was a long line of old stable blocks, to the right and behind the farmhouse were four large barns, some outhouses and milking parlours. Scattered behind the car were numerous machinery stores, yet only a single careworn Ferguson Tractor, parked at a skewed angle, directly indicated any farming activity. Looking around it was noticeable that there was no movement of any kind – the place seemed dead.

They sat looking at the farmhouse trying to see through slightly misted widows backed by net curtains. Any hope of immediately detecting signs of life proved futile, nothing was forthcoming. In the end Rennison opened his door and got out.

"Alex, Peter, round the back, check all the buildings – especially anything you can't get in to. I'm going to the farmhouse, we'll see if we can..."

As Rennison was leaning into the car giving his instructions the farmhouse door opened and a middle-aged man dressed in jeans and a blue checked open-neck shirt came out holding a single barrelled shotgun. As he appeared he pointed the weapon forward, directly at the car.

It was the sudden freezing of movement and change of gaze from Alex and himself that caused Rennison to halt in mid sentence and reach for his automatic. He felt Morton do the same, saying nothing as a Glok 19 appeared out of sight of the man with the shotgun.

Rennison suddenly backed away from the car door and turned, levelling his Browning at the man with the shotgun. At the same time Alex Morton leaned forward from his front passenger position and stretched across the drivers seat pointing his gun in the same direction.

"I hope you don't intend to use that on us." Rennison said as he ignored a few drops of rain splattering off his topcoat. "It would be a mistake, I guarantee I will get at least two rounds off in your direction before you fire."

"And I will certainly kill you regardless." Alex Morton added.

The man suddenly faltered and looked bewildered. He had nowhere to go and very slowly let the shotgun drop away.

"Please put the gun behind you and come forward. We are not here to harm you, we are looking for someone."

Rennison's ice-cold voice warmed, coaxing the man away from any hostile intentions.

The man turned, leaned the shotgun against the farmhouse

wall and then tentatively came forward three paces.

Rennison let his gun drop and then, pushing back his topcoat and jacket, returned it to his waist belt holster. He then walked forward and waited.

He'd watched this confrontation with bated breath, hoping that he was not going to get involved in yet another killing, either that of the man with the gun, or his own.

Morton turned and came erect from his prone position giving him a nod. "Lets get on with it Peter."

They both scrambled out of the car and gave themselves a few seconds to stretch and to wake up cramped muscles.

They allowed Rennison, now talking to a very nervous looking man, a last look and then walked towards the farm buildings.

"I'll take the rearward ones Peter, you go for the ones to the front here."

He confirmed with a nod. "Okay Alex, but remember I'm not armed and I don't have your training."

Morton stopped and walked back to him pulling at something in his topcoat pocket.

He offered a short-barrelled automatic pistol.

"Grab the slider by wrapping your hand over – oh, never mind."

He snapped back the slider and then slipped a small latch to one side.

"It's now loaded. You have eleven rounds in the magazine, if you have to fire on anyone count each round, they may fire back and you don't want to be left with an empty gun. This little lever is the safety. Move it down away from the letter 'S' to activate the gun. Okay? Just one thing, don't get trigger happy, I don't want you practising on me!"

As they broke away Rennison turned around from the man he was questioning.

"Hold on you two, Mr Snell here has something interesting to tell us."

He saw Alex Morton come to an immediate halt and he too turned to retrace his steps.

They covered the short distance to Rennison and the farmer rapidly; as they approached, Rennison looked towards them.

"Mr. Snell here is a tenant farmer – he's held the tenancy for, how long has it been Mr. Snell, fifteen years you say. Please tell these gentlemen what you have just told me."

The man, unshaven, grey flecked hair and somewhere in his forties, was obviously very nervous. His voice came out timidly and hardly above a whisper.

"I'm not the landowner, I just rent it from a family called the Ferguson's, they own pretty near everything here except my dairy herd, some machinery and the milking parlour. I've worked here for, yes, fifteen years, and hardly see the owners. As long as I pay my tithe they tend to leave me alone. Some months ago though, one of them, a woman, turned up and told me she wanted the use of one of the big winter feedstock barns. It wasn't a request, it was a demand, I had no choice. I had to transfer everything in the barn to leave it empty. Then some big transporters arrived very early one morning and I was told by the woman to make myself, and my farmhands, scarce. We had to drive away and not come back 'till the next day. When we did get back everything was quite, no one here, so I looked at the big barn and it had been fitted with fresh doors – steel ones with heavy padlocks. There was a note in the house there, on the kitchen table. I was not to attempt to access the barn or have my men or myself say anything about it to anyone otherwise we would be not get a renewal of the tenancy and would in other ways regret what we had done. That's all I can tell you."

Rennison turned to look at the barns opposite the farmhouse. "Which one is it Mr. Snell?"

"That one." The farmer pointed to the top of a large Dutch barn some thirty metres away.

"I take it you have an oxy-acetylene somewhere Mr. Snell."

"I do but I...!"

Rennison gave the farmer an intimidating look.

He stuttered. "It's...it's no good – my farmhands do all the cutting when necessary and they've all driven up to Salisbury to a Livestock market. I can't use the oxy-acetylene very well, I've got an eye condition and I can't see well through the safety mask."

Here was his chance to actually be useful.

"I can do it – I'm used to using an oxy-acetylene - one of my skills from the past."

Alex smiled, and Rennison turned to the Farmer.

"Where's the kit Mr. Snell – we need it now. Peter here will show you how it's done."

The padlocks cut away without any difficulty and apart from getting used to seeing the flame front through the visor again he had little trouble. The last of the four padlocks fell away with the red-hot remains of the hook sizzling as it hit the damp ground beneath it. He kicked it away and, slipping his fingers deeper into the protective leather gloves, immediately pulled back the hinges of the four clasps locking the door to the inset 'U' on the hasp and staple lock.

The heavy metal doors creaked back as the new hinges took the load. As they came open Rennison pushed his way in. As they all followed on they heard him curse.

The daylight flooded in from the open doors to reveal a completely empty space, there was only the residue of what had once been a barn full of cattle feed.

As all four bodies saw the vacant barn Snell exclaimed "But we thought they was already storing stuff...!"

Rennison turned violently, looking around as if demanding that someone would appear to express regret and assuage his wrath.

Apart from the farmer, who continued to mutter his disbelief, the trio remained shocked into silence.

Rennison took one last look, his whole stance expressing incredulity, and then walked out of the barn.

Alex Morton gave a low whistle and followed.

He too had one last look, noting how dry the barn was given all the recent rain, and followed the two SIS men out.

"What the hell is this?" Rennison hissed standing by the entrance, "We seem to be constantly on the wrong end of some kind of huge practical joke. How the hell are they able to lay so many false trails for us? It's as though they have some kind of prescience, as though they know what we are going to do next and simply lay a trap to frustrate us. It's not possible, but it's happening! Fuck it!"

The farmer Snell now stood by, listening to Rennison vent his anger. Just before the final explosive expletive left Rennison's mouth he interjected.

"Excuse me – I'm sorry, I forgot...my instructions...I was told that there may be more to come. I mean, I was told to stand by because there would be other deliveries."

He saw the colour instantly return to Rennison's face while Alex Morton gave a knowing smile.

"Other deliveries Mr. Snell, or the first delivery?"

"I...I don't know. Maybe the first delivery was just the barn doors. I'm not sure now."

He left it unspoken, but Morton made the observation that had occurred to everyone.

"Christ – you know what, I don't think the shipment is here yet. They have delayed for some reason and my guess is that they wanted to know what you were up to Emanuel, to determine if you were stuck in SIS on routine matters or still on their trail. They've left it late because you've been sniffing about all these months. Now they think everything has gone cold because of your daily attendance at SIS and it means the barn here is poised for a delivery. They'll probably move the stuff here because it will allow things to get colder and they can then ship it out. Given our location, Southampton docks isn't that far away. My guess is that if we wait, we'll nail them."

He waited for Rennison to reply but for a moment the man held his counsel.

With nothing forthcoming from the silent Rennison he decided to risk stating the obvious.

"If what you say is true Alex, we have to be here before they do, otherwise we'll lose the advantage."

Rennison turned with a questioning look. "Yeah? Why so Peter?"

"Because we've removed the padlocks to the barn. Unless Mr Snell here says otherwise, I suspect the opposition are the only ones with a second set of keys. If true, we can't simply replace the padlocks with new ones, it would stand out like a very sore thumb."

Morton shook his head in concern. "Yeah, you're right. It means we have to be here before they arrive but that we can't do – we have no idea when they are coming and we can't sit around the farm forever waiting for them to appear. It's a real pisser."

As the three of them stood pondering the reality of the situation

Snell started to speak.

"I get notice to vacate you know…er' they'll telephone me and give me 24 hours to get my herds under cover and myself and my help off the premises. If it happens again I could phone you. Look, I'm willing to help – what you have done today with the barn leaves me in a lot of shit with the Ferguson's. I need a way out."

Rennison looked down on the still anxious farmer.

"I'll make a deal with you Mr. Snell. Give us immediate notification that you have received a phone call to vacate and when all is said and done I will guarantee you immunity from prosecution. You have been very helpful so far; you may even get a ministerial commendation. More importantly, if things go the way I hope, you will be entirely free of any obligation to the Fergusons – in perpetuity."

Snell brightened. "You mean I won't have to negotiate the tenancy again?"

Ferguson looked slightly puzzled but replied "Something like that Mr. Snell, yes!"

37

It was a small dilemma, was he to make his way home for the interim, or stay with Emanuel Rennison in London? The latter had the advantage that he could instantly respond if wanted, but it also meant that he was twiddling his hands and toes while Rennison spent time in SIS. If he ventured home again there was a risk he would not be called up the moment Rennison was ready to move back to *Clear Spring Farm*. He had no real idea of the value Rennison set on his support but he would have resented hearing later that Rennison had wrapped up the whole business in his absence.

It was strange, but having seen so much of the investigation he was damned if he was going to be deprived of being instrumental in the final phases of it.

Was he crazy?

Of course he was, why on earth would he want to put himself at risk again? Hadn't he had enough traumas in the last few years to last a lifetime? Yes he had, but that argument had little influence on his sense of pride – he was not going to regret failing to see it all through because of a little bout of common sense and expediency.

The days dragged on and although he tried not to get in Emanuel Rennison's way it was becoming evident that he had almost outstayed his welcome. Furthermore, Catherine was starting to plead with him to give her a date when he would be back at the house. In the end he was compromised – by being stuck somewhere he shouldn't and not being somewhere he should.

He gave Emanuel Rennison forty-eight hours notice that he was returning to East Linkin and home, and that he could call him up for help instantly without notice. Rennison, in turn, expressed his thanks and deep gratitude for the support he had given so far and asked him to convey his thanks to Catherine for her fortitude and patience.

The next day he sat across the breakfast table assuring Rennison that he genuinely sensed it was the last lap of the investigation. Over a final coffee before his trip into SIS Rennison admitted that it was his experience that what appeared to be within reach was too often a case of so near yet so far, and that he never counted his chickens. Indeed, there seemed no reason to think that the Ferguson's, wherever they were, had not once again pulled the wool over everyone's eyes. Rennison said he was beginning to think that the farmer and his empty barn did really constitute another hilarious joke as far as the Ferguson's were concerned. Oh yes, wasn't it all very funny!

He deferred to Rennison's pessimism and because he could accompany Rennison on the tube going to Waterloo Station, he started the process of completing his packing. Then he heard the chimes of Rennison's mobile. There was a very short exchange of words and Rennison rushed into the spare bedroom where he was.

"We're on – Snell has just been told to vacate. He says he's leaving now and we can take over the farmhouse for as long as it takes. I'll get Alex lined up and some more backup if I can. Are you still game Peter, if so I need you!"

He didn't hesitate.

"Of course, anything I can do!"

Rennison smiled, "With luck we'll wrap this bloody business up. I'm beginning to think your sixth sense has merit."

It was a tense journey down to Twyford, neither he nor his two companions had much to say. It was on everyone's mind that the essence of the exercise was arriving before the opposition did. And yet Rennison drove with a kind of grim determination, hardly ever pushing the car above speed limits and being extraordinarily gracious to other drivers.

It was clear that his priority was arriving at *Clear Spring Farm* in one piece – it was no good getting the chance now on offer and then spoiling everything by getting involved in a road traffic accident or being stopped by the police for speeding.

As they inched up the dirt track leading to the farmhouse and its buildings there was no sign of life and each man began to realise that they had probably beaten the arrival of the expected shipment.

Rennison parked the car out of sight behind the main cowshed, the noise of the engine as they all dismounted being drowned out by the onset of mooing from a multitude of imprisoned cows.

"Barn first, farmhouse next." Rennison called out.

They circled the various sheds until they arrived at the steel doors of the food storage barn they had previously entered.

Morton pulled at the four closed clasps and pulled one door open.

"Nothing, still empty." he said, as he withdrew his head and started to close the doors.

"I suggest you leave them wide open." Morton said, "If the doors are pulled back it will delay them finding out that the padlocks have been cut away. Open doors on that empty barn could be construed as Mr. Snell's nosiness or negligence, not necessarily enemy action."

Everyone silently acquiesced and he pulled each of the doors flat up against the barn walls.

"Right, farmhouse."

Rennison flicked his head in the opposite direction and they began to walk towards the farmhouse. It was as they were about to cross the brick cobbled driveway separating the milking parlour and the farmhouse itself that all three froze.

He'd heard the sound, as had his companions – the low rumble of powerful engines moving towards them.

Rennison pulled back his jacket and his hand went into his waist–belt holster; instantly his automatic was in his hand. Alex Morton was equally quick and as he pulled Alex Morton's borrowed gun out he almost felt the equal of them.

"Can you use that thing?" Rennison hissed.

With only bravado to depend on he replied, "You point the thing and pull the trigger. Try me."

Rennison gave Morton a hard stare but then realised there was no time for debate.

"Alex, go right –stay hidden unless they make trouble. Peter, go to the Farmhouse, keep down and stay down unless called for. Go, be quick, the bastards are close."

He made a limping run across the mud–encrusted brickwork that had once served as pristine paving outside the farmhouse but had, over the years, suffered too much attrition. The surface was rutted and here and there portions of the brick had completely disappeared leaving large gaps in the ground like missing teeth. He was focused on the green painted farmhouse door that he prayed was not locked. His intention was not to retrace his steps but to break in if needed. With some relief he avoided tripping over the brickwork or stumbling from still imperfectly reformed feet.

As he burst in through the farmhouse door, he was immediately in the kitchen and overcome by a strange odour. It took a moment to realise that not too long past someone had fried bacon and perhaps fried bread – it took him back to another time, to a time before his tragedies. For a brief moment he remembered another life.

Wasn't life strange?

Here he was, armed, possibly soon to be involved in a firefight and living a life he could only have dreamed about a few years back.

He prayed that Betty, looking down on him, would be amused by what she saw and would try to protect him – he then thought of Catherine, wouldn't she be angry having to arrange his funeral. He smiled to himself; the usual joke came into his head – he would never hear the last of it from Catherine if he turned up dead.

Right now though he'd settle for a little wifely nagging. God knew he deserved it!

To the left of the kitchen door was a wood framed kitchen window with a low wide sill and a veil of net curtains hiding the glazing. He could see out, but having viewed the house from the outside, he knew no one could see in.

As he crouched down behind the window he heard the mingled exhaust notes of two heavy articulated trucks coming closer. In a few moments the massive engine bonnet and drivers cab of the first vehicle ran across his line of sight and the light coming into the kitchen dimmed as it blocked out the sky.

Almost immediately the cab door opened and the first vehicle's engine cut out followed by a distant second a few moments later.

Dressed in jeans and a grey roll neck sweater, the first driver clambered down and looked to his left and right but made no further move to explore, rather he dug into his pocket and pulled out a pack of cigarettes. He retrieved one and quickly lit it, inhaling the first drag with obvious pleasure. At the same time he flexed his legs, trying to remove stiffness from the ordeal of a long journey.

Seconds later another taller man joined the first, and he could make them out debating whether they had found the right address. It was as they had apparently agreed to knock on the farmhouse door to ask confirmation that Rennison appeared.

He waited, strictly adhering to Rennison's orders.

It seemed that the men were expecting to be met but had no idea who it would be, so Rennison's appearance did not result in any apparent adverse reaction. He watched them conversing, forming a three body triangle with Rennison forming the apex to the right.

Their voices outside were muffled and what was being said was less than distinct. After another brief exchange one of the men started to gesticulate and was clearly becoming agitated. He pointed at the name on the first cab and then pointed back, apparently indicating the same on the second. Then he searched his back pocket and withdrew a wallet. He opened it and offered Rennison a card which was taken and scrutinised. Rennison continued to listen as the second driver spoke up, emphasising his words with a thrusting head. Then he pulled a folded sheet of paper from his pocket and handed it over to Rennison. Again, Rennison inspected it while the first driver climbed back into his cab and leaned in, recovering something from the passenger seat. Rennison then took possession of a small clutch of keys which the first driver surrendered. He then stepped forward and opened the farmhouse door.

"Okay Peter, out you come."

Rennison immediately navigated around the first truck and called out.

"Alex, all clear."

He stood up and made his way to the outside, joining Rennison and the two drivers. Seconds later Alex Morton came up silently behind them and waited with his hand thrust into his jacket pocket – it was clear he was gripping his gun and was poised for any threat.

As they became surrounded, the two drivers shuffled nervously where they stood, clearly intimidated by their unexpected situation.

Rennison addressed Alex and himself.

"These men are part of a *bona fide* haulage operation – they were contracted to pick up the trailers and their loads at the port of Harwich would you believe, and ship them here. It seems they were instructed by phone. The client sent them notes on the pick up point, the routing, the destination and the payment; all by post and anonymously. They even got the keys for the padlocks on the storage barn – see!"

Rennison showed off the keys with a slightly metallic rattle.

"These gentlemen I'm sure would like to complete their task. As I understand it you are to back your trailers into the barn over there, decouple your cabs and then return home in the cabs leaving the trailers and their loads behind. Now, I have already warned you not to convey any part of this episode to your client. Remember, I know who and where you are. Should I find my warning has been ignored I will prosecute you under any number of different laws covering state security. Understood?"

He watched as the two, men voiced their compliance.

"Okay."

"Yeah we heard."

Rennison smiled.

"Good, so let's get to it, time is pressing."

The two men acknowledged again and broke away to get to their respective cabs. It took no more than twenty minutes for the two cabs to finish their manoeuvring and then to be unhitched.

Soon the two powerful units were on their way down the mud track leading away from the farm buildings. As the sound of their engines faded away he stood with Morton and Rennison staring at the two trailers now side by side in the barn.

"How do we know that this is the original shipment?" Alex Morton queried.

"Might it not be?" he then asked.

Rennison pursed his lips.

"I'm fairly certain that the outside is genuine, not sure about what we might find packed into the crates but we can't find out just yet, it's not going to change anything at the moment and, like the padlocks, if we started to break open any one of the containers it would immediately alert those we are expecting to arrive. However, one thing seems to be certain, assuming this lot is the original shipment to Estonia, it never got anywhere near Odessa! Again, the bastards just fabricated a nice plausible false trail that had us running in circles."

"But what about the missing padlocks?"

Morton raised his eyebrows and Rennison grinned.

"The thing is Peter, they were dependent on the haulage contractors – who is to say that those two guys didn't forget to lock up the barn. I suspect that with the shipment apparently sitting here intact, it will only cause a minor amount of consternation. Whoever it is turns up, we need them to show us what they intend to do with this lot – that way we roll the whole operation up. It's now our bait and we have to hope we will catch all the fish in one go. That said, back to our positions – we may not have a long wait."

As it turned out it was, or at least seemed to be, an interminable wait and he was beginning to long for a bit of whatever had been cooked for breakfast in the kitchen. The smell was as strong as when he had first detected it, and it was making his guts gurgle. Apart from his stomach he was beginning to feel the scar tissue on his back complaining. His store of analgesics had been left behind miles away and here in a strange farmhouse there was little chance of finding an aspirin let alone anything stronger. Not only that, not one of them had even the chance of a cup of coffee or tea since they had arrived, and he realised that sooner or later they would have to come out from cover and replenish their energies.

It was getting into the late afternoon when Rennison gave up. He suddenly appeared on the brick driveway and called out.

"Alex, Peter, we will have to call it quits."

Rennison's words were almost inaudible in the kitchen but he saw him through the window and assumed it was time to abandon the vigil. He lifted his bent knees and aching back stiffly from his crouched position and thanked God for Rennison's good sense and pragmatism.

As he opened the door he saw Alex slowly make his way to join Rennison. All three congregated nearer the farmhouse door than away from it and he hoped that Rennison had a refreshment-based reason for doing it.

He was wrong.

"Okay boys? I suspect that the arrival of the shipment today and the appearance of our targets, are on entirely different schedules. We could wait it out I suppose but I think we are wasting our time. We can't operate a direct 24/7 surveillance – but then, I don't think we need to. I am trusting to the fact that Snell will give us due notice when next he is ordered to vacate the farm. So all we can do is to go home and wait for the next…"

As Rennison abruptly halted his announcement they realised why. Coming down the track, but as yet out of sight, they heard the sound of an engine.

"Snell?" Morton asked.

"No – he's not due back until tomorrow morning. It could be our targets. Let's find our bolt holes again and see."

Rennison instantly turned away and Alex Morton followed. He too turned away towards the kitchen door, knowing that once again he had to face having to endure the delicious smell that pervaded the kitchen.

38

The BMW M5 appeared on the driveway very quickly. It came in fast and almost skidded to a halt. From the kitchen window he could just make out the number plate M50 OOO and it sent a chill down his spine.

So, now this was getting serious. If Charles Ferguson dismounted from the car all their worst suspicions would be confirmed and mayhem was likely to follow.

The driver's side of the car was facing his window but for an almost endless period of time the car door stayed shut. There was little doubt a man was driving, and there were two passengers in the rear seats. But the driver was talking avidly to someone in the passenger side and with his head turned away it was virtually impossible to determine who the passenger was. Neither the driver nor his passengers seemed to be in a hurry to leave the car and so he, like Morton and Rennison, had to be resigned to remaining hidden so as not to alert the car's occupants and scare them off or into offensive action.

At last the drivers door opened and as the man stepped out it was clear he had been wrong.

It was the masculine haircut that deceived him, and the beige suit had a masculine style, but there was no doubt, the driver was a woman. Her dark blonde hair complimented an almost flawless pale skin around her face. Her flattish chest and the lack of any makeup gave her the appearance of a youth.

As she alighted the other car doors came open and three men got out. One was tall and had a similar hair colour to the woman; the other two men were darker and powerfully built. It wasn't the sub-machine guns the two darker men carried that held his gaze, rather it was the woman's passenger, the one whose hair matched the woman's. There was no doubt; it was Charles Ferguson.

It was not a moment to fear or lament, rather he felt ashamed that he had been so gullible.

Ferguson had spun a web of deceit and falsehoods that had really taken him in, and he found it hard to accept that he had never once distrusted Ferguson after their first meeting. That Ferguson had fooled everyone else as well was no consolation – there was no escaping the fact that he had naively handed over the Eprom and even loaned the villain money and his beloved car. He supposed that he should be grateful that Ferguson had returned it, although he now suspected that even that gesture of honesty was part of Ferguson's misleading strategy.

Now he had a chance to even things up, but not of his own volition. He had to wait for Rennison or Alex Morton to initiate some kind of action and that needed the elimination of the two heavyweight guards.

As he waited he saw the woman say something to the two guards who then sauntered off towards the storage barn with Charles Ferguson behind them.

Soon, he knew, something would happen; it would not be long before they saw the arms shipment parked in open display in the storage barn. He prayed that Rennison and Morton could intercept and disarm them before the advantage of their own situation was compromised.

As he concentrated on the woman, now leaning her back against the other side of the BMW, the thee men disappeared around the side of the right hand cowhouse and for a short time he heard nothing.

Then, as if a small war had broken out, he heard the distant rattle of an automatic weapon and a long series of single shots interspersed with more bursts of automatic fire. This continued for what seemed a protracted period of time. As this took place he saw the woman open the passenger's car door and reach in. She withdrew and stood erect holding an assault rifle. She then turned and started to trot towards the sound of gunfire.

There was no choice; he had to ensure she did not join the fight, particularly if she was able to outflank Rennison and Morton.

Stiff as he was, the surging adrenalin meant he ignored his physical limitations and was out of the kitchen door virtually instantly. She had made nearly ten yards across the driveway by the time he had navigated around the BMW and had her clearly in sight.

"Stop...stop or I will open fire."

He prayed he had done exactly what Morton had told him about loading and unlocking the weapon's safety latch. He held the automatic with two hands and aimed at the woman's back.

But she was around in a flash, bringing the rifle's barrel up to a horizontal position and aiming it at him.

This he did not expect and for a brief second he suddenly felt panic. But he was damned if he was going to be bested again, not to mention that something inside of him demanded he stay alive.

He fired three panic driven shots in quick succession; not sure of anything other than that the recoil was unexpected and that his rounds were going in the woman's general direction. As the last cartridge case rang out on the brick driveway he stood agog as she let the rifle go and collapsed writhing to the ground holding her thigh.

Frozen to the spot, still with the gun pointing at her, he was entirely lost for anything to do next. She was moaning in pain and from somewhere in his shocked psyche he empathised with her suffering. He dropped the gun to his side feeling obliged to respond to her distress. Her hand was pressed hard on her upper right thigh but it was already covered in blood. He started to walk towards her but had only covered a few yards when a figure burst out from around the cowshed and ran towards him. He knew the man; it was Charles Ferguson, and he was armed.

Once again he trusted to luck, bringing the automatic up to the firing position.

And yet Ferguson did not appear to be intent on shooting at him. Ferguson's gun was held in his right hand and he was not even looking as though his next target was in front of him. Instead, as he dashed across the driveway he was staring at the woman, his face was contorted with anguish.

As he reached the woman he dropped the gun and bent down to her. He pulled her up into his arms and cradled her lovingly. She in turn lifted an arm to touch his but squirmed away as he tried to overlay her hand which was pressing down on her leg wound. He pulled a handkerchief from his top pocket and forced it between her hand and the bullet wound.

Ferguson looked up.

"Fuck you, you...Christ...Enfield? What the hell are you doing here?"

"I should ask you the same question Charles. I seem to remember being persuaded that you were innocent in all this."

Ferguson scowled.

"All's fair in love and war Peter and I had to take sides."

As this was said a sudden eerie silence descended over the whole area. A final gunshot receded into the distance and it was as though he had been abandoned by anything that could help him.

If Rennison and Morton had gone down he was on his own, and it wasn't a very warming prospect. He took a fatalistic attitude, if the worst came to the worst he would not give up – it was kismet and that was that. He had undertaken never again to be at the mercy of circumstances where otherwise he would have capitulated. This time he would go down fighting.

"Crap...I don't understand you – greed, treachery and treason is what you are talking about. You allied yourself to a criminal gang, you corrupted and exploited Fawly, and you weaved a complete web of falsehoods and distractions. I know where the war comes from – but hell, where is the love? I gave you shelter, I gave you money, I even gave you my car, but it was all a pretence wasn't it? I offered you friendship and you repaid it with treachery. You connived, fabricated, lied and schemed – you took my trust and good will and spat on it, all to suck me in to your conspiracy and deflect Rennison and the investigation. Christ Ferguson, I should have relied on my first impression of you – you're a first class shit."

Ferguson bent down and kissed the woman, giving no indication whatsoever that he was affected by the tirade. Then he lifted his head and replied.

"Well Enfield, here is part of it, my wounded wife and her morally wounded husband. Except for you all those I used came voluntarily – easy when their greed overrode their principles. But believe me, what I have done I did for her, it broke my heart but what else could I do? Tell me, don't you have something precious – a loving wife? Which of your principles would you deny to keep her?"

For a moment Ferguson's words hit a raw nerve. He momentarily thought of Catherine and all those he had loved and lost. Would he have sacrificed his honour and honesty for the woman or family he loved? It caused a huge vacillation in his mind. He had no immediate answer. It was a terrible dilemma that tore at his empathy. His past experiences made him think twice. He could not in all honesty be a hypocrite and condemn Ferguson out of hand. Maybe it was wrong but he decided on clemency.

"Okay, if this little war is over, we had better call an ambulance, that is if one can get out this far. No, on second thoughts better we drive her to the nearest hospital, it will be far quicker and she will suffer less."

Ferguson looked relieved and thankful.

"Thank you – I'm grateful."

"Don't be – you're lucky, I'm salving my conscience."

He looked beyond the sad tableau in front of him, wondering if either Morton or Rennison had survived. His answer came almost immediately.

From around the side of the cowshed, Morton limped into view with Rennison trailing behind. Morton stumbled forward still trailing his automatic in his right hand. A ripped trouser leg and a patch of dark blood indicated where a gunshot had penetrated his trouser leg. Open to view through the torn material was a bloodied pad of white tissue strapped to his leg by a waist belt.

As Morton approached him he let his gun drop, now certain that the two SIS men were able to give him cover.

As Morton closed the gap between himself and the two on the ground, Morton kicked away Ferguson's gun and then stopped to look down on the two bodies cuddling together. He gave a whistle of surprise.

"I'll be..."

Morton stopped as he came abreast.

Now, looking at the wounded woman, he thought he knew the value of the hidden room photographs.

"Yeah Alex, it's his sister, she wasn't killed in any air crash − that woman is the same one I saw in some family photos."

Ferguson stared up at him and snorted in disgust.

"Rubbish Enfield, my sister and her kids are dead and not by my doing. This woman is my wife."

Morton smiled knowingly and waited for Rennison to reach them.

"Guess who?" he asked.

Rennison, looking haggard, drawn and tired, simply shook his head.

Morton, almost in triumph, pointed down to the woman with the barrel of his gun.

"This my friends is Maureen Amanda Bennet, part of the Bennet criminal family and sister to Malcolm and Meridith Bennet. Now we have the link − Fawly, as my colleague Mr. Rennison here informed me, was rogue and in league with Ferguson and he, in turn, with the Bennet brothers. But Ferguson motivation wasn't the arms and the money; he was besotted with the sister. My guess is that greed broke up the family loyalties. As you noted, but wrongly Peter, Maureen here bears a definite and uncanny physical resemblance to Ferguson's sister. You can read into that what you like − but that, I'm afraid, is as far as it goes."

As he and the two SIS men surrounded the two Ferguson's wrapped together on the ground, he realised that he had been absolutely right, the explanation for all the false trails could be directed at Charles Ferguson who, for the love of a devious and criminally minded woman, had forsaken his principles and integrity and woven a deeply complex web of deceit, dishonesty and death. And yet he wondered again, with some sense of guilt, if he would have done the same.

What if he had been facing the loss of those he loved now, and had loved in the past? He remembered how resentful he had been at the funerals of Betty and Bobby, of how every time his fortunes had turned bad he would willingly have struck back by giving up his sincere and truthful life. What if he had been given a choice of following a criminal activity in order to save his family? It was a predicament he had no wish ever to encounter.

As he pondered on the morality of it all, Rennison looked at him.

"Peter, can you go inside and use the land line to get an ambulance..."

He objected to the request.

"No Emanuel, it will take too long. She's bleeding heavily, we should load her into a car and drive her to the nearest hospital."

Rennison hesitated and then relented

"Okay, but we take their car and ours. I will drive her in mine. Alex, you and Peter take Ferguson here in the BMW and make sure he's not going to..."

Ferguson almost spat.

"Stick it Rennison – I'm not going to run for it. It's all over."

Rennison shook his head.

"So you say, but we still want information that only you can give, so we would be very unhappy to lose you. Remember, I know how tricky you can be – with you it's once bitten, twice shy!"

Morton looked grim and gave Ferguson a nudge with his foot.

"On your feet and pick up your woman, the quicker we get out of here the better for all of us."

As if in slow motion Ferguson lifted himself upright and then bent to help his still bleeding wife. She had said nothing since the shooting and except for a small whimper as she came painfully to her feet she remained silent.

She staggered as she shifted all her weight onto her uninjured left leg and then put her left arm around her husband's shoulders.

She said something to him, too low to be audible but as she finished he gave her a long pleading look. She responded with a smile, a loving smile tinged with regret and farewell.

Abruptly, she rotated through a quarter circle and twisted away. She fell, and as she did so she stretched out, aiming herself at the handgun Morton had kicked back. Her aim was almost perfect and in an instant she had the automatic in hand. Pirouetting skilfully on one elbow she pointed it up, aiming at Morton.

Morton brought his automatic up but too late to stop her targeting him. He didn't stop moving, but was at least a second too slow and he could do nothing but watch as her finger started to squeeze the trigger. But she never made it – a single shot rang out and her head kicked forward as a bullet from Rennison punched through her skull and sent a plume of bone and brain onto the ground to her side.

As she toppled over Charles Ferguson gave a piteous cry of anguish and fell to his knees, his head drooping forward.

Morton looked at Rennison and slowly and sadly nodded his thanks; Rennison in turn looked completely defeated but said nothing.

For what seemed a long mournful period Morton and Rennison stood in silence, paralysed with shock. Morton then turned away and limped off for a few paces keeping his back to the horrific scene. The only sound was from the weeping, inconsolable Charles Ferguson; utterly broken by his loss. He now knelt over his wife's body with his head in his hands, his tears leaking between his fingers and dripping onto her body.

He stepped back as Morton had, but still morbidly fixated on the hideous scene laid out in front of him. It was too much, more than too much, and he felt tears come to his own eyes. He finally turned to escape what he saw and as he did so he heard Rennison shout out.

"No, don't be a fool, it's not..."

He half turned back and then instantly heard and felt the shock of another pistol shot.

As he came round to face the carnage he had wanted to wipe from his memory, he saw Charles Ferguson roll to his left with blood draining from his mouth and a bloody mess replacing the top of his head.

His dead hand relaxed its grip on the same gun his wife had used. Now it lay in his open palm as if to confess its guilt.

Being closer to the shot this time his ears had rung just as before, and they only recovered from the reverberating blast slowly. The first thing he heard as his hearing normalised was Morton blurting out "Oh dear Christ!"

Nobody moved for at least a minute, it was beyond anyone's emotional resilience. Then, as if he was physically divesting himself of the trauma of the last hour, Rennison shook his shoulders and walked towards the farmhouse.

"Come on Peter, I don't know about you but I could do with some tea.

The best he could do was to nod his head.

They had very little to say while sitting in the farmhouse kitchen. A sense of sorrow rather than triumph pervaded their stilted conversation and only a constant stream of over-brewed fresh tea succeeded in stopping the atmosphere from decaying into a morose and pessimistic funeral.

The only sound was the quietly voiced 'okay's' for a second and then a third mug of tea. Apart from this they were all withdrawn and unforthcoming. Rennison had called for an 'aftermath' clean up squad but it would not arrive for at least three hours. It was depressing to have to stay with the four bodies now parked in an empty tool shed at the side of the farmhouse, but protocol, he said, had to be observed.

Only Morton tried to lift everyone's spirits when he mentioned that they were unlikely to have to continue the investigation any more. For good or bad, he said, they had done all they could, and now it was done.

It was music to his ears, now he could think about Catherine again, about a routine life with zero chance of getting shot dead or ensnared into a test of his principles or morality. All he wanted was a return to normality, to cuddle Catherine, to drive Ella again, to face ordinary domestic problems – even if that meant arguing with the pool maintenance engineer.

It was as he gave a sigh of agreement that Rennison shook his head.

"What's up Emanuel – you don't think so?" Morton queried.

"Afraid not. As you blew the hell out of the last of Ferguson's heavies I was under fire in the barn. I got a lucky shot into the other bugger with the machine pistol and as he went down he had his finger on the trigger and kept firing. I saw the rounds go straight through the crate in front of me. The crate supposedly contained mortar rounds and in theory you should now be collecting bits of me in a bucket. After you made your way towards the farmhouse I found a tyre lever and lifted the lid off one of the crates."

"So?"

"It was empty, so were all the others, or at least all those where I removed the lids. They appeared to be new – no sign of any contents. As I previously proposed, at some point the arms were removed and repacked well before arrival here. Looks to me like whoever did it carefully replaced the lids and hammered them down giving no indication that they had ever been open. I believe this took place before Harwich, when the Fergusons had the freight parked in some other secure location. And no, I have no idea how it was accomplished. It wasn't the haulage contractors; I can't see them being able to plan an operation like this. Nor can I see the stuff disappearing before the shipment left the MOD compound; at the time it could only have been intercepted or diverted in transit. Yet, at some point the contents were snatched. So your guess is as good as mine. Seems not only us, but the Fergusons were conned, more fool them and more fool us!"

As Rennison finished he almost laughed, and would have if his back hadn't hurt so much and the whole bloody mess wasn't so serious. All that death hurt and heartache – all for nothing? So it appeared.

It occurred to him that the one thing he had a sneaky regret about was losing the Eprom. It was sad that Ferguson had used sleight of hand with it, now he would never be able to see the girl on the fake website again. He would forever wonder who she was and how she came to be featured by Bennet or whoever fabricated it. She had haunted his dreams for a while and he would forever have a soft spot for her. His Odessa Bride would always be ignorant of the fact that she had at least one ardent admirer.

He was tempted to disclose this little foible when next Catherine and he were having a cuddle on the settee at home. Yet there was an inherent risk in assuming it would be treated by Catherine as a neutral admission; more likely a passage to a reckless indulgence, and she might get very angry. It would be safer to tell the tale in simple understated terms, not revealing the dangerous bits. Shame really – but then, all things considered, Catherine would hardly believe the worst of it anyway, and she was not the type to see everything as black. However, he would give Isaac all the grimy details when he got back from the Lebanon – he was bound to want to know what happened.

Epilogue

Isaac Lahoud was enjoying the warming sun as it illuminated his upper story apartment in the Christian Gemmayze district in Beruit.

When Rennison had asked him to reconnoitre the movement of arms and money to the ISIL faction in Syria and Iraq he had at first refused, claiming that it was extremely hazardous and he was insufficiently experienced to give Rennison what he wanted. Rennison agreed, it was a long shot he had admitted, but he thought the lost arms shipment might turn up in the Lebanon on route to ISIL, the Islamic terrorists.

Rennison had cajoled and persuaded – virtually pleading for his help. Would he go?

Eventually he had agreed, on the face of it grudgingly and with deep reservations.

Yet, it was true what Rennison had said.

He was almost ideal for the mission. He was capable of speaking Arabic fluently and though a bit rusty had even brushed up on recent colloquials with some of his Arabic-speaking patients.

Though he seemed to be pressed into service, Rennison was not to know that the reluctance of his new-found agent was a sham. Isaac was overjoyed to get the chance – he had an ulterior motive for the trip. And so, pleased with his ruse, he cheerfully made his way to Beirut.

Rennison's failure to appreciate Isaac's true intentions was as misguided as his deduction that the arms shipment might be routed to Syria and Iraq via the Lebanon to ISIL. On the contrary, Rennison's expectation was the inverse of what Isaac intended.

In one sense Rennison was right, and closer to the truth than he could ever have imagined. He would have been astounded that the arms were actually destined to be smuggled across Lebanon –but not by the original hijackers – and even more astonished that the arms were now to be deliberately denied to ISIL.

Now Isaac was coming to the end of his stay and the end of his mission – a highly successful mission, and though not wholly in terms of what Rennison had expected, it was possible that though disappointed, he might have applauded the outcome.

It hadn't been easy; as he readied his packing he recalled all the stages of his deception. He had stumbled on the source of the hijacked arms shipment when Meredith Bennet and Fawly had been killed in Peter Enfield's house. He had tried to persuade Rennison that Meredith Bennet could not be working outside his family and that it was worth following that aspect up. However, at the time Rennison had his priorities elsewhere and seemed less than impressed with the suggestion; so Isaac was left to speculate on his own.

Fortunately one of his patients was a high-ranking police officer of long-standing and broad experience. He'd asked him casually, during a consultation, if there were any crime families in the UK like those in the USA. 'Certainly' came the reply, and without needing to prompt the officer anymore, he was given a complete run-down of all those families in the UK who based their livelihood on criminal activities. It took very little time and only a touch of friendly diplomacy to find out exactly where the Bennet family hailed from.

He'd spent some time in surveillance of the rather plush upmarket building which the Bennets enjoyed. It was situated in a very select area of London and consequently imposed a difficult surveillance operation. All the residents were virtually paranoid as regards house security, so after one particularly snotty challenge he was obliged to park away from the street itself and wait for movement by the Bennets in one of their cars.

Fortunately they invariably followed one particular route away from the house so as to more easily access the shorter road into town. As such, he simply waited for one of them to exit the house and pass him on the road junction. He would then follow. In a very short time he knew all their routines. Only a week after he had begun his vigil, he found himself on a ninety-minute journey following a lone female Bennet to the Harwich docks. This was intriguing since Rennison was certain that the Bennets had no daughters and only two male offspring, both of whom were certainly now dead.

At Harwich she stopped at what appeared to be a secure compound for custom bonded and private goods, comprising sheltered bays for private use and a barred warehouse for customs impounds.

She left her car and walked through the compound's security gates showing some papers and a security pass.

He stopped opposite the high chain link fencing of the compound, and using binoculars could see the woman walking down the various bays, all housing crates and goods free of customs restrictions.

At one she halted and looked in; it was an open bay holding two flatbed trailers, all with drab olive or khaki painted crates stacked on them. She walked into the bay and for a moment disappeared along one side of a trailer. As she reappeared he knew that what she was inspecting was the arms shipment.

What better place to have it? Snug in a secure compound and

unrecognised by anyone. But now he grasped the solution, all he had to do was find a way of getting to the trailers and moving the contents of the crates to another place. Thereafter it was he who would determine where they ended up.

As he carefully packed his bags, ready for the flight back to England, his mind ran over the night he had actually hijacked the shipment.

In every sense it had been too easy.

First he acquired a range of different sized crates and had them variously painted in khaki and drab olive. He paid to have the job given priority status and they were finished in 36 hours.

He then hired two flat bed trailers fitted with cranes, along with their motor cabs and two drivers, from a rundown haulage firm near the A120. The firm and the drivers were paid handsomely not to ask questions. They picked up the new crates, loaded them on to the flatbeds and then waited for instructions.

He subsequently visited the secure compound in the docks and hired a sheltered bay for a week, telling them that two flatbed trailers with cargo would be arriving the next night and that some unloading would take place. To his relief the movement of cargo, day or night, was taken as a routine occurrence and the registration officer raised no objections, simply grunting his approval.

The following night he was passenger in the first flatbed to arrive and they were waved through the moment he showed them the passes and registration papers. Less than a minute later they drew up opposite the two trailers carrying the arms. Thirty minutes later, thankfully working under dim and obfuscating lighting, they had exchanged one set of khaki and drab olive crates for another.

He then had his trailers move down the road and back into the sheltered bay designated for them. His two drivers were then despatched to search for a takeaway meal. They returned with kebabs and chips, which he recalled was definitely to his taste.

That night they slept in their respective motor cabs, there being ample room and facilities. Next morning they drove out, no one the wiser because the night staff was off duty and the new day shift had no reason to suspect that what was going out had not come in.

What for him was even more perfect was that the cargo ship SS *Emelia*, on route to the Port of Beirut, had room in her hold for a lot more cargo. His shipment was loaded as part of the usual freight manifest, declared as machine parts.

The ship was due in Beirut in 24 days, which gave him more than enough time to fly in and arrange for collection and sea transportation of the crates along the Lebanon and Syrian coast to Turkey – there to be smuggled into Iraqi Kurdistan. It was a tense period but it was not long before he was notified that the shipment had arrived at its intended destination. It was Isaac's triumph, for he had successfully moved the whole arms shipment to the Peshmerga – the sworn enemies of ISIL.

He felt contentment, a total exhilaration; he had now fulfilled his promise to his last foster parents – that he would always support, in every way he could, the fight against the evil fanatics who had killed their first born. It did not matter that it was not the PLO that was the current enemy, the ones the Peshmerga fighters were engaged with were, if anything, more evil then the animals who had killed both his foster parent's children, and were more evil than the brutes the youthful Isaac had endured and destroyed.

It was to him a moral crusade, instilled in him by his foster parents who had wept with joy when they first saw him and his brother because they was so like the children they had lost.

Furthermore, his first set of adopted parents was to be revenged too – by honouring the one, he had honoured all.

Yes, they would be looking down on him now, joyous from seeing him as a humane and successful doctor but equally happy that he was the bringer of death to the beasts that plagued civilised mankind.

As he zipped up his holdall and locked his suitcase he thought how strange it would be to get back to a routine medics life. He hoped that nothing too much had changed other than the fact that unbeknown to his government in the UK, they had unintentionally made a strong contribution to the war against ISIL. He momentarily realised that the loss of the arms was a distinct cost to the UK exchequer and someone would have to pay for it.

But he was comforted by the recognition that the defence budget was already due for a top up and the arms now being used against ISIL was a drop in the ocean compared to the full UK defence budget.

If he were wrong, it might conceivably mean pressure to increase taxes, but if so he for one would gladly pay it. After all, he had already effectively subsidised the UK should they ever do officially what he had just done illegally; for he had already spent heavily in transporting the arms. He had disposed of most of his foster parent's substantial legacy in arranging all the concealment, carriers and agents handling the arms shipment. The biggest expense had been in the Lebanon – he could never be sure if he had been paying for transport or for silence.

He grinned as he finalised the packing. He wondered if given his massive outlay over the last month the Inland Revenue might not give him a rebate.

Five hundred metres away the assassin had brought the inside of the bedroom into focus on his telescopic sight. The rifle had already been sighted in a desert location and was aligned for very low windage and deflection. He lay prostrate on the roof of a five-story apartment block outside of the Christian Gemmayze district, an area he would willingly have demolished and decimated had he been able. He feared nothing in this life other than the wrath of Allah for not doing his duty. His teaching from the Koran by his elders had been explicit *'make war upon the Jews and Christians – fight and slay the Pagans wherever you find them. O ye who believe – take not the Jews and Christians for friends'*.

His target now was not only an unbeliever, but also a foreigner who had successfully contrived to move arms to the enemy of his people; arms that would kill his brothers. For that crime the infidel was to suffer death.

He waited until the man closed the lid on his suitcase and was fully covered by the cross hairs. Then he softly squeezed the trigger.